### About *The Salacia Project*

*The Salacia Project* is an action-packed thrill ride that races along the bleeding edges of technology and covert operations. Set in the near future, *The Salacia Project* begins with a harrowing covert helicopter ride through the mountains of Afghanistan, and ends with a spectacular gun battle between US and Chinese intelligence operatives in Virginia. The Salacia technology, over which these two nations are fighting, could keep US naval forces and the land-based military units they support indomitable for decades. Developed by a brilliant young researcher at the Brystol Foundation, the technology essentially "moves water out of the way" of ships as they traverse the open sea, more than doubling their speed. But if it falls into enemy hands, it could cost America its naval superiority in a matter of months. US and Chinese intelligence communities are pitted against one another in a winner-takes-all contest of wits and firepower. Murders, assassinations, kidnappings, and daring rescues sweep the reader along in a high-stakes adventure filled with intrigue and moral dilemmas.

### Praise for *The Salacia Project*

"Bill Duncan's new page-turner, *The Salacia Project*, is a fast-paced suspense novel that combines thriller, espionage, spy, and drama that delivers a gripping tale readers won't be able to put down." – A. Saenz Review: (5 out of 5 Stars)

"I could not put this book down, definitely a page turner. Also, I love that Bill Duncan is not afraid to kill people. Crazy, but I love it." - Daniale via Goodreads Reviews: (5 out of 5 Stars)

### About *The Angelia Project*

A devastating new cyber warfare technology known as Angelia has been stolen from the Mossad, and it's being weaponized. In enemy hands, Angelia will enable the destruction of national economies and disable strategic military defenses. An international team of spies is embedding these weapons in the world's most secret facilities, and by the time the truth is discovered, the Middle East has been brought to the brink of war. Racing against the clock, a team of covert operatives led by Ben Dawson must wrest the technology away and stop the man about to trigger Armageddon. But to succeed, Dawson must enlist the aid of the former assassin who was responsible for the death of his close friend, and tried to kill Dawson as well. *The Angelia Project* is a powerful story of technology and trust, risk and redemption. It sweeps the reader across four continents through tense covert operations and frenetic gun battles to a climax that leaves us breathless, awaiting the next Ben Dawson adventure.

### Praise for *The Angelia Project*

"Great storyline, believable dialogue, and details that bring the story to life. It is an absolute delight to read. Another adventure that you just can't put down!" – CPMC Review: (5 out of 5 Stars)

"*The Angelia Project* was a very sophisticated and interesting read. It delves into a present day type of warfare which I had not yet even fathomed. Not to mention, it was well written and exciting. Well worth the read!" – N. Keel Review from Amazon Books: (5 out of 5 Stars)

# THE ICARUS PROJECT

A BEN DAWSON NOVEL

## BILL DUNCAN

BRYSTOL
FOUNDATION

Published in the United States by Brystol Foundation, LLC
St. Louis, MO

This is a work of fiction. Any resemblance to actual events or persons, living or dead, is merely coincidental, and names, characters, and incidents are either the products of the author's imagination or are used fictitiously.

More information, photographs, and background about the author's experiences that inspired *The Icarus Project* can be viewed at www.bill-duncan.com. Additional copies can be purchased there as well.

ISBN: 0991121341
ISBN 13: 9780991121342
Library of Congress Control Number: 2015916466
Brystol Foundation, Manchester, MO

This book is dedicated to a great editor, and even better friend, Tony Vlamis.

Thank you, Tony, for all your invaluable counsel, help, and friendship over the years.

And, as always, God bless the United States of America.

Bill Duncan
St. Louis, MO

# THE ICARUS PROJECT

In ancient Greek mythology, Icarus escaped his earthly captivity with the assistance of bird-like wings until he flew too high, where the wings were destroyed by the heat of the sun.

But to the international intelligence community, Icarus represented the opportunity to transport armies and their equipment with incredible scale and speed. It was a game changer for governments looking for ways to shift the balance of power, and no price was too high.

# CHAPTER 1

Siberian summers are painfully brief. The snows linger into May, and cold weather returns again in September, transforming the terrain into a desolate still life. The endless forests of straggly pine and birch are peppered with hibernating bears and ravenous wolves, and the wind is utterly cruel. The Siberian forest stretches over five million square miles from the furthest tip of Russia's arctic regions to points as far south as Mongolia. It reaches from the Urals in the west to the Pacific in the east. With the exception of just a few towns, that vast area of wilderness is home to only a few thousand people.

Ben Dawson and Jim "Chief" Romero clambered through the foothills of the steep-sided Ural Mountains approaching an off-limits Russian R&D facility near Mezhgorye. For two days, the men had been negotiating trails and back roads along white water rivers that ran in torrents through local valleys while skirting slick, icy bogs. The weather had been favorable and they had made good progress. But Dawson was increasingly wary, alert to the possibility of being discovered as they grew closer to their target. The last few miles went more slowly as the men carefully picked their way along, avoiding obvious choke points. Choke points—narrow openings between boulders and trees—afforded placement opportunities for concealed tripwires, motion sensors, electric eyes, and other remote sensing equipment.

Dawson and Romero both wore mountain camouflage and substantial backpacks, laden with electronic gear and weapons that would have been impossible to explain if they were captured. Consequently, the backpacks themselves were rigged to explode and utterly destroy their contents if they were removed from the bodies of their bearers without the entry of a preassigned four-digit code within thirty seconds. Dawson was a former operative of the US National Security Agency, and still worked closely with the NSA on assignments as a part of his official "day job" at a research and development firm called the Brystol Foundation. The Brystol Foundation developed world-changing technologies, often with strong US national security dimensions, and most often under contract with US intelligence agencies. Usually, these technologies were discovered and developed through typical research or through outright purchase. But on some occasions, when the technology was found to be under development by entities unfriendly to the West, less traditional means were employed to acquire them. That happened when the technology was perceived to be extremely dangerous to western interests and to US national security interests in particular. This excursion represented one such event.

Dawson was not as worried about direct human observation. Even in the colder months, the forest in this area was thick enough to swallow whole armies of foot patrols, and his recon man, Billy Winger, was well out ahead of them. Winger was a former Delta Force operator who worked for the NSA in Eastern Europe and Soviet satellite countries for several years. Then he was reassigned to Kabul and Baghdad through the "noisy" period between 2003 and 2009. He left the agency after nearly a decade to marry, and regretted the union almost immediately. The marriage lasted only a year, but Winger had burned some bridges with his abrupt departure and never looked back. He worked freelance contract assignments for the CIA and FBI for a short time thereafter, when Ben Dawson began to use him for Brystol Foundation work. Since those events in 2011, the men had become close friends. These days, Winger was a member of a private security outfit called Kelly & Gerard Enterprises, LLP. Romero, a recently retired US Army Ranger, also worked for the firm. Lily Gerard, who ran the small security company, was Dawson's paramour and confidant, and Dawson—as security director for the Brystol Foundation—was Kelly & Gerard Enterprises' primary client.

As they crested a rise about two miles from the target facility, Dawson and Romero both heard a series of chirps in their earbuds. Two steady chirps followed by three short chirps, each one tone higher in pitch than the preceding tone. Winger had arrived at their destination. Dawson and Romero smiled at one another momentarily and moved on. The GPS-based device on Dawson's wrist indicated they were close and headed in the right direction. The forest was still thick as they remained well below the timberline, but the terrain was leveling off which made breathing a lot easier. Dawson was still in good physical condition, but he was fifty years old and carrying a substantial load. As the air got thinner, he and Romero could feel the effects of the two days on rocky inclines in their lungs and legs. They were both looking forward to shedding their backpacks for a while.

Dusk was falling, and the canopy of leaves and pine needles hastened darkness in the forest. Romero was the first to spot the ancient hunter's cabin where Winger was already setting up shop. As they approached, Dawson could see why the intel guys from Langley had been so high on this location. Getting the information had required his friend and former boss at NSA, Charles Jennings, to call in a favor from CIA Deputy Director John Deering. The intel was solid, and Dawson couldn't help smiling as he thought about how the cabin would sound in a travel brochure. *Unspoiled rustic beauty set in a pristine paradise,* he thought. *Personally, I'd prefer running water and electricity.* But this was exactly where they needed to be, and given the blanket of overhanging branches, the tiny thermal signature from their small chemical heating unit would be undetectable from airborne surveillance drones. He could see one such drone tethered to the ground in the distance, fixed in position a thousand feet in the air above the facility. There were also two towers on the site, bristling with antennae and camera arrays. There was no direct line of sight from the cabin, but the view was unobstructed from an outcropping just a few yards away.

"Zdravstvujtye!" Winger said, greeting Romero and Dawson as they entered the cabin. Winger was the only man on the team who spoke Russian, and he readily admitted he was quite rusty at that. But with any luck the men wouldn't need to converse with the locals on this mission. The cabin was in better shape inside than it appeared from the exterior. The bottom two feet of each wall was stone which gave way to rough-hewn timbers reaching to the low, vine-and-moss-covered roof. Patches of what had once been a wolf pelt adorned one wall, and a crude stone fireplace stood in one corner. The building had one small window with no glass, and the sagging door had old rusty hinges that looked like they could disintegrate at any moment. A latch was fashioned from a piece of leather and a wooden peg.

Winger had been setting up camp. He'd stretched a thin metallic sheet into an arc shape just in front of the fireplace over the stones and placed their chemical heater on the floor there. He was just putting together a crude table from a rotting, discarded plank, using some fallen tree branches for somewhat precarious legs. Dawson and Romero gratefully shed their cargo, carefully entering the appropriate codes to disengage the self-destruct devices, and then began to help. Within a few minutes, the men had a workable base camp with heat, light, and bedding laid out for the night. Then they walked outside to survey the surrounding area.

The outcropping was the most advantageous observation post but was also the place where detection would be easiest from the vantage point of the drones or the tower-based cameras. Off to one side there was a stand of pine trees forming a thick wall of visual cover, and Romero dragged a couple of suitable stones into position to form seats beneath the boughs of the tallest tree. By the time he finished, Dawson and Winger were already scanning the valley in front of them with binoculars, shifting back and forth between normal and night vision modes owing to the twilight.

Dawson could see men entering and leaving a high-bay, flat-roofed structure with oversized doors. The foot traffic seemed to be picking up there, while it diminished around the other buildings. The lights over a small parking area and along a chain-link fence surrounding the site came to life, and Dawson was able to count two sentries along each fence line, one of which was accompanied by a German shepherd. The fence was topped with razor wire. All of the sentries wore Russian Army uniforms, and they were armed with AK-74 rifles and automatic pistols. "Hmpf," Winger wondered aloud, "when did they start carrying Strizh pistols?"

"What's amazing is you can make that out from here, Billy," Dawson said. "I can tell they have pistols, but I sure can't tell what kind."

"The grip is different than their old 443 Grachs," Winger continued. "Steeper rake. I've seen 'em before but never fired one."

"Well," Dawson said, "if the intel is correct, the show should be starting in about an hour. I guess we might as well eat. Who wants first shift?"

"I had a Clif Bar on the trail a while back, so I'm fine," Romero replied. "I'll keep an eye out." He settled in on one of the newly acquired rocks and raised his binoculars to peer out from beneath the branches.

"OK. Thanks, Chief," Dawson said, and he returned with Winger to the cabin. They broke open stripped-down Meals, Ready-to-Eat—MREs—and used the chemical packets to heat their food. "Teriyaki chicken," Winger smiled. "Not bad!"

After about thirty minutes, Dawson headed back outside with a cup of coffee for Romero while Winger began to set up equipment on the makeshift table. Romero hadn't moved, and reminded Dawson of a statue he once saw of Indian Chief Black Hawk looking out over the Mississippi River Valley in Rock Island, Illinois. It made the moniker of "Chief" even more fitting. Romero earned the name "Chief" when he was coming up through the Army and it had stuck. He was a tough, grizzled fifty-one-year-old widower with a salt-and-pepper crew cut and tanned, chiseled features. He was a serious man and quiet most of the time, but the thing Dawson loved about him was he was as predictable as the sunrise. He never flinched, never wavered, and always did exactly as he said he would do. About two years earlier, Romero had gritted his teeth and helped Dawson and Winger rescue a badly wounded soldier from Iran, even after his own ribs had been cracked by the concussive force of a grenade. "Hey, Boss," he said, still looking out through the binoculars. "They're about to bring something out of that big building down there." Then noticing the hot coffee, he said: "Thanks," and handed the field glasses over.

Dawson could see Romero was right. The Russian soldiers had rolled back the wide, heavy doors. Technicians wearing civilian coats were hustling in and out, talking and calling out to one another while making arrangements of some kind. While Dawson watched, Winger approached from the cabin. "Go ahead and grab an MRE if you want, Chief," he said. He was carrying a short tripod and a small electronic device to mount atop it. Winger unfolded the tripod and got it assembled, and Dawson stopped looking through the binoculars long enough to assist with the balance of the setup. Thin fiberglass rods were bent into hoops forming three concentric circles of different sizes, the largest of which was about two feet in diameter. Then they were arranged by Winger and attached to connecting support strips forming a cone-shaped frame. The frame was then fitted with a set of heavy duty foil sheets, interconnecting in a curved pattern and producing a parabolic dish. One coaxial wire attached the dish to the electronic device Winger had carried out of the cabin with him, and another connected the camera beneath it. Winger flipped a switch on the side of the unit. In a matter of minutes, they had established a powerful ground-based surveillance station with a compact night vision camera and a parabolic microphone pointed toward the scene unfolding on the ground below. Winger watched the meter on the top of the electronic module as it displayed signal strength while he adjusted the dish in small increments, swinging it back and forth until he had achieved the best reception. Then he began to listen in earnest through a headset. The device connected to the parabolic microphone began to monitor and record the conversations almost a half mile below them. Between the electronic signal boosting and filtering capabilities of the device, the fidelity of the sound was startling. He could decipher some of the phrases, but many of the snippets were scientific in nature and meaningless to him.

About thirty minutes elapsed before they heard a big diesel engine rumble to life, and a Russian T-72 tank crawled slowly out of the building and stopped a few yards away. When it appeared, Romero issued a low whistle.

"What have we here?" Winger added.

Dawson saw the reason for their surprise immediately. The tank had undergone some major modifications. It had always had relatively low ground clearance—about nineteen inches—and stood just over seven feet at its tallest point. But this vehicle looked to be well over ten feet in height—perhaps closer to eleven. The lower body of the tank had been extended by roughly three feet in height. Dawson couldn't imagine what could be considered so valuable that it warranted such a design change. It would have been exceptionally expensive; it shifted the center of gravity to a much higher position, and it substantially altered the vertical opening requirement for transport vehicles. What could be worth that kind of investment? Tanks were recognized to be falling behind in terms of their value as a war-fighting tool in the face of airborne weapon systems and cyber warfare. It was hard to imagine why anyone would pour a great deal more into R&D on such an aging platform.

But as they watched, another sound—the crackle of electrical arcing—reached them, and all of the ground technicians stepped back from the tank. What happened next was an event that all three men would remember for the rest of their lives.

# CHAPTER 2

As Dawson, Winger, and Romero looked on, the crackling sound seemed to smooth out into a kind of flickering hum. And as the hum became perceptible, the T-72 lifted off, hovering almost ten inches from the ground. The three men were utterly incredulous. None of them could immediately believe what they were seeing. After about thirty seconds, Dawson asked aloud: "How much does a Russian T-72 weigh?"

"Forty-one tons and change, Boss," Romero said. None of them could tear their eyes away from what they were witnessing.

"So, are you seeing a forty-one ton Russian tank floating a foot off the ground down there?" Dawson asked.

"Yeah, Boss," Romero replied again. "Are you sure it was just coffee you gave me?"

A man who was standing toward the front of the tank signaled the technicians, and two of them moved to positions at the side of the vehicle and immediately to the rear. They each held short rods—they looked like aluminum or possibly a polymer of some kind—and lifted them into casual positions as though preparing to take their turn at billiards. In tandem, they gave the vehicle a shove and it rotated in front of them, basically spinning in a circle in mid-air. After about fifteen seconds though, the tank began to wobble, and the crackling sound occurred again. About three seconds into the crackle, the vehicle lurched several inches to one side and fell unceremoniously back to the ground with an earth-shaking crash. Then a hatch opened on the top and three men scrambled out amidst sparks and smoke. One of the technicians rushed forward in a gas mask and shot a monoammonium phosphate-based fire extinguisher into the open hatch, expunging the flames and ending the smoke emission.

The man near the front of the vehicle, who Dawson surmised was the lead technician, seemed unsurprised and unperturbed at the course of events. He signaled the team, and they began working immediately to get the vehicle operational again. When that didn't happen quickly, a special crane-lift vehicle was summoned from another part of the facility, and the disabled tank was hoisted into position aboard a low-slung transport truck, and carried back into the building from which it had emerged.

"Was that what you were expecting?" Winger asked Dawson, speaking for the first time since the event started.

"No," Dawson replied, "I wasn't expecting to see any flying tanks today, Billy. Something about the expression 'when pigs fly' comes to mind."

They continued watching, and about an hour later another vehicle emerged from the hangar-like building. This time the vehicle was a long squatty truck with eight axles and a narrow cab which was clearly designed for only a driver. It sat next to the business end of a very long tubular object more than sixty-six feet in length.

"Holy moley, guacamole!" Winger exclaimed quietly. "Guys, that's a YARS RS-24 mobile launcher. Only I've never seen one like it. And it's not the YARS that's different, it's the launcher. It's been modified like that T-72."

Winger was right. The YARS RS-24 is a Russian Intercontinental Ballistic Missile—ICBM. Capable of delivering nuclear warheads, the weapon was developed to counter western Star Wars defense technologies, and launch from both static silos and mobile ground-based units like the MZKT-79221 truck that now sat, engine idling, in the compound below.

"Any idea what the weight of this unit is?" Dawson asked. "I have no clue."

"Well, if it wasn't for the modifications, I'd say the vehicle and the ICBM it's carrying would weigh in at about 364,000 pounds, Boss," Winger replied. "But the way it's built up, and the way those tires are bulging, I'd say there's another—oh, I don't know—maybe 5,000 pounds. So I'd guesstimate about 370,000 pounds altogether."

At that moment, the headlights of two Mercedes SUVs broke through the trees as they rounded a sharp turn, and rolled toward the gates of the Russian site. The first vehicle was black or dark blue—it was impossible to be sure using the night vision equipment—and the second was silver. There was a flurry of activity at the smaller building, which appeared to be comprised of offices, and several low-to-mid-level officers emerged, some of them still donning their overcoats against the cold. The sky was clear and the darkness was deepening. Even though it was late April, the nighttime temperatures in this area often dropped into the teens. A moment later, from another building on the far side of the compound, a man appearing to be the senior officer at the facility could be seen hustling across the grounds toward the area where the YARS unit sat, surrounded by technicians and soldiers.

"This ought to be interesting," Romero muttered. "Looks like a surprise inspection to me." Over his military career, Romero had been on the receiving end of many of them, and he knew them when he saw them.

The two Mercedes were admitted through the gate, and drove directly to the testing ground, pulling up about ten yards from the side of the YARS unit. The drivers of each vehicle emerged hastily and rounded their respective vehicles to open the passenger doors in the back. When the passengers emerged from their vehicles, Romero once again made a low whistling sound. "Boss," he asked, "is that who I think it is?"

Dawson nodded in the affirmative. "Chief of the Soviet Operations and Technology Directorate, Vadim Shelepin. One of the primary faces of Russia's new Federal Security Service—formerly known to all of us old-timers as the KGB."

Dawson could see Winger smiling on the other side of Romero. "You feelin' old tonight, Boss?" he asked. "You schlepped eighty plus pounds of gear across twenty miles of rocky wilderness at some altitude the last two days, and I didn't hear any complaints. That's not bad for an old man."

"It's all relative, Billy," Dawson smiled back, "but none of us is getting any younger."

"I'm not so sure, Boss," Winger continued to grin, this time with an air of mischief. "I notice Lily has a real spring in her step these days, and you're smiling a lot easier than you used to. ..."

Dawson cleared his throat and wondered how—even now—he could still be made to blush, and whether his face glowed in the dark. Even Romero had to smile at Dawson's discomfort.

"So, returning to the matter at hand, who is the other VIP down there?" Dawson asked. As they watched, a short, portly man basically rolled out of the other Mercedes, and the vehicle actually sprung back perceptibly as he disembarked.

"My, my, my," Winger said, all humor having fled the new turn of events. "If it isn't our old friend Professor Jürgen Bleckhaus from the Technische Universität Berlin. Boss, this must be our lucky day; I thought we'd never see this particular rascal again."

"I know what you mean," Dawson agreed.

"Makes me wish I had my SR25," Winger said, referring to his sniper rifle. "I could do the world a whole lot of good from right here."

"Man, you sound more like Max Kelly every day, Billy," Dawson said. Kelly had been Dawson's close friend, and at the time of his death, had been Gerard's partner—both on and off duty. He was killed in a shootout related to an earlier Brystol Foundation matter known as the Salacia Project. They all missed him dearly, but none as profoundly as Dawson. Now, almost two years later, he harbored a deep-seated feeling he should have done something differently to prevent Kelly's demise, though he had no idea what he could have done. He wondered sometimes whether his feelings stemmed from the fact that he was with Gerard now, but he pushed it aside. He loved Gerard beyond words and no twinge of remorse about Kelly would cause that to change.

As they continued to watch, it became clear the VIPs were there to see some magic, and they weren't willing to be disappointed. Winger listened closely to his headset, then said: "Shelepin says he's paying for this program, and he's not leaving until he sees a demonstration." The junior officers and technicians went into overdrive, swarming around the area like bees. It took almost an hour, with junior officers fetching cups of hot coffee out from the barracks every ten or fifteen minutes to the VIPs, and they were ready to go.

The site's senior officer signaled everyone to withdraw, and they stepped back to a distance of about twenty yards. Then he spoke into a radio, and the electrical crackling sound began again. This time, Dawson thought he could see some kind of minor arcing along the base at one corner near the back end of the vehicle, but then it disappeared. The crackling once again turned into a hum and the base, along with the ICBM itself, began to move. The truck remained on the ground; it had obviously been decoupled from the cradling device. It looked as though the ICBM and the cradle in which it was lying were levitating about a foot above its original location on the truck.

Again, the senior officer barked an order into the radio. The humming sound became just a little louder, and the device basically began to float like a dirigible into the sky. As it ascended, two large spotlights mounted atop buildings situated at the end of the testing ground were trained on the ICBM.

"Billy, is our camera picking this up or did it ascend out of the camera's frame?" Dawson asked.

"I'm zooming out now, Boss," Winger replied, adjusting the camera's focus. "Looks like it's about even with us so it must be over a quarter mile up at this point."

Again, the senior officer barked a command into the radio, and the airborne ICBM with cradle began to slowly descend to its original position. As it got to within several inches of the truck bed, the site commander spoke again into his radio, and the device halted in position, where it appeared to wobble just slightly. Four technicians approached with short rods and carefully nudged the massive object, which appeared completely weightless, until it was precisely where they wanted it to be. Then another command into the radio brought the device fully back onto the truck. Dawson observed that the bulge in the tires Winger had pointed out earlier had returned. The test had been a success, and Dawson could almost feel the relief in the site commander. Have a T-72 fall a couple of feet was one thing. But had the ICBM fallen from a point nearly a quarter mile in the air right in front of the Chief of the Directorate, it would likely have been a career-ending event at the very least. Dawson surmised the warheads were likely missing or at least disarmed, but even so, the point these researchers were making was clear, and would be especially obvious to this particular set of VIPs.

All three men watched the activity below for another hour, but the evening's demonstrations had evidently ended. Dawson thought about what to do next. Their mission was purely information gathering, but allowing Bleckhaus to get loose again without being able to understand the nature of his involvement would be a tragedy. He needed to extend the surveillance if possible.

"Billy," he said as they walked back into the hunting cabin, "do you suppose the PAASS would work on a car?" PAASS—the Pneumatically Applied Auditory Surveillance System—was invented by some contract technicians working for the National Security Agency late in 2014. Surprisingly, it had remained an undiscovered tool of selected US intelligence agencies since then, and had met with remarkable success.

"Sure it would," Winger replied, "if we can get close enough to use it. But anybody inside the car would hear the impact when it was delivered."

"True enough," Dawson said, "but not if they're distracted. I think Bleckhaus' vehicle is going to have a flat tire."

Winger smiled. "And just when I thought things were gonna get boring," he said. Winger grabbed a small plastic case from his backpack and each of the men retrieved night vision goggles and their sidearms. Dawson and Winger left Romero in charge of the equipment and headed out immediately, swinging in a wide arc around the compound in order to avoid any hidden motion detectors and other surveillance devices. Before they left, Dawson asked Romero to signal them with three decreasing tones when Bleckhaus' silver Mercedes departed the compound.

After about sixty minutes, they found a likely position at the sharp bend in the road. Dawson and Winger deployed at two separate locations—one on each side of the road, with Winger about fifty feet further down the road than Dawson, both concealed in the trees about twenty feet from the actual roadway. Winger found a fallen tree and used its trunk as both cover and a firing bench. He knelt in the pine needles blanketing the ground and screwed the sound suppressor onto the end of his FN Five seveN, and prepared to sight in on the vehicle when it approached.

Dawson established a higher position with a somewhat better vantage point, but he was more exposed. He was seated—quite uncomfortably—on the third branch of a large birch tree. He wouldn't be easily seen, but he also knew rapid escape was unlikely if something went wrong. He sat there in the dark, muttering quietly to himself about fifty-year-old men having no business in trees, while he unpacked the small plastic case Winger had grabbed from his backpack at the cabin. He extracted a small pistol the size of a soldering gun, a compressed air cartridge about half the size of the standard $CO_2$ cartridge used for air pistols in the US, and two small paintballs resembling those used by gamers. The first paintball was white and the second was black. He loaded the weapon and made himself as comfortable as possible while he waited. Another thirty minutes went by, and the earbuds of Winger and Dawson chirped in the expected pattern; Bleckhaus was on his way. Dawson and Winger both prepared themselves. Dawson's extremities were becoming numb from the cold so he rubbed his hands together to generate some warmth from the friction.

It took the Mercedes about three minutes to arrive at the sharp bend in the road. As it approached, Winger sighted in at an angle that would enable him to fire into the tread of the tire rather than the sidewall, making immediate identification of the puncture as a bullet hole very difficult. He fired a single round, and the tire began immediately to hiss loudly. As soon as the shot struck the tire, Dawson fired at the top corner of the rear window with his pneumatic pistol. Both men had struck within an inch of their respective targets. Dawson quickly revectored his aim and hit the rear bumper with the second projectile from his tiny air gun. There was a flat tire for the driver to deal with, and on the back window it appeared as though an owl or some other large bird has emptied its bowels on the unfortunate window. However, within the messy deposit resembling bird excrement were three beads that looked like seeds. They were actually microphones, and the gelatinous substance growing more viscous around them would hold them in position against the glass until the vehicle was washed, removing all traces. While they were in place, an extraordinary carbon-fiber antenna comprised of fibers roughly the diameter of a human hair unwound themselves in a spider web-like pattern, and attracted energy from incoming radio signals. The signals were overlaid against the sound waves produced inside the vehicle to produce a net-effect or null signal, causing a transmission to be emanated back into the airwaves.

The delta—or null—signal was amplified by a high-powered nano-crystal transmission device enmeshed within the viscous liquid of the second shot, a smear similar to the one on the window that contained the system's microphones. However, the second device, because it would be discernible at some point, was designed to disintegrate by virtue of an embedded acid pack within 120 minutes of deployment. It was a nearly perfect audio surveillance system when attached effectively. If they had been close enough with a ground-based receiver, they could literally have listened in on Bleckhaus. But in this case, no such opportunity existed. So the second device merely provided a uniquely encrypted beacon. It should be enough for the NSA to find Bleckhaus' mobile signal, which was all Dawson was looking for.

While the driver did his normal recovery routine, radioing back to the compound for assistance and then beginning to remove the tire himself, Winger and Dawson slipped away and headed back to the cabin. When they arrived, Romero was still attentive but reported almost no significant activity had occurred since they left. A support vehicle had been dispatched to assist Bleckhaus' driver, but Romero indicated only two soldiers were in the vehicle; there was no sign they believed anything untoward was happening.

Dawson sat down in the cabin and began to compose a communiqué for Diane Maretti at the Brystol Foundation. Maretti was Dr. Kenneth Brystol's administrative assistant and personal security detail. She also coordinated the travel of Brystol's key staff members, including Dawson.

In the communiqué, Dawson directed her to contact Daniel Winters via Charles Jennings, informing him that a PAASS device had been installed on a vehicle transporting Bleckhaus. Winters would need to lock in on Bleckhaus' location and comms ASAP, since the PAASS would only be functional for another ninety minutes. He then stated the attached audio-video file contained important information for Brystol.

They compressed and attached a copy of the critical minutes of the surveillance they had captured of both the T-72 and the ICBM. At precisely two minutes after the hour, Dawson uploaded the information via an encrypted sat-phone. Then he took over sentry duty for Romero, so he and Winger could get some sleep. Winger took the following shift while Dawson slept, and by ten a.m. the following morning, all three men were rested, fed, and ready to perform their final surveillance tasks.

The first step was installation of an Arbor-lite surveillance camera high in the boughs of one of the fir trees overlooking the R&D compound. The device was about the size of a softball, and camouflage in coloration. It contained a camera with solid state memory, a small CPU for processing instructions related to image capture, upload, and deletion, and an internal battery. Winger mounted it on the trunk of the tree facing the compound, fastening it with zip-ties. Connected to the two plugs on the outside of the unit were a separate solar panel about fourteen inches by ten inches, and an antenna array designed to look like a small, bare tree branch. The night-vision-equipped camera's lens provided a 200 power zoom, and it could be repositioned by remote signal in a sixty degree arc. Winger secured the solar panel to another branch where it would capture maximum daylight. While Winger made final adjustments to the camera position and secured the solar panel and antenna, Romero kept watch with his binoculars. Dawson verified everything was in working order, and notified Winters back in DC that the device was in position and operational. His communication was a quick, asymmetrical encrypted burst designed to provide almost no traceable electronic footprint. Then the three men broke camp and headed due east about three quarters of a mile.

They established a likely location for their returning rendezvous, and Dawson took up a sentry position. He remained with the balance of their equipment while Romero and Winger started out again, this time to see how close they could get to the compound. They belly-crawled through the brush to an edge of undergrowth closest to the headquarters building without being detected. Both men carried their pistols, with sound suppressors attached, and wore radios. Winger also toted the small plastic case containing the PAASS device in the oversized pocket of his camouflage cargo pants.

Dawson watched the two men disappear from sight, then began his regimen of shifting position and continually scanning for threats. It was nearly three hours when Winger and Romero returned. "He nailed it, Boss!" Romero reported, beaming.

Winger sheepishly added: "Took me two shots, Boss. I admit I'm probably slipping some, but holy cow—can't we get the guys back in the lab to add one more inch to the barrel on these things? I mean the target was over forty feet away."

Dawson smiled and shook his head. Without a word he pulled the transmitter from his backpack and coded another burst. It read: "PAASS on stationary target. Popping smoke."

Winger had hit the widow glass on one of the offices in the headquarters building. Until it was washed away, the tiny seed-like microphones would pick up and transmit the sounds from inside the office to the remote repeater/booster concealed by Romero just a few feet inside the nearby foliage. So for some period of time—until the window was washed off, or until the small con-cealed transmitter's battery died—whatever was spoken inside that particular office would be directed to equipment in an NSA lab in Maryland.

It was time to head for home.

# CHAPTER 3

At NSA headquarters, Daniel Winters' telephone rang. Winters was peering at a Java script he had been working on, and was barely paying attention when he punched the speaker option on the desk phone, hoping it was something quick so he could get back to what he was doing. "Daniel Winters," he said, still staring at the monitor in front of him.

"Daniel, this is Diane Maretti," a voice said. "Please take me off of speaker."

Winters knew Maretti, the administrative assistant and sometimes personal security officer for Dr. Kenneth Brystol, CEO of the Brystol Foundation. Maretti was a US Marine Corps reservist and did not suffer fools. If she was asking him to pick up his handset, Winters knew there was a good reason for it, and he did so immediately. "Hi, Diane, what's up?"

"I'm sending you a secure communication from our friends in the ice box," she responded. "You and your boss are both going to want to see this ASAP."

"Understood," Winters replied. "I'm on it. Thanks, Diane." Winters signed off and sighed, saved his latest version of the Java script, and began to download the file from Ben Dawson. It sounded like Dawson was at it again, and when that happened, Winters found he might as well set aside whatever else he was working on; his full attention was going to be required.

Daniel Winters, an up-and-coming thirty-something department lead, was one of the NSA's brightest young analysts in the realm of computer hacking, wiretapping, and just about every other form of high-tech surveillance. He lived for the chase as long as it led him through a maze of electronics. His boss, Deputy NSA Director Charles Jennings, had found when it came to this kind of work, there were few who were more skilled than Winters.

Understanding the urgency of Dawson's request, Winters peeled off the audio/video file of the T-72 tank and the ICBM and forwarded them on to his boss. Then he went to work on isolating and tracking the cell signal which corresponded in position to the PAASS device Dawson had attached to Bleckhaus' vehicle. When he had the signal of the cell, he initiated a search on all records the NSA had related to the specific signal to see what communications could be retrieved, and began a monitoring track on all conversations going forward.

As soon as he had it set up, he buzzed through to one of his lead analysts, Mickey Wahl. Wahl hit the "accept" button on his desktop and Winters could see Wahl's thin, unkempt-looking bearded face appear in one corner of his screen. "What's up, Boss?" Wahl asked.

Winters ran through a quick summary of what he needed Wahl to do, and jumped off the interoffice video conference again to refocus his efforts on the PAASS signal from the R&D building in Siberia. Again, he set up a monitoring track, this time engaging a translation and transcription routine to document events as they were captured, along with related time and date stamps.

Fifteen minutes later, Charles Jennings buzzed his administrative assistant, Gloria Treadway, and directed her to set up a meeting with Kenneth Brystol in two hours, then get his driver to pick him up in ten minutes to head to the Brystol Foundation. After reviewing Dawson's footage, he wanted to waste no time getting Brystol's personal assessment.

Before leaving, Jennings called Winters and said: "Daniel, I need you to pull out every face from the crowd in the compound on Dawson's video. I need whatever information we have on those personnel—both military and civilian, but especially the civilians. Put whoever you need on it; we have a new top priority."

"Understood, Sir," Winters replied. Just as he had suspected, another Ben Dawson adventure was about to unfold.

* * * *

At eleven a.m., Jennings' driver pulled up to the front gate at the Brystol Foundation outside of Arlington, not far off Highway 50. Minutes later, Diane Maretti ushered him into the office of Dr. Kenneth Brystol, where he was greeted warmly by his old friend. Brystol resembled a more sophisticated version of Christopher Lloyd's character from *Back to the Future*, with snowy hair and sparkling eyes, and the air of a showman in spite of his impeccable academic credentials. His friend Charles Jennings was more worldly and formal in appearance, fond of tweed jackets and bearing a striking resemblance to Donald Sutherland.

Settling into a comfortable leather chair, Jennings graciously declined Maretti's offer of tea and got down to business almost immediately. "I take it you reviewed Ben's communiqué?" he asked.

"Yes," Brystol replied. "It looks as though our friends at the Russian Ministry of Education and Science have been holding out on us."

Jennings frowned. "I don't think so," he said. "I think one of us—probably both of us—would have heard about it by now if this had come from the civilian sector. No, this has the earmarks of the old Soviet Military Industrial Commission—the Voenno-promyshlennaia komissiia; the VPK."

"I thought they had been disbanded along with the rest of the Soviet directorates," Brystol said. "I should have known better. A rose by any other name."

"Just so," Jennings replied. "And so now we find ourselves in a rather precarious position. As you can see from Ben's video, the Russians have made significant progress on this front. I take it they are well ahead of your people?"

Brystol sighed heavily. "I'm afraid you're right, Charles," Brystol replied. "It's disappointing. We do have a program running along these lines. Obviously, the Russians are well out in front. I'm really surprised they were able to get this far along without detection by either of us."

"Will Ben's intelligence help you?"

"Yes, it's helpful," Brystol responded, "but only in a parametric way. It holds clues as to how they have approached the problem, and how advanced they are. We can gage the approximate size of their device, and from the combination of its container dimensions and the minor electrical arcing, we can certainly tell they have followed the Kammler path—known as such because of its inventor, General Kammler of the Third Reich—rather than either of the known alternative approaches. Our own project is pursuing similar work. I often find it disquieting to reflect on how close the Nazis came to ultimate success. The technologies they were developing were a hundred years or more ahead of their time."

"It was a close thing," Jennings agreed. "Thank God they were stopped; this would be a very different world otherwise. Along with his technological leadership, General Kammler also killed roughly 20,000 slave workers while creating that complex the SS hacked out under the Hartz Mountains in Germany, where he oversaw production of V1 rockets. One day in March 1945, the guards hanged fifty-two people in one of the underground galleries, tying a dozen at a time to a beam, which was then pulled up by a crane. Those next in line were forced to watch."

"It's a grim story," Brystol agreed. "An incredible testament to the ability of some men to simultaneously reach the heights of intellect and the depths of moral depravity. During Kammler's work, various plants and animals were exposed to what he was doing. Rapid decay set in and people who helped conduct the experiments suffered from sleep problems, memory loss, and muscle spasms. Several terms were coined to describe the effects, including 'vortex compression' and 'magnetic fields separation.' I found it interesting that Ben's video shows three men evacuating the tank; I cannot imagine it was a healthy environment for them even *before* the device failed. And I noticed even those who moved the tank around only touched it with rods—never directly with their hands—while the gravitics device was engaged."

"I wondered about that as well," Jennings said.

"So we could try to identify the source of their seminal work, perhaps beginning with the 'Bell' device from Kammler's team. It was discovered along the border of Czechoslovakia immediately after the war. But given what we have just seen, I'm afraid even by overlaying our framework here at the Foundation, we won't be able to overtake them in time to render their initial deployment moot."

"Yes, that was my fear as well," Jennings said. "If the Russians build a deployable device first, it would certainly be destabilizing. It would move them from a distant third to first place in terms of force deployment. In addition, the ability to transport weapon systems so efficiently would leave everyone else at a distinct disadvantage. It sounds to me as though we are going to have to get John Deering, and perhaps the Pentagon involved here."

Brystol agreed. "Perhaps John can bring something new to light," he said. "I am often surprised by what the CIA knows … and sometimes just as surprised at what they *don't* know."

Jennings nodded. "I understand completely," he said. "I wonder whether the CIA *does* know about this. The Kammler Bell was removed by a special SS evacuation team just before the Russians arrived. More than sixty scientists working on the experiment were then ruthlessly killed to preserve the secrets associated with the project. The Bell was shipped out, but no records indicate where it went. Then Kammler dropped completely out of sight in mid-April of 1945. There has been a lot of speculation about whether the US recruited him for his scientific skills and provided him with anonymity in exchange for his service and cooperation. It would have happened during the days of the Office of Strategic Services, the predecessor to our current Central Intelligence Agency. Kammler is surely dead by now, no matter where he went. But if it's true, then someone at the CIA would almost certainly have some knowledge of it. Things like this are currently handled by the Agency in Gary Pellar's shop, I think. Of course, John doesn't know about every ongoing project at CIA, and there was a lot of activity back in OSS days that hasn't been fully revealed to the current CIA administration. But John has saved us from ignominy more than once. I'll give him a call this afternoon and see what he can do."

# CHAPTER 4

The trek back out of Mezhgorye on foot was slow, and complicated on the second day by a brief snowstorm as they approached the small tribal village from which they began their journey. Snow bursts were unusual so late in the spring but not unheard of. Their contact was Grigol Orlov, a local man whose family had been ousted from their home and eventually killed by Soviet soldiers when the secret military complex was being constructed. Orlov was only twelve years old at the time, and now—in his forties—his anger still burned fiercely. Over the years, he had been identified and recruited by the CIA. Agency contacts ensured he was provided with opportunities to make an adequate living, and funded his flight training. He transported businessmen and hunters around the Siberian forests, enabling him to travel unharassed around the countryside.

Orlov was a large, bearded and gregarious man who had never married. He was popular among local residents, in spite of the tribal nature of many of the Siberian communities. He was waiting for Dawson's team with hot cabbage soup, fresh bread, and hot water for bathing, all of which were a welcome relief. They ate and then got some rest.

The following night Orlov led them out onto a clearing high above his village, where a small plane awaited them. The aircraft was an old Chernov Che-25—an amphibious craft Dawson could see had been well maintained.

It was hangared in a small building at the end of a runway comprised of dirt in the summer and hard-packed snow the rest of the year. Orlov proved to be a skilled pilot, but he rarely stopped talking as he ferried them between three different lakes on their way to Ankara, Turkey.

Owing to their need to remain undetected, it took Dawson and his crew almost a week to arrive in Ankara, and from there regular commercial airlines were able to get them back into Dulles about twenty-four hours later. The sheer vastness of the expanse of Siberia was astonishing, especially to Romero, who had never been to Russia. All of the men agreed it was not a place they were eager to visit again.

*  *  *  *

At NSA headquarters, Winters and Wahl worked through the night after receiving Dawson's uploaded file and attached PAASS system alerts. The PAASS device remained in place on the glass of the window of the building of the R&D compound for nearly a month before it was washed away by a maintenance crew, yielding important information about project plans and personnel involved. When the information had been translated and transcribed, Jennings reviewed it and then decided to share it with John Deering to cross-check against any intelligence CIA might have related specifically to names, dates, and other critical elements contained in the transcription.

About an hour after sending the information to Langley via a secure network connection, Jennings' desk phone buzzed. It was Jennings' administrative assistant, Gloria Treadway.

"Yes, Gloria?" Jennings answered.

"Assistant Director Deering for you, Sir," Treadway replied. Then she put him through and disconnected.

"Good afternoon, John," Jennings said.

"Hello, Charles. I received your communiqué; I think it might be useful for us to chat, if you have time this evening."

"All right, I think I can make it work," Jennings said, popping his online calendar up in front of him. "Want to make it dinner at our usual place? I can have Gloria arrange for a table." Their "usual place" was the Taft Dining Room at the Washington University Club. They both liked the privacy, the atmosphere, and the cuisine. Best of all, the taxpayers covered the tab since it was a business meeting.

"Sounds good," Deering agreed. "Six o'clock?"

"Absolutely," Jennings replied. "I'll see you there."

In the meantime, Mickey Wahl had been following the trail of the PAASS signal attached by Dawson to Bleckhaus' vehicle. Using the signal boosting device affixed to the bumper via the second "paintball," Wahl was able to immediately identify and locate two cell signals; the cell phone belonging to Jürgen Bleckhaus, and another one belonging to his driver. The driver's cell signal was a real bonus. Bleckhaus had only recently decided to employ a full-time driver/ bodyguard after some activities surrounding the Angelia project in China had left him persona non grata for some months with the Chinese MSS. Having a bead on two cell signals provided some additional assurance that Winters' organization would be able to track Bleckhaus, even if Bleckhaus switched phones. VIPs rarely maintained the same level of discipline around the mobile phones of their staff members that they exercise with their own.

As a result, Wahl was able to capture some of the conversations directly from Bleckhaus' mobile for the next three days—at which time he switched phones. Then, tracking the signals in close proximity to the driver's mobile, he again identified the signal from Bleckhaus' new phone, basically defeating the defense mechanisms of switching SIM cards or phones. He could continue this pattern of surveillance with some occasional tweaking indefinitely until Bleckhaus' driver/bodyguard replaced his mobile phone. Even thereafter, if Wahl remained vigilant, he could do the same thing in reverse if the driver's phone changed at a time when Bleckhaus' did not. Finally, with the continuous locating of both phones, even if Bleckhaus' phone was exchanged for a new one and he was not in the same location as the driver/bodyguard, he might still be tracked. If Bleckhaus immediately began a conversation from his new phone at the same location where the old phone was discarded, Wahl had a good chance of identifying the new signal. To do that, he would use a voice and linguistic pattern recognition application the NSA had developed not long after 9/11.

Using this with the combination of numbers Bleckhaus called or was called from over the next several days, a number of patterns emerged which made Wahl confident he could find Bleckhaus again if he needed to. While these patterns faded over time, as Bleckhaus' contacts also changed communication devices, it was like watching fireworks disburse in the sky. Wahl could almost see the touchpoints from one pattern as they slowly disappeared and successors formed in their places.

These techniques and others enabled the NSA to build an interesting compendium of Bleckhaus' locations, contacts, and conversations. Even though Bleckhaus was careful to be brief and cryptic, repetitive phrases appeared, often referring to people and locations. The result presented its own macro level patterns, and Winters recognized their value immediately. He identified many of these patterns from the body of Wahl's aggregated work, and constantly amended and updated a profile on Bleckhaus with them. Based on what he was seeing, Winters felt certain someone would eventually decide to interdict Bleckhaus for one reason or another. When that time came, he knew the information they were gathering would be invaluable.

When Dawson landed at Dulles on Friday morning, he found a message waiting. His attendance was requested at a meeting—along with Brystol and Jennings—at CIA headquarters in Langley, Virginia. While waiting to go through customs, Dawson, Romero, and Winger were discussing the coming weekend.

Winger was looking at the messages on his phone and said: "Looks like Bi-shou has a new pistol she wants to try out. So I'm thinking tomorrow morning will be firing range time for me. How about you guys?"

Bi-shou, a former assassin of some renown, had received a presidential pardon for her activities as a result of working with Dawson's team on a recent adventure called the Angelia Project. A highly skilled marksman and political operative, she knew her way around the Washington, DC Beltway and still assisted with occasional personal security work and intelligence work as a freelance operative. But during her time working with Dawson's team on Angelia, she and Billy Winger had fallen in love. Neither of them ever said that—at least not in those terms—even to one another. But it was utterly obvious to those around them, and it suited Dawson just fine. He liked it a lot better when Bi-shou was on his side.

As it worked out, Dawson and Bi-shou earned each other's respect and trust only after Bi-shou had tried to kill Dawson, and landed in a US federal penitentiary. It was quite a story, and one result was that—although she tolerated Bi-shou—Lily Gerard was still not a fan. She suspected one day Bi-shou would revert to her former ways, and one of their team members would have their throat slit by the woman.

"Sounds like fun," Romero said. "I mostly have things to catch up on at home. Exotic stuff, you know, like laundry. How about you, Boss?"

"Oh, I imagine Lily will have something in mind," Dawson said, "but if not, I think I'll catch up on some personal research projects. Given our activity these last couple of weeks, at least I'm not feeling like I need to spend a lot of time at the gym."

"Roger that," Romero agreed. "My legs are still sore. That countryside was pretty unforgiving."

At the baggage claim, the men shook hands and parted ways for the weekend.

As was his custom, Dawson rented a car at the airport. Driving toward Langley, Dawson put a call through to Lily Gerard.

"Hi, stranger," Gerard said, delighted to know he had returned safely. "Are you on your way home?"

"Not quite yet," he replied. "I have to stop down at Langley. Shouldn't be too long, though. How have you been?"

"Bored," Gerard replied.

"How did the tournament go?" he asked.

"Pretty much like all of them these days," she replied. "You win some and you lose some, I guess."

"Ah, I see," Dawson smiled. "You won again, didn't you?"

"There's just not much competition at my weight these days," she said. "You know, Ben, if you would just feed me better ..."

"Lily, taking you to better restaurants so you can fight at a higher weight class is really not a great idea, and besides, you know it wouldn't work anyway. You'd just beat bigger people."

Lily Gerard was an accomplished martial arts figure in the greater Washington, DC area, and rarely lost a match. A fiery redhead, Gerard was equal parts beautiful and lethal. Now forty-six, she still regularly bested almost everyone local in her weight range, a pattern stemming from her days at the Boston Police Department.

"You say the nicest things," she retorted. "So when will I see you?"

"I'll text you when I'm headed home. I'm guessing it will be around four."

"Sounds good," she said. "I have light duty here today, so I'll get there ahead of time and cook for you tonight."

"Great idea," Dawson said. "I'll make sure I get out of town early this evening."

*　*　*　*

About ninety minutes later, Dawson was granted access at the gate in front of CIA headquarters, and drove to the appropriate parking area. Eight minutes after that he was escorted into a small conference room adjacent to the office of Deputy Director John Deering. Brystol and Jennings were already there, and after a brief session of small talk, the men got down to business. Deering asked Dawson to recount the events of his excursion for them, and he took about thirty minutes to do so, with occasional interruptions for clarification by either Jennings or Deering. Brystol indicated he would wait to ask questions of a more technical nature on the following Monday, when Dawson reported for work at the Foundation. Most of the questions Deering and Jennings posed were related to security, observations of personnel, the logistics of the mission, and Dawson's impressions of the maturity of the technology he saw.

After an hour or so, Brystol withdrew for the day to return to the Foundation where he had other meetings to attend. Dawson remained behind at Deering's request. They were joined by a stocky man in his early fifties with close-cropped salt-and-pepper hair and a gravelly voice. He had bright blue eyes and an expressionless face. *This guy would be a great poker player,* Dawson thought.

"Ben, this is Gary Pellar," Deering said as the men shook hands. "Gary's department handles several rather unique research projects for us, mostly around technologies that haven't born fruit but look especially promising. It's a long gestation period for most things, but Gary is a patient man."

"Sounds interesting," Dawson replied.

"It's not very glamorous," Pellar replied stoically, "but we've managed to make a contribution here and there."

"First of all, Ben, I want to thank you again for an excellent job," Deering said. "Getting those PAASS units in place, especially the unit on Bleckhaus' vehicle, was truly outstanding work. Please pass along my personal thanks to your compatriots as well."

"I will, Sir, thank you," Dawson replied.

"In fact, Ben," Jennings picked up the thread of conversation from Deering, "the information we have obtained as a result has illuminated some very dark corners for us. One of the things we discovered is a possible way to get this technology away from the Russians, or at least to catch up with them."

"Oh?" Dawson said with genuine surprise. "How is that, Sir?"

"One of the people you picked up on video out there at the R&D facility is a deep cover asset of ours," Deering said. "He fell off the grid almost two years ago, and we've been worried about him; he is among their top researchers, and was feeding us extremely valuable intel. We thought perhaps he had been blown, but now we see what happened." At this point, Dawson detected a slight stiffening in Pellar—just microexpressions and a barely detectable straightening of the spine. He wondered momentarily whether Pellar had been responsible in some way for the loss of contact with their asset.

Deering pulled a photograph out of his breast pocket and placed it in front of Dawson on the conference table. It was a little grainy and taken from a great distance—undoubtedly through the surveillance array Winger had set up in the trees above the R&D compound just outside of Mezhgorye.

"Gary," Deering nodded to Pellar, "please educate Ben and Charles about Dr. Antonov."

"Yes, Sir," Pellar replied evenly. Then, turning to Dawson, he said: "His name is Sergei Antonov. Antonov was born in 1956 in Vladikavkaz—then known as Ordzhonikidze. He grew up in Semipalatinsk, in the Soviet Kazakhstan. He later worked at the Institute of Physics of the USSR Academy of Sciences, and at the Physics Institute in Vladivostok. Even though the Soviet Union operated a large number of research facilities on a worldwide scale, the authorities decided Antonov was not eligible for any overseas assignments, either because of the critical nature of his research, or because his grandfather had been a prisoner of war during WWII, or because of Antonov's 'foreign connection;' his sister had married an Indian citizen and immigrated to India, then later to Canada. Antonov's field work, therefore, was restricted to Russia's domestic facilities, and as you can see from the placement of the Mezhgorye facility, they are taking no chances with him. A few years ago, one of my operatives was able to recruit Antonov after he came to resent the Russian government even more. Two of his team's most promising projects were canceled, one after the other."

"How did you lose track of him?" Dawson asked.

"He attended a physics conference in Moscow about eighteen months ago," Pellar replied, "and never returned home. It seems his sister, who is his only close living relative, was told by government officials he was doing important research, and would be out of touch indefinitely. Because she was given no more information than that, we had no opportunity to pursue him since then. We only became aware of the Mezhgorye facility a couple of months ago, and yours was the first mission to the site."

"I see," Dawson replied. Then he turned back to Deering. "And so now you are thinking if you can get Antonov away from them, he would defect to the US and go to work for us at the Foundation?"

"That is the broad strokes of what we are thinking, yes," Deering said.

Dawson exhaled slowly, thinking back over the travails of exiting the mountains of Siberia.

"How confident are you he would even want to leave?" Dawson asked.

Deering and Pellar looked at each other, and then Deering said: "About seventy percent, Ben. I wish the odds were higher, but I'm not going to lie to you about it. Gary had just returned from a multi-year assignment in Islamabad when Antonov was being recruited. He was barely in his new role here, and we weren't as skillful with the process as we should have been." Pellar looked uncomfortable, but said nothing.

"John," Jennings asked, "do you think we would be able to get the Russians to bring Antonov back from Mezhgorye to Moscow or Kiev, or somewhere else where it would be easier for us to work?"

"Not to interrupt, Sir," Dawson interjected, "but I'm pretty sure the answer is 'No.' This guy is their lead technician—I could see that from the way he was coordinating the efforts of the rest of the team on the ground. With the technology close to completion, they won't let this guy go flying off to some conference. Besides, as you could see, the top guy in their chain of command, Vadim Shelepin, came out there to see his work. They didn't bring Antonov or the work to him. I don't think Antonov is going anywhere anytime soon."

Deering's eyes were sparkling. "You know, Ben, I'd make it worth your while if you ever decided to come to work for me here at the Agency. We need those analytical skills of yours every bit as much as Charles needs your field work."

Again, Dawson thought he detected a microexpression in Pellar's face reflecting disdain, but it vanished immediately. Dawson chalked it up to professional jealousy.

Jennings wasn't happy to hear Deering openly recruiting his top operative, either. "You know very well, John, Ben's combination of tradecraft, scientific acumen, and analytical skills make him uniquely valuable to *all* of us. Boxing him up in an office would just diminish his value."

"Yes, I suppose you're right, Charles," Deering replied resignedly, but turned to Dawson again and said: "Just remember, Ben, when you get tired of field work, you have other options."

"Thank you, Sir. I'm sure the time will come; I'm not getting any younger."

"Now," Jennings huffed, "to get back to the point. If we can't get Antonov transported out of the middle of Siberia by the Russians, how do we get him? It is, after all, the middle of Siberia!"

"Do you have assets other than Grigol Orlov on the ground in that neck of the woods—no pun intended?" Dawson asked.

"We would need to bring most of a team in from elsewhere," Deering responded without revealing any more detail than necessary.

"I know you're aware of this, Sir," Dawson said, "but this is literally in the middle of nowhere. No large airports, no shipping lanes, no public or private transportation the way we think of transportation. There is barely a road to the compound. It took three of us over a week to slip out of there, just getting as far as Turkey, and no one was after us. An assisted escape—which might turn into an unassisted abduction—from Mezhgorye without starting an armed conflict will be very tough. And a kinetic exchange of any size would trigger enormous repercussions. How are you thinking of going about it?"

Deering leaned forward, removing the "cheater" spectacles from the bridge of his nose and placing them next to him on the table. Placing his elbows on the table and frowning across at Dawson, he said: "I haven't the vaguest idea, Ben. I was hoping you could help me with that."

# CHAPTER 5

The Turkey Run Shooting Range in Fairfax, Virginia was still sparsely populated at seven thirty a.m. on Saturday morning. Bi-shou had arrived at seven, just as the range was opening, and so she was already in position and firing when Winger arrived. As he donned his hearing protection and goggles on the other side of the bullet-resistant polymer doors, Winger stared through the door at the serene face of Bi-shou as she fired off round after round from her Beretta 71 .22 caliber semi-automatic pistol. Bi-shou was extraordinarily attractive, even in a t-shirt and jeans, and Winger enjoyed just watching her move.

Most of the other shooters who frequented Turkey Run used larger calibers ranging from .38s to .44 magnums. The most common caliber fired was the 9mm, and many shooters regarded the .22 as a starter weapon, something to train amateurs with. None of the people around her realized Bi-shou was a skilled assassin. At not yet forty years of age, she had already taken the lives of dozens of people—more than half of them with .22 caliber firearms.

Bi-shou was fully capable with a wide variety of weapons, including her own body. In fact, she had essentially saved Ben Dawson's life less than two years earlier using a 9mm pistol under less than ideal conditions. But she had learned early on that "stopping power" was not the primary concern of an assassin. She needed a weapon that was easy to conceal, sufficiently deadly when properly aimed, readily sound-suppressed, and utterly reliable. The Beretta Model 71, Bi-shou's personal weapon of choice, loaded with .22 Long Rifle ammunition, has virtually no recoil and can be easily controlled in rapid fire. It is easy to disassemble and maintain, and designed to be carried with the hammer on safe, fully cocked, and ready to fire. Weighing only seventeen ounces empty, the weapon was an ideal choice for a slender woman's hand, and even though Bi-shou had ample physical strength, she just loved the way it gripped.

Bi-shou noticed Winger as he opened the door, and gracefully finished off her magazine before engaging her safety and turning to smile at him. As he approached, she left her weapon on the table and leapt into his arms.

"Miss me?" Winger grinned.

"Yes, I did," she purred, "and I have a surprise for you!" Disengaging herself, she turned and retrieved a small Pelican case from the floor beside her and held it out to him. "Happy birthday," she said.

"All right, who told you?" Winger asked, incredulous that she would know such detail.

"Does it matter?" she asked coquettishly. "I have my sources, you know."

Winger sighed, knowing it was hopeless. He balanced the small case on his left forearm, and carefully opened it with his right hand. "Whoa!" he said. "What's this?"

"This, Mr. Winger, is the M45A1 Close Quarters Battle Pistol—CQBP— more commonly known as the Colt Marine Pistol."

"Very nice," Winger smiled even more broadly, then shifted the case a bit on his arm. "It's heavy," he remarked. "I bet that helps with recoil."

"Yes, it is," she replied. "Forty-two and one half ounces, to be exact; it looks to me as though most of the added weight is around the slide. Extremely rugged, and uses any kind of .45 ACP ammunition. Flat desert tan so it won't reflect much light, and given your propensity for field work, it just seemed like it fit you. It has a black polymer finger pad, cocking serrations on both sides, beveled ejection port, and I got you the Novak LoMount sights complete with Trijicon's tritium highlights. But the best feature is the Colt National Match barrel. The way you use a weapon, this seems like the perfect extension of yourself. I suppose that sounds odd in English but it is the best way I can think of to phrase what I mean."

"I've heard of this weapon," Winger said, "but I haven't seen it in the field yet. Not even on marines."

"Not many marines have them," Bi-shou said. "They have only been issued to MARSOC, the Marine Special Operations Command, a small unit who work directly for the Department of Defense and theatre commanders.

"Yes, I know MARSOC. And you got this one for me how?" Winger asked.

"Never look at the teeth of a freely given horse," she responded.

It took just a moment for Winger to register what he had just heard, but then realized "gift horse" was likely a term with which Bi-shou was more technically than linguistically familiar.

"Well, it's amazing, sweetheart; thank you," he replied. "This is, I think, the best birthday gift I ever got. It's a beauty."

"So give it a try," Bi-shou said, stepping back and motioning toward her bench position. She strode over with him and inserted a new target, then pressed the button to return it to the far end of the lane.

Winger injected the magazine, which Bi-shou had already loaded for him, and chambered the first round. Then Bi-shou stepped back, and watched as Winger fired off the first several rounds. She could see the muscles flex along his forearm and in his shoulder. The weapon did indeed have significant recoil. But she knew Winger wouldn't mind. He was very strong, and the weapon had combat-level stopping power which was important in Winger's line of work. He was primarily a field agent, not an assassin. If he needed to do that, it would most likely be done with a sniper rifle.

Winger reeled the target back in, and examined it with Bi-shou. The grouping was tight, but consistently a half-inch to the right. Bi-shou handed him a small flat-bladed screwdriver and he made the appropriate adjustment. Then they replaced the target, and Winger repeated the process. The second target showed the same tight grouping, but this time the shots were all in the center of the black bullseye.

"Perfect," Winger smiled, and Bi-shou beamed up at him. He ensured the rear sight was tight in its adjusted position, and returned the weapon to its Pelican case. "When you said you had a new pistol you wanted to try out, I thought you meant a new pistol for yourself. I didn't realize you were bringing one for *me*."

"It is your birthday," she replied. "Everyone should have something to unwrap on his birthday."

"I do love the way you think," he replied. "What shall we do with the rest of our day?"

"I have a few things in mind," she said. They packed up Bi-shou's remaining gear and headed back through the office on the way to their vehicles. "I'll meet you at your place," Bi-shou called out, and a minute later they drove away.

Across the street, a man in running clothes and a navy blue hoodie with "U2" emblazoned across the chest leaned against the post of a traffic signal and sipped from a Starbucks cup, watching Winger and Bi-shou. As they walked through the parking lot, the observer surreptitiously snapped several photos of them with a small Nikon, and of their vehicles as they drove away. When they were both out of sight, he drained the last of his coffee and tossed the empty cup into the back of a random pickup truck parked on the street as he walked back to his own car.

The man was in his mid-fifties, wore a couple of days' worth of beard, and stood an even six feet tall. Patrick Burke, a former member of the Provincial Irish Republican Army—PIRA—had been living and working in Canada for over a decade, and operating as an independent contractor doing the odd surveillance and assassination job when one came his way. On this occasion, he was ostensibly on a fishing trip in upstate New York. He had been contacted for this assignment by an intermediary who was anonymously representing the Chinese Ministry of State Security—MSS. His job was to identify and gather intelligence about the woman Bi-shou, and about anyone with whom she associated over the next thirty days.

Unknown to Burke or his intermediary, the MSS was looking for a way to learn about NSA work on Internet security. They had received information from their own mole in the NSA that the agency was working to gain access to the Internet's domain naming system—DNS. The Chinese MSS had been working hard on it for almost a decade. Teng-hui had directed his chief of operations, Hu Li, to see whether Bi-shou could be convinced to help. Bi-shou's relationship with Ben Dawson and his team could prove to be a tremendous advantage—if the MSS could recruit her again—and if Bi-shou's previously amoral, anything-for-money internal compass still held sway.

After he returned to his room at the Doubletree, Burke uploaded the images from his Nikon into his laptop, popped open his photo editing software, and put together a brief report, including the photos. He logged in to an encrypted network and deposited the file in an electronic drop box, then logged off again.

Burke's contact, an intermediary named Bertha Lyman, worked during the day shift at the US Library of Congress—LOC. She had no trouble handling her regular job duties along with her entrepreneurial endeavors related to passing along specific information between prescribed parties. In most cases, she didn't know who the parties even were, and didn't care. In this case, she had only an inkling of the customer's identity, but she did know Patrick Burke by reputation and work history. In fact, she had recommended him.

Lyman had been doing this work since the early 1980s, and she'd kept track of the agents engaged in past assignments by contact information and by category of work performed. So when a potential customer had approached her via encrypted email for this engagement, she passed along a name and the customer evidently did their own background check from there. Four days later, she had received the authorization to place Burke under contract along with the background file to pass along to him. She was the "cut-out" in criminal parlance, essentially insulating the customer from the agent, and she was paid well for performing the task.

The only daughter of a low-level New York mafia member who had died under what the NYPD termed "suspicious circumstances" in 1989, Lyman found herself an educated and divorced woman with a decent job at the LOC, and no remaining interest in men or raising a family. She had fallen into her line of work naturally enough, utilizing contacts from her teenage years—when she was still attractive and curious—among the associates of her father. Her degree in Library Science from Queens College, her work at LOC, and her rather colorful list of family friends all equipped her with the skills and background for her current work. She already had enough money to retire comfortably, she reasoned, but she enjoyed her life and especially the intermediary work. It was exciting to know that in some small but critical way, she was enabling hidden events which changed things on a much grander scale than she even knew. It was intriguing, and just dangerous enough to be exhilarating.

Lyman suspected the MSS was her customer, based on the phrasing of the request and its similarity to other requests that occasionally came through for surveillance targets which later appeared in the news. However, she was always careful not to express any overt interest in the identity of the customer or the target, and ignored any requests by the parties involved for information. It always had the potential to reveal her identity or the identity of her customer.

Lyman's customer for this engagement was, in fact, Lee Teng-hui, the MSS Station Chief for Washington, DC. Teng-hui had used Bi-shou on many occasions for delicate work, especially in North America, including a number of assassinations. Since then, however, Bi-shou had refused all MSS related engagement offers, following a deal struck with Ben Dawson that included a presidential pardon.

After those events, Bi-shou had accepted only assignments she considered unrelated to the interests of the United States, and did not involve killing US citizens on US soil. As a result, she became essentially unavailable to Teng-hui, and in so doing, denied him access to his most valuable independent agent. In addition, a rumor had recently surfaced related to events surrounding an explosion and fire at a secret MSS facility in Shanghai the previous year, indicating Bi-shou might have been involved.

Normally Teng-hui would have given no credence to such rumors. But, although it was impossible to tell with certainty about the timing, it might have been just possible Bi-shou's release from prison coincided with those events. If Bi-shou had, in fact, been involved, it was of no particular concern to Teng-hui. He was not on good terms with his superiors at the Ministry, and secretly wished them ill fortune anyway as long as it did not reflect upon him. Still, it was a card he would like to hold; such information, if true, could prove to be an effective tool in convincing Bi-shou to accept engagements for him again. He knew blackmail was a device Bi-shou understood very well. But Teng-hui had decided to tread carefully. Bi-shou had killed three separate teams of assassins sent for her on previous occasions; she was not someone to be trifled with.

When Teng-hui received the information from Burke, he reviewed it and then called in his chief of operations; a young and ambitious new arrival from Beijing called Hu Li. He explained to Li that he needed to identify the individual with Bi-shou, and any information he could discreetly turn up about residences, contact numbers, etc. for them both. By noon on the same day, Teng-hui had a report in his hands listing the identity of Billy Winger, his current address, and the address listed for the license plates on Bi-shou's vehicle.

Just after one p.m., David Winters received a call on his cell from Mickey Wahl.

"Hey, Boss, I hate to bother you on a Saturday …" Wahl began.

"No problem, Mickey. All you're interrupting is laundry. What's up?" Winters responded.

"You remember the list of information we have flagged for Dawson's team? Plate numbers, phone numbers, credit cards, and so on?"

Winters, who had been about to step into the elevator of his apartment building with a basket of laundry, stopped and let the elevator go. "Yeah, I remember. What about it?" he asked.

"Well, somebody just ran a trace on the plates for a vehicle owned by Billy Winger and another leased by Bi-shou. Then there were credit check inquiries run on both of them within thirty minutes. I think something's going on." Winters stood fixed in position for a minute, thinking. Finally Wahl said, "You still there, Boss?"

"Yeah, Mickey. Still here; just thinking. Track the inquiries back as far as you can. It'll take me an hour or two to get finished up here and I'll drive in. Sounds like things are about to heat up."

"OK. Sorry to bother you, but I just thought you'd want to know," Wahl replied.

"You did exactly right, Mickey. I *did* want to know, and I appreciate it. See you soon." Winters ended the call and pushed the elevator button again. Then he changed his mind and decided his laundry could wait. He turned and started back for his apartment.

By the time he arrived at NSA headquarters in Fort Meade, Wahl had already assembled an impressive pattern and had it displayed on a wall-size smart board. On the left of the display about midway up was a circle named Bleckhaus. Immediately below was another smaller circle named Krauss Driver. There was a line extending between Bleckhaus and Krauss. Inside each of the circles was a telephone number—in Bleckhaus' case, there was a series of three numbers— each of which included an area code. Winters surmised each additional telephone number in the Bleckhaus circle indicated he had changed phones. Thus far Bleckhaus' driver, Krauss, had not. At least one call from two of the three phone numbers used by Bleckhaus had gone to the same number in Germany, and Wahl had the number highlighted in red. That number, represented by another circle closer to the bottom of the monitor, read "Shelepin_FSS."

"This is interesting," Winters said, pointing to the Shelepin node.

"Yeah, I thought so, too," Wahl replied. "I have Hal working on it now."

"Hal" was Wahl's euphemistic name for an algorithmic set of artificial intelligence programs he had bundled together to trace the contacts between telephone numbers of interest and identify patterns. It was some kind of homage to the artificial intelligence depicted in Stanley Kubrick's *2001: A Space Odyssey.*

"In the meantime, though, I have been tracking this." With a couple of mouse clicks, the screen repainted itself with a similar image, this time starting with a circle reading "Lyman." That circle was connected to two other circles; one was the personal telephone number designated: "Lyman_PC_ Peterson_VA_DMV," which Winters understood as belonging to a personal contact of someone named Peterson who was associated with the State of Virginia Department of Motor Vehicles. Winters understood this was likely the contact that was providing the residential addresses and other critical information requested as a part of "running the license plates" from the vehicles of Winger and Bi-shou. The other circle looked as though it was another personal number. That number was listed as "Lyman_PC_2_Experian." This one, Winters knew, must be someone at the credit rating agency who was being paid or coerced in some way by the individual shown as Lyman to provide personal information such as financial statuses.

"Who is this Lyman person?" Winters asked Wahl. "Looks like they have a pretty extensive network. A private detective?"

"Nope," Wahl replied. "An employee at the Library of Congress, oddly enough. Her name is Bertha Lyman. Age fifty-nine, five feet five inches tall, one hundred forty-five pounds, brown hair, brown eyes, divorced in 1989, and no children. No criminal record. Originally from New York City—the Bronx, specifically. Her father was Benny Lyman, a small-time gangster, and her mother, Jane Armstrong, was a nurse at a local walk-in clinic. Father was killed in 1985 in the parking lot of a night club—either a bizarre accident or a hit-and-run. She has lived down here for almost twenty years, but still makes a lot of calls between here and the New York City area. She also makes and receives calls from a lot of other places. Some are international. Because she is at the LOC so much, I have a feeling a lot of them emanate from there as well, but I have no idea—yet, anyway, what her extension is over there. I'll work on that as soon as I can; since it's a US government line, it should be pretty straightforward to get into those records. But I'm reasonably sure these two calls," he pointed to the two circles to which her circle was connected on the monitor, "were the ones that initiated the background checks from the license plates and credit bureaus on Winger and Bi-shou. I'm not absolutely certain, but they were both initiated as a result of the same query. I'm pretty sure it was an uploaded encrypted file ..." Wahl continued, scrolling down through a list of calls on his computer, "... right here."

"How'd you get that?" Winters asked. "I thought you were just looking at phone traffic."

"Daniel, you gotta be kidding," Wahl replied, looking hurt. "You know I never do anything one-dimensionally. As soon as I have an identity I start looking for associated email and social media links, and backtrace as far as I can. Well, actually Hal does it. Anyway, looking purely at timing, this is just too close to be coincidental. The likelihood the file transfer was causal here is well over eighty-five percent."

Winters could see it looked as though it was an encrypted attachment. It had been run through an electronic drop box and uploaded by Lyman within eight minutes of the first call she placed looking for a background check on the license plates.

"Can you tell who sent the file, or get a look at the contents?" Winters asked, but he already knew the answer.

"You bet," Wahl grinned, "just as soon as we have a court order."

"Yeah, I'm not sure why I even asked. Wishful thinking, I suppose," Winters said. "We don't have anything here that justifies a warrant. Now, we *could* go after Lyman's two contacts—the ones who ran the background checks without any official reason. Of course," he continued to think out loud, "it would get them fired, and maybe even some kind of small-time 'illegal use of government property' rap, but it wouldn't get us any closer to who was running the trace or why."

Winters came back from his reverie to see Wahl shaking his head. "Small fish anyway, Boss," Wahl continued grinning. "I haven't shown you the most interesting part yet."

"Holding out on me, Mickey?" Winters asked. "You know annual raises don't come out for months. What've you got?"

"I looked at the numbers called by Lyman within thirty minutes of completing the background check inquiries," Wahl replied, "and the longest call, followed immediately by an outgoing data transfer, was to a number I didn't even have to look up. We know this series of numbers very well indeed."

Winters looked at the line Wahl was referring to and released a long, low whistle.

"Yup," Wahl said, leaning back in his chair, "our old friends at the Chinese embassy—almost certainly the MSS."

"I wonder whether she knew who she was speaking with on the other end of this call," Winters wondered aloud.

"I doubt it, based on the calling pattern," Wahl responded, "but I can't really tell from what we have here."

"I'd better let the boss know," Winters said, referring to Charles Jennings. "He's gonna want to alert Ben Dawson right away. Looks like Teng-hui is at it again."

# CHAPTER 6

As he walked from his condo to the car, Dawson pulled his cell phone out and thumbed a number. In his address book, the name listed was Tom Bradley - office. The name was fictitious, but a lot of calls occurred between Dawson's phone and that number. On the other end of the line, the phone rang once and then was disconnected. About thirty seconds later, Dawson's phone buzzed and he hit "Accept." The voice on the other end of the line was mellow and cultured. "Benjamin," Charles Jennings said, "I'm glad you called. Daniel has been discovering some interesting activities, and it would be good to bring you 'up to speed,' as he puts it. Can you swing by, or would you prefer to meet somewhere more convenient?"

"If you don't mind, I'd like to meet at our usual place," Dawson replied. "I need to get back out to the Foundation right now to check on my day job. Could we meet near the end of the work day—say, five or so?"

"I think so," Jennings said. "Give me a moment." About thirty seconds later he came back on the line. "Yes, that would be fine," he said. "Please plan for a couple of hours, though; there is a great deal to cover."

"Understood," Dawson said. He drove to the Foundation, checked in with Diane Maretti, and then headed for his own office to catch up on the small mountain of paperwork and email accumulating since he had last been in his office, nearly a month before.

After a few hours he had most of it squared away, and he began to scan satellite images of the area surrounding the Russian R&D facility near Mezhgorye. His satellite images were classified captures from US spy satellites, and so there were no screens imposed on the commercial images available to the general public. As a result, he was able to pick out the small landing strip from which Grigol Orlov operated his aircraft.

However, even when Dawson knew what to look for and where, he had a difficult time finding it. Scanning the area surrounding Mezhgorye, Dawson searched for other similar clearings that might represent paths of ingress or egress. He finally realized even in good weather the spots he could see were either so small as to make parachuting in—something he never looked forward to in any case—too dangerous, or too close to the city, making them likely to be observed. The closest commercial airport seemed to be the one located at Beloretsk. It would require significant time to reach even by road, and roads were few in that area of Siberia; they would be easy to monitor.

Dawson took a break, and met Gerard for lunch at a local restaurant called Sweetwater. Time with Gerard was always a pleasant distraction. Dawson thought it might help him recharge mentally, and cause him to look at the problem from a different angle. But when he returned to his office, no new perspectives presented themselves.

The problem seemed intractable. There were several surface roads in the area as well as one highway, but all of them could be closely monitored except for trails through the forests and mountains, like the ones Dawson, Winger, and Romero had traversed in the previous weeks. Once Antonov was discovered to be missing, a manhunt of incredible proportions would be launched. It was unlikely anyone could get through the net the Russians would cast. Only two possibilities presented themselves to Dawson, and he hated them both just about equally. Nonetheless, he sketched them both out along with the pros and cons, timing and cost.

Finally, as he was finishing up, something else occurred to him. *I wonder where the K-MAX II project is by now,* he thought. He made a call to an old friend at the Pentagon, arranged for a quick meeting, and headed out the door.

\* \* \* \*

At Fort Meade, Winters and Wahl were continuing to work the surveillance issues. While Hal was running additional analyses, they poured over the final intercept that came through from the PAASS unit attached to the office window at the Mezhgorye R&D compound. The conversation was between Bleckhaus and Shelepin, and it had occurred on the night Dawson and Winger observed the demonstration—just before Bleckhaus left the compound.

The transcript, after translation, read:

Bleckhaus: "Director, this is better than I had imagined. You have come very far since we last spoke about this."

Shelepin: "Yes, we have more than enough now to make the technology attractive. It is time to move ahead with our operation, I think. If we do not act soon, it will be too late—the technology will have passed the last significant hurdles, and the opportunity for exclusive ownership will be lost."

Bleckhaus: "How long do you think we have?"

Shelepin: "I would say thirty days; forty-five at the longest. No more than that."

Bleckhaus: (garbled) "... so soon. I will have to move much faster than I thought. I have three parties who will want to bid on this, when they have seen the video, I am sure. Is there any reason to suspect anyone else knows about what is going on here?"

Shelepin: "I have told you before, Herr Bleckhaus; I have this under control. No one finds out what is going on here without coming through me, including my own government. No one who has been assigned to my unit has ever left—alive, in any case. This is another reason why we need to move quickly."

Bleckhaus: "I understand, Director, I will leave immediately and get the bidding under way. I will let you know where we stand as soon as I have initial offers."

Shelepin: "Very well. As I said before, I will not accept less than five million euros."

Bleckhaus: "With this video from tonight's demonstration, Director, I do not think it will be a problem. But as I explained, economic times—especially in one of the countries which has expressed an interest—have been challenging of late. We shall see what the market bares."

When Winters brought the transcript to his boss, Jennings was reaching for his coat; he had been about to depart for his meeting with Dawson at their "usual place," which was the Rock Quarry Tavern in Silver Spring. However, when he saw the transcript he literally sat down again at his desk. "Oh my," was all Jennings could say at first. He read the transcript three times. "Are we certain about this transcription?" Jennings asked Winters.

"Yes, Sir," Winters replied. "I can try to get the garbled words cleaned up, but the length of the words and voice inflections make it pretty obvious he was saying something like 'I had no idea it would be so soon.' Anyway, I will get it for you if we can clean it up any more, but I can't imagine it will change the context of what we are seeing here."

"No," Jennings agreed. "I can't either. This is very interesting, Daniel. Thank you for bringing it to me immediately. Is there more?"

"We have subsequent comms between Bleckhaus and Shelepin after this event, Sir, and they are in work now. But this is the last one we have between them from the stationary PAASS unit."

"Very well," Jennings said, standing again to retrieve his coat and head to the garage. "Please bring me anything like this as soon as you have it—day or night."

"Yes, Sir; I will," Winters replied.

★  ★  ★  ★

The Rock Quarry Tavern in Silver Spring was rarely crowded in the early evening, especially on a week night. That, and its nearly equidistant location between the Foundation and Jennings' route home from Fort Meade, had made it a logical meeting place for Jennings and Dawson over the years. In this instance, owing partly to the delay just before Jennings left his office, Dawson had arrived first. By the time Jennings was seated, Dawson was half-way through his first iced tea, and had a glass of Bordeaux waiting for his former boss. Jennings exhaled and smiled at Dawson in appreciation.

"How are you, Charles?" Dawson said as Jennings sipped his wine. "You seem a bit unsettled."

Jennings smiled again as he replaced his glass on the table, and glanced around one more time to assure their privacy. "I am well, Benjamin. Thank you for asking," he replied. "I have some news. Things are moving along quite rapidly. But first, how are you progressing with the matter John laid out the other day?"

Dawson frowned heavily. "Not well," he replied. "I have two ideas, and they are both terrible. I wouldn't bet money on either of them."

"Really," Jennings asked. "What are they?"

"Well," Dawson replied, lowering his voice even further, "the first is a scorched-earth approach, where we essentially level the place, making it impossible to tell Antonov is missing. Of course, that kills a lot of people—most of whom, I'm guessing, don't deserve killing. The second approach is to build a blind someplace close to the compound—probably underground. Then get him out of the compound on foot and into the blind, and wait until the tumult subsides. Eventually, we walk him out to Orlov's aircraft or some similar means of transport. Lots of downsides there. It will take us a while to get in and construct the blind unobserved. We'll have to make sure not even the guard dogs they have deployed around the compound can unearth the place, and we'll need to stock it like a doomsday bunker. Frankly, I just don't like going underground; that blast from the RPG when I dived into the karez over in Afghanistan a couple of years back left me with an aversion to holes in the ground. Spending a week or so inside of one doesn't sound like much fun to me."

Jennings pursed his lips and nodded in agreement. "There are a few airstrips and roads around the area," he said.

"Yes," Dawson answered, "but those will be under intense scrutiny, and the closest commercial airport is in Beloretsk, which is hundreds of miles away by automobile. It's just ugly. I did finally have another brainstorm, and I am running a trapline on it now. It might help us get back out of the woods over there, but it's too soon to know. I'll keep working it, Charles, but right now—as I said—it's looking pretty ugly."

"Benjamin, I agree with your assessment," Jennings said, "and it makes my news especially well timed, I think. The reason I was a bit late arriving this evening is, just before I left my office, Daniel came in and handed me this." He retrieved the paper copy of the transcribed conversation between Bleckhaus and Shelepin, and passed it across the table to Dawson, facedown.

Dawson picked up the paper and read it slowly twice. When he finished, he passed it back across the table again, also facedown, and Jennings returned it to his pocket.

"Two things surprise me," Dawson said. "First of all, I'm surprised you have that on paper. Dangerous thing to do, as you know."

"Yes, I wouldn't have printed it, of course, but Daniel delivered it to me in this form and I was basically walking out the door," Jennings said. "Don't worry; it will go immediately into the fire from here. What's the second thing?" As he was speaking, Jennings' smartphone began to buzz. Jennings retrieved it, but didn't look at the display until Dawson responded.

"The second thing that surprises me is these guys are going to try to sell the technical data without the inventor. As long as Antonov is still alive, the data is noncurrent at best, because his work will continue. The information will grow staler with each passing day, diminishing its value in a very tangible way, unless Antonov dies."

"Interesting point," Jennings responded. Then he looked down at the readout, saw it was an encrypted message from Winters, and said, "Pardon me for a moment." He hit a couple more buttons with his thumb and read for a minute, then put the device away.

"It seems you're not the only person thinking along those lines, Benjamin," Jennings said, taking another sip of his Bordeaux. Dawson waited while he slowly swallowed, and then smiled. "Apparently, in a call between these same two parties about," he glanced at his watch and frowned, "six hours ago, our German friend told our Russian friend he has a high bid of three million euros for the technical data alone. But an inquiry has been made about whether the inventor could be included as part of the bargain, in which case the customer would be willing to double their offer."

"So someone is willing to pay six million euros for Antonov along with the data?" Dawson asked.

"Exactly," Jennings replied.

Dawson sat quietly and thought for a minute. Then he said, "Charles, I need to go up to Fort Meade and sit down with Winters and his team. I have an idea."

"Ah, I do like the sound of that," Jennings said, smiling again. "I'll ensure he makes himself available. But before you leave, I have asked someone to meet us here in …" he looked at his watch again, "… about ten minutes. I'd like to introduce you."

"Oh?" Dawson said.

"Yes, this is an operator out of John Deering's organization named Rick Potter. His team of field operatives in Eastern Europe infiltrates and monitors various organizations over there. I think he may be able to help us. Anyway, he is someone John wants you to know, in case you need help in his AO—area of operations."

"Sounds good," Dawson said. "I could use some help."

"There is one other thing," Jennings said. "Daniel's team has discovered our old friend Teng-hui has been running a loose surveillance on Winger and Bi-shou. We have no idea yet what specific motives are at this point, and there is no indication yet of a termination order or anything similar. But it's not a good sign, and I wanted you to know."

"Thanks, Charles—I appreciate it," Dawson replied. "I'll alert Billy and Bi-shou, but by the time I do they will probably have discovered it on their own. These two are both experienced operators, and their tradecraft is pretty good."

He and Jennings continued to discuss other matters while Jennings sent along a message to Winters asking him to remain in the office until Dawson arrived. About fifteen minutes went by before John Deering entered the tavern, accompanied by a tall, lean man with dark features. The tall man went immediately to the bar and ordered two beers while Deering walked over to the table where Jennings and Dawson were seated. After introductions, Deering explained why he thought Dawson and Potter should meet.

"I've asked Rick to provide any assistance he can to you for this mission," Deering said. "Interagency cooperation at the field level is sometimes challenging, as we all know, but I try to make sure that's not a factor where my team is concerned. Still, owing to your current status as a civilian, Ben, I just want to make sure you know how to avail yourself of Agency help in the target area if you should need it. Our resources there are limited, but we do have a few assets on the ground."

"Thank you, Sir," Dawson replied. He noticed Potter, even while joining them and shaking hands with him and Jennings, had kept a watchful eye on the door and the few other patrons at the bar. *Good SA—situational awareness—* Dawson thought. *I think I'm gonna like this guy.*

Deering said, "Rick, why don't you explain your mission parameters to Ben, here."

"Yes, Sir," Potter replied. Then he turned to Dawson and adopted a quieter tone. "Sir, I have a team embedded with various groups who oppose the Russian government all over that part of the continent. Most of them are in the northern caucuses, areas like Ukraine, the Republic of Adygea, Karachay-Cherkessia, Kabardino-Balkaria, North Ossetia-Alania, Ingushetia, Chechnya, and the Republic of Dagestan. A few of the groups we have infiltrated are pure terrorists or terrorist wannabes. They do things like bomb civilian targets in major Russian cities. But most are just run-of-the mill thugs. As I'm sure you realize, the Agency has other assets inside the Russian government, and whenever we can do so without exposing our own people, we pass along intelligence that could save the lives of innocent Russians through those assets. But usually it's just not possible."

Potter paused to take a drink of his beer, glancing around the room again, and then returned to his narrative. "Our AO in Russia's Northern Caucasus, is turning into one of the most volatile, lawless regions in the world. These days, it's a breeding ground for international terrorist activity in spite of decades of Russian military operations against them. Over the last thirty-six months or so, as Russia has continued to lose control of the region, it has become a significant base for Islamist terrorists and organized crime. Our agency is worried it may ignite an even broader terrorist campaign inside Russia and beyond."

"ISIS?" Dawson asked.

"Yes, and we expect more of them soon," Potter replied. "We are doing our best to get into these groups and figure out where the worst of it will be happening and when, so we can stay out in front of it. At some point we may be able to shape it enough to render it benign, but it's doubtful. What we can do, though, is gather intel related to any likely moves against US or allied interests. Anyway, the bottom line is these guys despise the Russian government. So if there is any way you can make use of them, or of our contacts in the region, I'm willing to try. My boss here says what you're working on is top priority, so I'll do whatever I can."

"Thank you, Rick. I appreciate it," Dawson replied. "It would be good to have friendlies in the area if we have to go back in there. Tell me, do you have any assets further south and west, say in the Urals and central Siberia?"

"I have a small contingent there, Sir; not much, I'm afraid." Potter replied.

"I understand," Dawson said. "So, how can I get in touch with you, Rick?"

Potter slid a business card across the table to Dawson. It simply had his name, telephone number, and email address. No company name, no job title, no logos. This guy was all business. Dawson liked him better all the time.

"Thank you," Dawson said. "It's going to take me a day or two to sort out next steps here, but as soon as I do, I'll be in contact. I really appreciate your offer, Rick, and the introduction, Sir," Dawson said, turning briefly to look at Deering. Returning his gaze to Potter, he said: "I recognize the value of these assets, and I won't take your offer lightly."

"Thank you, Sir. That's excellent. We'll do what we can," Potter replied. The meeting broke up, as everyone drained their glasses, and Dawson headed for the door to make his way out to Fort Meade.

# CHAPTER 7

It was after eight p.m. when Dawson finally got into the office at Fort Meade. Finding Winters and Wahl both hunched over computers in Wahl's lab area, he plopped down a box of hot pizza and a six pack of cold Diet Coke, then dropped into a nearby chair.

"If you gentlemen can take turns chewing and talking, I'd be very interested to review your progress," Dawson said.

Winters and Wahl were already descending on the pizza. With the click of a few buttons, Wahl started the transcripts of recent intercepts slowly scrolling up the screen of the large monitor where they could all see them. Dawson read while Winters and Wahl consumed their dinner. The transcripts were in chronological order and each speaker was noted at the beginning of their respective sentences, which made things pretty self-explanatory. When the transcripts had scrolled through and Winters and Wahl had each consumed several pieces of pizza, Wahl popped the network diagrams he had been building up on the monitor in their place.

"So, here's what we have," Winters said, looking first at the network containing Bertha Lyman. "As you can see, the transcripts here indicate a Canadian independent operative named Burke was hired through an intermediary named Bertha Lyman to perform surveillance on Bi-shou, and the customer is almost certainly Teng-hui or one of his guys at MSS. That's the first thing."

"Nothing indicates the purpose of the surveillance?" Dawson asked.

"No, Sir," Winters replied. "We'd need a warrant to look at the actual content of emails and any recorded conversations of a US citizen like Ms. Lyman, and we don't have one. However, we have no such restrictions around MSS personnel or around Canadian citizens. So we can still piece a lot of this together. Before too long, we should be able to present what we have to the FISA Court and get to Lyman's records as well."

"And nothing we have so far is indicative of actions planned for going forward?" Dawson asked.

"No, Sir, nothing we have seen," Wahl replied, since Winters had a mouthful of pizza.

"OK, I've got it," Dawson replied. "Where are we on the other problem?"

"Ah," Winters replied, "now that is more interesting!" Again, he changed the network diagram on the large monitor and started pointing. "It looks to me as though the bids are coming in from North Korea, Iran, and Pakistan."

"Nothing from the MSS?" Dawson asked, incredulous.

"Nope. It doesn't appear, based on what I have seen here, that China was even contacted with an offer. We could have missed it, but I don't think so," Winters replied.

"Well, it is possible—after the loss of the Angelia technology recently—the MSS has decided to stay away from these things for a while," Dawson opined. "More likely, though, Professor Bleckhaus has decided it might be prudent to stay away from the MSS, at least for now. Interesting." He thought about it for a moment, and then said: "Oh, that's really *very* interesting!"

Winters and Wahl just looked at each other, Wahl still chewing on pizza. Finally, Winters said: "You think you can use that?"

"I sure hope so," Dawson replied, "but it depends entirely on you guys."

Wahl finished the last of his pizza, wiped his hands on a napkin, and was all business again. "What do you need, Sir?" he asked.

"Here is what I'm thinking, guys. But it cannot leave this room, with the exception of Deputy Director Jennings. Do either of you have any problem with that?"

"No, Sir," they both replied simultaneously.

"OK then. Here's what I think we need to do. I want to set Bi-shou up as a representative of the MSS. She's going to reach out to the intermediary

Teng-hui is using ..." he glanced up at the network diagram and then turned back to Winters and Wahl, "... Bertha Lyman, right?"

"Right," Wahl replied.

"So Bi-shou will send a communiqué to Lyman using whatever Teng-hui's normal method is, but she'll tell her—for purposes of this matter only—she is to shift to a new communication channel with a different phone number, contact protocol, IP address, etc. And she will instruct Lyman to contact Bleckhaus, and tell him MSS has found out about the offer he has out to various other entities, and MSS is not pleased to have been omitted from the bidding. She will strongly suggest to Bleckhaus that he reconsider. Bi-shou can pull this off, I believe, because of her long association with Teng-hui and the MSS. When Bleckhaus opens up the bidding to MSS by responding, which I have great confidence he will do, we'll have Bi-shou outbid the others significantly, but insist Antonov be delivered, along with the technical data for the technology, completely unharmed. Following me so far?"

Winters and Wahl both nodded in the affirmative.

"OK," Dawson continued, "now here's the tricky part. And I need you guys to really think hard about this because I gotta believe what I am about to suggest is completely illegal. When Bi-shou wins the bid, they are going to want her to transfer funds electronically to some bank account. Could be Switzerland, but more likely the Caymans or some similar monetary refuge. So I need to be able to transfer funds—or else make it look like I'm transferring funds—into whatever that account is, get the deal done and Antonov to safety, and then recover those funds electronically. In fact, if there are additional funds in the account, I'd like to transfer them out as well."

The room was quiet, with only the soft whoosh of the air handling unit filling the audible void. This time it was primarily Winters and Wahl that were thinking. It remained quiet for almost a minute before Winters finally broke the silence.

"So, Ben, I realize we're speaking hypothetically here because we're dealing with international banking laws, and I know you would never ask us to do anything illegal ..."

"Exactly. Purely hypothetical," Dawson said, following Winters' lead.

"Because even if I were to agree to something like this, I'm Mickey's boss and they could lock me up and throw away the key, and Mickey as well. I would never agree to put Mickey at risk, even if I was to put *myself* out there that way."

"I understand," Dawson replied. Wahl remained silent, his eyes wide.

"So let's just say—hypothetically—someone wanted to do this. Here is how I think it might be done." Winters, Dawson, and Wahl leaned in and lowered their voices even though there was no one else in the room. Over an hour later, Dawson had the framework of a plan. The risk level, especially for Winters, was off the charts. But as he had just casually pointed out, he had a lot of personal leave time coming and a lot of frequent flyer miles banked. Winters was thinking about taking some time off anyway. If he sold back some of his vacation time, then took an official leave of absence, he would not really be an active employee of the US government for a while. The legality of the plan was very weak but it was the best he could come up with on the spur of the moment. If he was caught, it should protect Wahl, at least.

"Sounds just about perfect," Dawson replied.

"Just about?" Winters said. "What did I miss?"

"We've just talked about potential repercussions from official authorities and from the Russians," Dawson replied. "But there is someone else who will likely become involved here. The danger is far greater than I think you realize."

# CHAPTER 8

Just after one p.m., Burke was waiting in a commercial parking garage almost directly across the street from Bi-shou's condo building when she and Winger returned from lunch. He was parked on the third level of the six-story structure, and because it was a Saturday, there were only a few other cars, even on that level. As he watched the main entrance to the condo through a pair of Nikon Aculon binoculars, Winger dropped Bi-shou at the curb and then went on to park his pickup around the corner. Owing to the time of day, the sun was high overhead, which left Burke in deep shadow just a couple of feet back from the edge of the waist-high wall surrounding each floor of the parking garage. However, as he was tracking Bi-shou with his binoculars, he inadvertently allowed the front lenses of the device to slip out from the shadows. It was only for a couple of seconds, but the strong overhead sunlight glinted off the glass of the lenses just as Bi-shou looked back at Winger. Catching the double glint, she immediately recognized the source was almost certainly binoculars rather than a rifle scope. She decided to let Winger move off into traffic rather than keep him in a position where he would be vulnerable to sniper fire from the opposite side of the vehicle, through the driver's side window. But as soon as she cleared the truck, Bi-shou moved immediately behind the large metal post in front of her building, leaning casually against it—out of any direct line of sight from the position where she had seen the glint—and putting her mobile phone to her ear. Winger was just pulling into a spot on the street around the corner when his cell buzzed.

Winger saw it was Bi-shou's number. "Did you leave something in the truck?" he asked, glancing around the cabin as he spoke.

"I think we have a tail," Bi-shou replied. "Third floor of the parking garage across the street from my condo. I am pretty sure I caught a reflection from binoculars when I got out of the truck, so I ducked behind a big metal post here on the street where you left me."

"Got it," Winger replied. "I haven't parked yet. I'll swing out again and drive around to enter the back of the garage. Give me a couple of minutes— I'll let you know when I'm there." Circling the block and the one across from Bi-shou's building, Winger pulled into the parking garage from the opposite side and cruised the first and second floors looking for something out of place. Seeing nothing on those floors, he parked the truck on the second level and mounted the stairs on the backside of the structure quietly, slowing near the top. He sent a quick text to Bi-shou indicating he was in the garage and nearly in position, then put the phone on silent and removed his weapon from its holster.

Slipping around the corner, Winger edged out just far enough to get a look around the corner of the pillar at the edge of the stairway. Because there were only a few cars on that level, Burke's silhouette was clear on the opposite side of the floor. He had edged back just a bit, so the front edge of the binoculars no longer reflected sunlight downward, but from Winger's perspective he was starkly outlined against the sunny exterior. Winger withdrew, redialed Bi-shou, and said quietly: "He appears to be alone and has no exposed weapon. Just watching you. Give me one minute to get in closer to him, then come on across the street."

Bi-shou did as instructed. As soon as she turned toward the curb to head across the street to the parking structure, Burke began to retreat from his position and return to his vehicle. However, by then Winger had moved carefully and silently up behind him. When Burke turned fully, he found Winger standing right in front of him, weapon raised, pointed right at the center of his chest.

"Ease the binoculars to the ground and put your hands behind your head," Winger growled.

Burke did as he was told, saying: "No law against bird watching, mate."

"I'm not a cop," Winger replied. "Just stand easy for a minute."

Bi-shou appeared a minute later and immediately frisked the man. She found a Glock 9mm pistol in his belt and some cash, but no ID. There were rental car keys though, and they matched a late model Ford; one of the three cars parked on their level. In the console of the car, Bi-shou found a wallet and passport identifying the man as Patrick Burke. Burke had a Toronto street address and nothing seemed out of the ordinary. Based on the passport, it looked as though he had entered the United States a half dozen times in the last eighteen months and rarely stayed longer than two weeks.

"Today is your lucky day, Mr. Burke," Winger finally told him. "We're going to hang on to your weapon for you. It will help you to stay out of trouble since I see nothing in your wallet indicating you are permitted to carry a concealed weapon in the United States. It would appear 'bird watching' is a more dangerous hobby than I realized. Anyway, here's the punch line. I'm not going to bother asking you why you're spying on us, or who paid you; we can find the answers to those questions without exerting ourselves to get them out of you directly. So I'm just going to say this: you're walking away alive and uninjured today with just a warning. It won't happen a second time. If you would like to remain healthy, you need to leave both of us alone."

"I've been threatened before," Burke replied impassively. "And yet, here I am."

"Ah," Winger replied, detecting the distinctive though subtle remnants of Burke's speech pattern. "Irish. Former PIRA, I'm guessing. Well, Mr. Burke, that's not a threat. I'm just telling you what's going to happen. Frankly, I don't care one way or another. My friend here, who I am guessing is the 'bird' you were actually sent to 'watch,' would likely have already killed you if I wasn't here. So the choice is entirely yours."

Winger holstered his weapon and walked with Bi-shou back to the stairwell and down to the second level. They climbed back into Winger's truck, drove out to the street, and parked it again.

When they got up to Bi-shou's condo, Winger thumbed open his cell and punched in Dawson's number.

Winger told Dawson what had just transpired, and Dawson asked Winger to put him on speaker so he could speak to both Winger and Bi-shou. Winger punched the speaker button and laid the phone on a coffee table between himself and Bi-shou.

"Bi-shou," Dawson said, "our people here in the office have been tracking communications that popped up related to both you and Billy. The name of this guy you just discovered came to my attention last night. But it didn't sound as though there is a contract out, just a surveillance order. I was going to alert you both about it today anyway, but I'm not surprised you already discovered the guy. Looks like he's working alone, and while I can't be absolutely certain yet, our guys think there's a high probability it's your old friend Tenghui at the source. He's using a cut-out, though, so it's taking us a while to piece it together."

"We had a talk with him," Bi-shou replied. "I do not think he took us seriously, though. Many people make that mistake." Bi-shou was seated in a lotus position on her sofa, perfectly erect, a serene smile on her face. She looked as though she might be discussing something as innocuous as the weather.

"I think he might be former Provincial IRA, Boss," Winger added. "They don't scare easy, and this guy sure fits the bill. Anyway, we just took his weapon and let him go. I even allowed him to keep his field glasses."

"I'll ask Lily and Chief to see whether he remains an annoyance," Dawson said. "I have some other work I need your help with, if you're available, Bi-shou."

"Oh?" Bi-shou responded. "All right. When do you want to talk about it? I have plans for the birthday boy today, but anytime starting tomorrow …"

"Oh!" Dawson exclaimed. "That's right! Happy birthday, Billy! It had completely escaped me that today is the day. Let's see—are you looking into assisted living yet?"

"Very funny, Boss," Winger retorted. "As I recall, you're only a year behind me."

"All too true," Dawson laughed.

"I would say Billy is very well preserved for his advanced age," Bi-shou smiled.

"There are some things I think I'm just going to take your word for, Bi-shou," Dawson said with a chuckle. "But back to your question. I think Monday morning is soon enough. Can you and Romero swing by my office at the Foundation—something like 0900?"

"Sure, Boss," Winger replied.

"Hey, Boss, I assume Lily knows about this? I mean technically, I do work for her these days and ..."

"Yes, you're absolutely right, Billy," Dawson interrupted, "and no, she doesn't know yet but she will before I see you on Monday."

"Fair enough," Winger replied.

After a few more pleasantries, they ended the call.

\* \* \* \*

Even though it was a Saturday, Winters and Wahl started work about eight a.m. By noon, they had managed to clone the communications channel and incorporate an electronic "trap"—a bypass that rerouted communications between the numbers Bertha Lyman and Teng-hui had been using to contact one another. Winters printed out examples of some of the historical messaging to understand typical syntax and sentence structures used by both Teng-hui and Lyman. By three thirty in the afternoon, Winters felt they were ready to go and made the system operational.

As soon as he stood up the new system, Winters sent a message to Dawson saying the communications package he'd ordered had been built and was installed. He placed the note in the drafts folder of Dawson's Gmail account. Then he sent a text message to Dawson which simply said: "Check your mail."

Within twenty minutes, Dawson had read the note from Winters and arranged to meet Winters and Bi-shou at a small coffee house on the edge of Old Town Alexandria the following afternoon.

\* \* \* \*

The late May afternoon was warm but there was a strong breeze out of the southeast. Dawson parked a couple of blocks from the coffee house—easy to do on a Sunday—and made his way down the sidewalk in no particular hurry, drinking in the sunshine on his skin as it spilled around his dark sunglasses. Dressed in a windbreaker and jeans, he smiled at passers-by and glanced in the windows of the shops, pausing occasionally to check his six—the area behind him—as he strolled.

He had picked up simple elements of what the intelligence community referred to as tradecraft over the years from his colleagues and friends on hundreds of missions. At this point in his life, Dawson understood he would never be as skilled as a professional, full-time field operative. On the other hand, full-time field operatives had no opportunity to explore the wide array of leading-edge technologies and high-tech investigative techniques that were a big part of his working life. Dawson counted himself fortunate to be able to move between those worlds, associating with some of the best in both communities and learning from all of them.

One of the tools he had acquired in his field work over the years was an instinctive recognition of patterns and outliers. In a crowd of people, Dawson was especially good at identifying the person who didn't belong there, and represented a potential threat. He recognized anomalies and anomalous behavior. The human resource technicians at the National Security Agency had described it in more technical terms. However, Dawson always thought of it as a kind of figure vs. field perspective, and when he discovered the advantages it offered, he began to hone it. Supervisors and colleagues sometimes referred to the skill as "instinct," and Dawson supposed there was an innate aspect of it. But he knew it got better with practice, and so he concluded it was as much skill as talent. Over more than two decades, it had served him well. He found this capacity for pattern recognition was beneficial in a myriad of diverse ways, from scouring financial transactions for commonalities and trends, to spotting a surveillance "tail" among the pedestrians on a crowded street. Today was one of those days.

As he approached the coffee shop where he was to meet with Bi-shou and Winters, Dawson saw Bi-shou approaching from the opposite direction. Dressed in casual weekend attire, Bi-shou was still strikingly beautiful. Watching her move evoked the lyrics of a hit song from 1961 called "Poetry in Motion." Several male pedestrians cast admiring glances her way as she strolled down the sidewalk, and there was nothing unusual about that. But Dawson noticed that one head remained nearly fixed, and as he watched, the man appeared to be focused exclusively on Bi-shou. He was careful about it, but there it was. Dawson turned toward the glass shop window on his left and punched in Gerard's number.

"Hi, handsome," Gerard answered, "I thought you were on your way to a meeting."

"I'm nearly there. Just spotted Bi-shou heading this way, and she has a tail. We're headed into the Grape + Bean coffee house on Royal. I'm pretty sure it's Burke; evidently Billy and Bi-shou didn't quite get through to him. Can you take care of it?"

"Sure thing," Gerard replied. "I'll be down there in twenty minutes or so. I expect your meeting will take longer than that."

"Yes, I think so. An hour at least. You're welcome to join us if you'd like."

"Thanks, but I'll pass," Gerard said. "I have some other errands to run. I'll just catch up with you at dinner."

Dawson smiled and shrugged. Gerard simply didn't trust Bi-shou, even now after Bi-shou had saved Dawson's life, and he didn't know whether it would ever change. The fact that Bi-shou was so attractive probably wasn't helping the situation, either. *It just is what it is,* he thought. *She'll have to get over it—or not—in her own way.* "OK, sweetheart. See you around six then," he said, and signed off. With that, Dawson turned back toward the coffee shop and followed Bi-shou inside.

# CHAPTER 9

Dawson found Bi-shou waiting in line at the counter and fell in alongside her. Although Bi-shou didn't know Winters, Dawson spotted him already seated at a small table in one corner of the shop engrossed in something on his iPad.

When they had each ordered and received their drinks, Dawson led Bi-shou over to Winters' table and introduced them. Winters did his best to be professional but he was clearly in awe of the former MSS assassin. He was overly polite and deferential. He cleared his throat frequently and seemed nervous throughout the conversation. All of this made both Dawson and Bi-shou smile. Accustomed to the fawning attention of men in general, Bi-shou handled it with practiced grace.

"It looks like the MSS usually contacts Bertha Lyman through Teng-hui's chief of operations, Hu Li," Winters explained. "The contact is made via encrypted email and the email is disguised as junk mail. It's really pretty cool. The MSS has developed a piece of junk email that looks like an offer from a credit card company. The message is accompanied by a trigger that is included as the initial credit card number. The numerical sequence of the credit card number refers to a cipher key embedded in a website for the credit card company. At the receiving end, the reader clicks on the site, types the account number into the appropriate field to 'activate the card,' and an algorithm is downloaded to the client—the reader's computer. The cipher code is unique to that message. The algorithm is downloaded to the reader's computer and immediately erased from the hosting website. It works on the reader's own computer, identifies the words embedded in the email in the appropriate sequence, and forms the words of the message in the proper order for the reader."

Winters paused to take another sip of his drink, and Dawson said: "Interesting approach. It sounds like a 'SAAS—Software As A Service' concept; don't bring the data to the software, take the software to the data. Are there other peculiarities surrounding the communications?"

"Funny you'd ask," Winters beamed. "There is one other element strengthening the security here. It's timing. The cipher code is only available once, and then only for three minutes. If the reader doesn't enter the code on the website within the three-minute window, the key is lost forever. The reader presumably has to notify the sender, saying they failed to get the message. It doesn't make a lot of sense but I haven't come across an occurrence of that yet, so I'm not sure how it's done."

"And how are the communications handled going the other direction?" Bi-shou asked.

"Excellent question!" Winters effused. "Actually, because the algorithm generating these theoretically random cipher codes is housed at an independent website, the communications process can be bisynchronous."

"So," Bi-shou continued, "the response is sent back disguised in the form of a junk email as well?"

"Exactly!" Winters responded. "One of the markers that makes this anomalous enough to identify is …"

"Is the fact it is theoretically a spam message but it's only sent to one recipient," Dawson interrupted.

"Right," Winters replied, just a shade disappointed because Dawson had seen it so quickly. "When the message is read, the live algorithm produces a window asking whether there is a reply. If there is, the reader types a reply in; it's embedded in a spam message along with a cipher key number and sent back. If not, the original message and the cipher key are automatically erased."

Bi-shou thought about this, and asked: "And what enables the first message to be produced?"

"The website, I'm surmising," Dawson replied.

"Right again," Winters said. "You really ought to be in my department, Ben."

"Nonsense," Dawson smiled back at him. "I learned this stuff by watching you, Daniel. I'm just trying to keep up."

This apparently made Winters feel better, and he carried on: "Anyway, the person wanting to send the first message logs on to the website, and 'applies' for a 'credit card.' A temporary password is provided, cross-checked to make sure the IP address matches one in the database of prior users, and the algorithm is downloaded to the originator. How the IP address gets into the database initially is something we're still working on. In fact, I'm working on 'another line of inquiry,' as my boss would say, and I think it will likely shed some light on it." He paused and glanced around, then continued in a lower tone: "It's related to the Internet Corporation for Assigned Names and Numbers—ICANN—the organization that manages the Internet's domain name system, or DNS. This is the Internet's version of a telephone directory—a series of registers linking web addresses to a series of numbers, called IP addresses. Those guys literally have the keys to the Internet."

"I see," Bi-shou replied. "But the question is, can you inject a communication which looks as though it is coming from Hu Li to Bertha, and intercept the responses without MSS becoming aware of these events?"

"Exactly," Winters said. "And the answer is yes. Ben actually came up with the idea initially. He said something about directing Bertha to communicate with a different recipient on all matters related to this activity, and I think it will help us minimize the risk of discovery. Once we start up the new website emulating the old website, the rest should be a piece of cake. Reverse engineering the algorithm is the hard work, and we're almost there. We are building another website with an almost identical set of processes and simply naming it for a different credit card. The junk mail, sign-in process, and so on will work exactly the same way. So from a 'look-and-feel' perspective, Bertha should be very comfortable. That's where my work on the ICANN thing has proven especially useful."

"When can we be rolling on this?" Dawson asked.

"I think it will be ready to go sometime tomorrow afternoon," Winters replied. "The communications window opens at four fifty-seven p.m., and closes at five p.m. Eastern time every second day. But of course I need to know exactly what you want the messages to say, and we'll have to time their delivery in the same manner as the old communications, so it appears to be a continuation of the old pattern rather than a departure from it."

Dawson's phone buzzed and he paused to read a message from Gerard. He smiled, typed in a brief reply, and returned the phone to his pocket.

Over the following ninety minutes, Dawson, Winters, and Bi-shou worked out the details. On Tuesday during the prescribed time window, Lyman would receive a message from the account of Hu Li embedded within the junk email typically used by the MSS for that purpose. The message would include a cryptic warning saying China would be very disappointed if they were not permitted to bid on the new technology about to be brokered to potential competitors. It would also direct Lyman to respond—on this matter only—to the new website address. It was risky, but Winters was confident the continuity of the "look-and-feel," would overcome any potential suspicions about the source of the email, and Dawson reasoned the "carrot-and-stick" combination of the fake MSS warning and offer to raise the stakes of the bidding would carry the day.

*   *   *   *

Across the street, Lily Gerard arrived to find Patrick Burke seated on a bench at a bus stop and watching the door of the coffee shop where Dawson's team was meeting. She drove past the location and parked her car down the block, unnoticed by Burke. Gerard fed the meter for a thirty-minute period, deposited her purse inside the trunk, and dropped her car keys into the front pocket of her jeans. Watching the pedestrians, she strolled slowly up the sidewalk on Burke's side of the street, approaching behind him and remaining largely out of sight concealed by signage and traffic signal poles.

When she saw a lull in pedestrian traffic, Gerard finally closed the remaining distance. She swung around the end of the bench, and just as Burke noticed a figure coming up on his left, she connected with the right side of his face delivering a vicious, open-handed slap. The force of the blow was jarring and the shock registered in the man's eyes as he sprang to his feet, a picture of confusion and anger. Seeing his assailant was an unknown and attractive woman, apparently alone, only exacerbated both feelings.

"What the …" Burke began.

"Shut up!" Gerard interrupted. "Evidently you paid no heed to the warning you got yesterday. You're still tailing my friends. This is your second warning and you only get two of them. If any of us see you again, you're going to jail or going someplace far less pleasant."

"What are ye thinking, lass?" he finally got out. "I have a mind to knock your pretty head off."

"Exactly how thickheaded are you?" Gerard demanded, getting up in his face. "You do understand English, right? You're familiar with the terms 'jail' and 'less pleasant?'"

Then Burke made his first mistake. He was about to tell Gerard to shove off, and intended to emphasize his words with a physical shove to her shoulder. But when his palm reached the spot where Gerard's shoulder had been, there was only air. He had less than a second to recognize that fact because the missing shoulder had left him off-balance slightly, in a forward lean. Gerard had capitalized on the kinetic motion. She pivoted, turned, and grasped his extended wrist. Burke continued forward over Gerard's body, and crashed heavily to the curb. Gerard wheeled and brought the startled man's wrist up behind him, flipping him to a facedown position with her knee in the small of his back.

Burke, a trained fighter and a bit of a bully, was suffering a substantial blow to his ego by then. He was several inches taller than Gerard, and fifty pounds heavier. "All right," he groaned, anger rising in him like a crimson tide, "I'm having enough of this from you."

He lunged hard to one side. Sheer physical mass caused a gap to open between the two bodies, pushing Gerard's knee aside enough to gain Burke his freedom. Both Burke and Gerard sprang to their feet, and Burke made his second mistake. With his right shoulder still aching from his initial trip to the pavement, Burke launched a hard jab, aiming for Gerard's face with his left hand. This time Gerard spun like a blurring top, kicking Burke's legs out from beneath him and sending him careening backward. As she came erect out of her spin, she slammed the heel of her right hand upward into Burke's chin, which was already tilted upward as he succumbed to the force of gravity pulling him backward. In the end, the back of Burke's skull made unfortunate contact with the front edge of the composite bus bench on his way to the pavement. He was unconscious before he hit the concrete for the second time.

The entire encounter had only taken less than two minutes, but a few onlookers had seen the events and paused on the opposite side of the street. They continued to watch as Gerard got her arms up under Burke's and lifted him back into a seated position on the bench. The back of his head was bleeding a little, but it didn't look serious. Gerard ignored the onlookers and walked back to her car. She drove away, circled the block, and parked around the opposite corner where she could watch what transpired. While she was waiting for Burke to regain consciousness, she sent a text message to Dawson which read: "Target is still in position but out of commission for the time being. He will likely be pissed when he wakes up, but I think he's got the message now. XO"

About ten minutes went by and Burke awakened. Evidently the curious pedestrians across the street had shrugged the matter off and continued on their way, because no police cars rolled up and no one walked over to assist Burke. Lolling on the bench, Burke looked to other passers-by as though he might simply be intoxicated and passed out on the bench, slouched and leaning to one side.

When he came to life again, Gerard could see him wince and feel the back of his head. He sat there for a couple of minutes, regaining his bearings, and then walked a half block in her general direction. He stopped about thirty yards away and got into a rental car. Falling heavily onto the seat, he finally got a key in the ignition and pointed the car toward the street. In another minute he was gone.

Gerard had noted the make, model, and license plate number from the rental he was driving. She followed him, giving him a wide berth, preferring to err on the side of losing him rather than alerting him that he was now under surveillance himself.

Burke seemed to pay no attention at all to whether he might be followed, probably owing to the pain and humiliation he had just suffered, and drove directly back to his hotel. It was a Marriott about seven miles from the place of the altercation, and Burke went directly to his room.

After noting where he was staying, Gerard broke off her surveillance and returned to her condo. She had just enough time to get ready for her dinner date with Dawson.

Back in his room, Burke applied a cold, wet compress to the back of his head and leaned back in the easy chair. When he felt reasonably normal again, he headed downstairs to the bar. He figured it was going to take at least two Jamesons to get this all straight in his mind. *Bested by a girl,* he thought. *Definitely not my best day.*

# CHAPTER 10

As promised, Winger and Romero appeared in Dawson's office at the Foundation. Dawson brought the two men up to speed on the general outline of the overall plan, without saying more than necessary in case one or both of them was captured and subjected to interrogation. Then he went through the plans for their next assignment.

"If you fly back in the same way we came out last time, it will probably arouse the least suspicion," Dawson said. "I know it will take longer, but under the circumstances …"

"Is Orlov still flyin' around up there?" Winger asked.

"Yes," Dawson replied. "I checked with Deering's office. Deering was out on PTO, but one of his top staffers, Gary Pellar, approved it; we can still use him. He'll pick you guys up in Ankara."

"The high points, then," Winger summarized, "are these: We meet Potter in Turkey, arrange another excursion out through the woods and into Mezhgorye, this time taking Potter's crew in with us. While you're getting Antonov and the technology away from the Russians, we're destroying the technical specs, documentation, and equipment so their program is set back. Then we turn the compound over to Potter's team and get outa Dodge. Is that about it?"

"That's about it," Dawson agreed.

"Seems straightforward enough," Winger said.

"What do you think, Chief?" Dawson asked Romero.

Romero ran his hand through his crew cut. "Well, the job is clear enough, Boss," he said respectfully, "but there's a world of difference between simple and easy."

Dawson smiled. Romero was a man of few words, but one of the things Dawson liked most about him was that he didn't waste any of them.

"True enough," Dawson replied. "I know a guy who often says 'everything's easy if you know how.' I finally told him, 'I know how to dig ditches, but it's still backbreaking work.' I think he's stopped saying that now. But what's got you worried about this one?"

Romero sat back a bit, forming up his thoughts, and said: "Off the top of my head, Sir, here are three things. First of all, we only have Potter's word for the availability, willingness, and capability of his people over there on the ground. Second, this is going to require more equipment, which means more visibility. And finally, now there are more people in the loop. We've had some real problems with mission security in the past, once things were known by other agencies. It seems to me we now have NSA, CIA, and some covert ops team of Eastern European rebels involved so far. That's a very long string to pull, and the longer the string, the more likely it is the vibrations along that string will get noticed."

Romero was right. Twice before, once with the Salacia technology, and again with a project known as Angelia, enemy operatives within US intelligence agencies had brought about near-disastrous consequences, costing American lives. The set of risks here was higher still; there were more moving parts, and their dependency on unknown operators reduced the odds of success dramatically.

"I can't argue with your assessment, Chief," Dawson said. "It's spot on. So let's talk about risk mitigation. What can we do to improve your odds of getting back here in one piece?"

Over the next ninety minutes, the three men covered travel contingencies, evasion and escape planning, and communications. Dawson provided a photo of Potter, asking both men to memorize the face. They also covered ordnance requirements and intellectual property acquisition, reviewing what types of equipment should be confiscated, which types should be photographed, which types should be tested, and so on. Finally, Dawson explained a refresher list of these elements would be sent to them via email as soon as they texted or emailed him the appropriate code, indicating they were in position and prepared to execute the acquisition processes. They agreed Winger and Romero would be airborne and headed for Ankara in about three days.

All in all, the meeting took most of the morning; when the men shook hands and went their separate ways, it was just before noon. Dawson decided to swing by Brystol's office just to tell him things were in motion—Brystol never wanted to know too much detail—before departing for Fort Meade.

When Dawson dropped in on Brystol, he could see the scientist was mentally involved in something serious. He had only seen Brystol personally engaged in research a few times in the years they had known one another. But each time Brystol had worn the same expression. It was as though the man had mentally closed all of his doors and windows, and the only remaining connection to the outside world was focused exclusively on the problem before him. Brystol had no idea he had even entered the room, and so Dawson simply retreated quietly back out again. As he did so, though, he noticed Brystol was gazing at the ancient blackboard he wheeled in from his closet occasionally. On the blackboard were several equations and phrases Dawson had not seen before, such as "Gravitons = $<10^{-33}$ electronvolts." There were several of these, and at first glance, they appeared to be grouped around topics like "Hadamard condition," "photon emission," and "high-energy y-rays." Even though Dawson was no stranger to quantum physics, and had made minor contributions of his own to research projects on occasion, all of this was well beyond him.

When Dawson arrived at NSA headquarters, Winters was working on an algorithm designed to rapidly produce a draft of the "junk email" required to communicate between Dawson and Bertha Lyman, in order to dupe Lyman into believing she was receiving instructions from Hu Li.

"Basically," Winters explained, "you just tell the algorithm what the message is, and it develops the appropriate code, embeds it in the text of the email, assigns the appropriate decryption code, and produces the independent script for download to the client. Then the combination of the junk email and the activated download deciphers the email at Lyman's end and voilà! Ms. Lyman believes she is speaking with Hu Li. Once we have shifted her to our own site, we're home."

"Outstanding work as always," Dawson said. "Can we get started right now?"

"Absolutely," Winters grinned. "No time like the present, as my Mom used to say."

It took about ten minutes for Dawson and Winters to develop the appropriate email, and set it to send at the prescribed time that afternoon. Then they went to work on drafts of responses related to bidding for the new technology. When Lyman's instructions for bidding came in, they needed to respond quickly and appropriately. Soon, Winters would have to go "on leave," and begin setting up offshore accounts and other related shell mechanisms.

While they were waiting for the email to be launched, Dawson spoke with Winters about another matter. "Daniel," he asked, "do you remember the analytical device we went into Afghanistan with when we recovered the mineral for Salacia?"

"Sure," Winters replied with a smile. "Some of that particular contractor's best work, I think. It included an industrial laser, a spectrum analyzer, an uplink for the findings, and a couple of other goodies. The entire device was about the size of a shoebox. As I recall, you weaponized it while you were over there."

"That's a bit of a stretch," Dawson said. "Actually I just used the laser as a weapon briefly. It required no modification. Anyway, I think our team heading east could use something like it. But in this case, I'm interested in metallurgical properties more than mineral ones, and would like to attach or build in an electromagnetic field detection and analysis device as well."

Winters' brow furrowed. "Are we talking about amperes per meter—A/m—or flux density? Or if it's magnetic fields we're talking about here," he continued, clearly thinking aloud, "then we probably need to be considering a gauss meter—maybe even something that picks up readings in the milligauss range."

"The problem is, I just don't know," Dawson admitted. "We need to scan for everything. Any clue at all could at least get the team over at the Foundation pointed in the right direction. Right now we're all pretty much shooting in the dark."

"And whatever they find, you want to be uploaded via sat-link almost immediately, I assume?" Winters asked.

"That's the idea, yes," Dawson confirmed.

"And our guys need this by?"

"They are wheels-up in three days," Dawson responded.

"Holy cow, Ben. Three days?"

"I know, Daniel. I'd give you more notice if I could. Think it can be done?"

"Sure it can be done," Winters said. "It's just gonna be expensive. The components are all off-the-shelf. The tricky part is integration with the on-board transmission and recording equipment. Integration is always on the critical path in a project like this. I'll walk downstairs and get our contractor engaged as soon as we're done here."

"Thanks, Daniel," Dawson said. "Just remember, they can't take much more equipment with them in terms of weight and form factor. If the additional capability can be built into the same box, it would be ideal."

"I understand; we'll try, but you realize you're asking a lot here, right?"

Dawson smiled and said: "I never bring you the easy stuff, Daniel, because you're the best there is. And the best guys never pull easy duty."

"Just keep bringing us pizza," Mickey Wahl said, entering the room unannounced, "and we'll do whatever you need. Hi, Ben."

"Hi, Mickey. Good to see you," Dawson replied. Then he turned back to finish the point he was making with Winters. "Anyway, we won't need to take PAASS units and some of the other surveillance equipment in with us this time, which will save a little room, but the smaller the form factor the better."

"I understand, Ben; we'll do our best," Winters replied.

* * * *

A short while later, the time window for email exchanges hit and the counterfeit junk email was transmitted to Bertha Lyman. If she took the bait, Dawson knew, they were on their way.

Lyman was attentively waiting at her terminal in the Library of Congress and saw the email when it hit her inbox. The transmission looked identical to previous transmissions from this client, though the trigger to download had changed just slightly in terms of its position on the screen. This was almost unnoticeable and Lyman paid no attention to it at all. However, the message itself, shifting her responses going forward to a slightly different website for purposes of this set of communications, made her a little nervous. She saw no reason for it. She thought about this for several minutes and finally decided she would go along. This particular client had always paid promptly and in full, unlike some others. So although it made her just a little uneasy, if they wanted isolation for this specific project, she couldn't really see any harm in it. She reformatted the message as her usual process dictated and sent it along to the recipient, who in this case was Bleckhaus.

# CHAPTER 11

It was well into the evening in Berlin and things had finally begun to settle down at the campus. When Bleckhaus received the email, the message was clear enough. He was working through the night in his office at the Technische Universität Berlin. He had forestalled his departure in order to begin preparations for bidding on the new Russian technology, and now this new message placed everything in a somewhat different light. Although it never mentioned the MSS, there was no doubt in his mind about who had authored it. The MSS was going to be a part of the bidding, or else they would find another way to acquire the technology that would leave Bleckhaus out of the game entirely, and his commission from the brokering arrangement would evaporate.

The worst case scenario, from his perspective, was one where Bleckhaus himself might disappear. If MSS was the successful bidder, his fees would be larger. If they lost the bidding or decided to decline after looking at the technology, the bidding might go higher and would likely be no lower in any case. If they were left out of the bidding, however, it was likely the technology would simply be taken by force, and Bleckhaus might well be dead. In his view, the timing could scarcely be better.

Bleckhaus developed a response which basically said the new client was welcome to participate, and details about the technology demonstration and bidding would be provided through this same mechanism within forty-eight hours. The message would be relayed again during the next communication window.

Lyman's acceptance of the message to Bleckhaus was the trigger for Daniel Winters to request his leave and begin preparations. Winters decided to operate from Hyderabad, India. Hyderabad, the capital and largest city of the southern Indian state of Andhra Pradesh, had a population of nearly seven million people, and a metropolitan area population of nearly eight million, making it the fourth most populous city and sixth most populous urban agglomeration in India. In addition, Hyderabad was the home of corporate headquarters for some of the world's largest high tech consulting and IT service desk firms. There were more than 1,300 information technology firms doing business in Hyderabad, including global conglomerates such as Microsoft—operating its largest R&D campus outside the US—Google, IBM, Yahoo!, Dell, Facebook, Tech Mahindra, Infosys, Tata Consultancy Services, Genpact, and Wipro. Winters knew it was an ideal place to get lost in the dense cloud of technological traffic.

As a part of his preparations, Winters created a set of travel documents and credit cards for himself based on a recently deceased man of his approximate physical dimensions and age. This was easy for him to do, given his broad US government database access and prodigious technological skills. He memorized a few pertinent facts about the man whose identity he was assuming, a Mr. David Volmer. Next he set up bank accounts in Volmer's name, and arranged with a longtime friend in Salt Lake City to check the mail at the address each day to ensure any correspondence from the bank was intercepted and forwarded to Winters. Until a future resident showed up, this would cause no alarm, and afterward Winters would simply close out the account by withdrawing all funds. Then he hacked the Canadian immigration system and listed Volmer as having entered Canada one week prior, identifying the purpose as a vacation with an expected duration of two weeks.

Working through an international travel agency, he leased both sides of a two-tenant vacation home—a structure often referred to as a duplex in the United States—in the hilly outskirts of Hyderabad, overlooking the Hussain Sagar Lake. He leased each side of the two occupancies under different names, telling the relocation agency his sister and her family would be occupying the other residence. He then arranged for three separate shipments to the address via Federal Express. Using the last residence of the late David Volmer in Salt Lake City as the "ship from" location, Winters sent ahead generic personal items such as toiletries and clothing from ubiquitous department stores, computer and telecommunications equipment, and some generic food on which he could survive in a pinch including Clif Bars and cereals.

The last thing Winters did in preparation was lease a mid-size boat from a company called Avanigadda for cruising on Hussain Sagar Lake. The lake had been off-limits to private vessels until recently, but a few months earlier the number and variety of watercraft had grown to the point where one more would raise no suspicion. The boat was already moored at the lake, and Winters had some ideas about using it as both an operating platform and an escape vehicle if he needed one. His family had done some sailing in his teenage years, and he had continued boating into his twenties so he knew what he was looking for. He'd selected a Sea Ray 290 Sun Sport and paid to have it outfitted with extra fuel and a portable generator.

Winters' last meeting with Mickey Wahl before leaving on "vacation" was to iron out any remaining questions about the communications and transactions anticipated between Bleckhaus, Lyman, and the person they both thought was Hu Li. He also presented Wahl with the mobile numbers for eight burner phones and a schedule for when he planned to activate each of them during his travels.

"I have to say I'm a little jealous," Wahl said. "But at the same time, I'm glad it's not me, you know? I mean this is a little crazy, and if the guys Ben Dawson was telling us about manage to track you down ..."

"Yeah, I'm trying not to think about that," Winters grinned. "But why should Ben have all the fun? I want stories to tell my grandkids too."

"Grandkids," Wahl smiled back at him through a scruffy beard, "you don't even date anybody! Where are you going to find time for grandkids?"

"Well, you know—someday," Winters replied. "Anyway, getting back to the job, do you have any other questions before I skate out of here?"

"I think I have most of this down," Wahl said. "Now about the stuff for Winger and Romero ..."

"Oh yeah," Winters responded, "I almost forgot. I've set up with Sandra Anderson over at CIA to assemble the special gear they want. Their contractor

turned out to be available and has the components we needed. She's been working with Tina Gosbee downstairs, and the equipment is just about finished.
Tina has the complete list, including the self-destructing backpacks and all the
rest, and is supposed to have it ready for Ben to pick up tomorrow." Winters
paused to scratch out a telephone extension on a post-it note and handed it
over to Wahl. "Here's Tina's extension. You OK with all the rest of this stuff?"

"I guess so," Wahl replied uncertainly.

"Don't worry," Winters said, "you'll be fine. I'll check in every day and if
something comes up, we can work through it then." With that, he waved at
Wahl and headed out the door. In a small valise was a three terabyte external
hard drive, but he left anything related to the Agency or to him personally behind at his desk or at his condo. Starting out at the Ottawa airport a few days
later, he would no longer be Daniel Winters. *I'll be David Volmer,* he thought,
*and I'll be on my own.*

Winters traveled to Ottawa under his own name. After leaving the secure
area of the airport, he went to the men's restroom and changed out his passport and other ID papers. He then walked to the ticket counter, checked his
bags, and retrieved his new boarding pass as David Volmer. His flight to New
Delhi took nearly a day, giving Winters plenty of time to review his plans and
mentally prepare. Once on the ground in Delhi, he had a short layover before
transferring to his one-hour flight on Jet Airways India for Hyderabad. When
he arrived at the lakeside residence, he was met by a coordinator from the travel agency who showed him around and presented the keys to both residences.
The coordinator was also pleased to point out local markets and restaurants,
which Winters appreciated, but he was most interested in the broadband access. The coordinator assured him the broadband coverage in both residences
was excellent, even though it came from two separate providers; a situation
Winters also preferred. When the coordinator had finally left, Winters went
shopping for bottled water and basic household supplies, then returned to the
condo and settled in for a few hours of sleep.

He was awakened by the sound of the doorbell. He padded down the hall
to his front door, still rubbing the sleep from his eyes, and found his three
Federal Express shipments awaiting him just outside. Two of the packages
were pretty manageable, but the third box—containing the bulk of his electronics—was quite large and heavy. Winters finally decided the smart thing to

do was break it down where it stood, carrying the individual components in as he removed them.

He set up the residences with the highest speed Internet connection, creating an office and telecommunications center. Then he ran a cable through the vent from the clothes dryer to the outside of the structure, attaching it as discreetly as possible along one corner. At the eaves, he duct-taped it securely to the underside of the gutter and then ran it to the roof. From the upstairs bedroom window, he carefully climbed onto the roof and mounted two small parabolic dishes similar to satellite television apparatuses, with one pointed toward the northern sky and the other pointed directly toward the center of Hussain Sagar Lake. Since they were on the side of the structure facing the lake, they were barely visible from the street.

Inside the reconfigured living room he set up the large, flat-screen monitors from both bedrooms alongside the living room unit and rerouted the wiring so they worked as monitors for his computers rather than television sets. Then he set up laptops from the shipments and attached one to each of the three monitors. He placed a "Go Bag" with clothing and travel toiletries near the door, along with another empty computer bag with enough capacity to carry the three laptops.

Finally, he extracted the external hard drive he had brought into the country with him and plugged it into the center laptop. The laptop to the left was attached to the cable connected to the skyward-facing satellite dish, and the one on the right was connected to the cable attached to the lake-facing dish. He placed a wireless router with dual-level, sixteen bit encryption in the corner of the room and connected the three laptops wirelessly to it, and to one another. Then he spent a couple of hours loading and configuring the software from his external hard drive onto the three laptops, and finally engaged a special self-destruct firmware package of Angelia-based security measures on each unit. The Angelia firmware was developed by the Brystol Foundation more than a year earlier and could be programmed to execute almost any instruction set with complete lack of detectability. By then, it was almost nine p.m., and Winters was exhausted. He broke down the empty shipping containers and moved them inside, then went to bed.

After a light breakfast the following morning, Winters fired up the various pieces of equipment he had assembled the previous day, checked them out to ensure they were working properly, dialed in the satellite dish position, then powered all of them down again except the laptop attached to the lake-facing dish. It was time to check out the boat.

The Sea Ray was docked at the end of a community pier about two hundred yards from the residences Winters had leased, and adjacent to Lumbini Park. The walkway along the lakefront was easy enough to negotiate. Winters had double-lined the small wheeled trash container from the condo and loaded the supplies he needed into it. He pulled it behind him to the dock and transferred the cargo to the below-deck cabin. It took him about an hour to get things stowed and the electronics set up as he wanted them there. Then he fired up the Sea Ray and took a spin around the lake. The boat he had leased was one of the larger craft on the lake, but not out of place. The man-made lake was big enough for him to avoid being continuously visible from any vantage point, and afforded several locations around its shoreline where he could dock, including at least two different marinas with fuel.

Winters discovered a sixty foot tall statue of Gautama Buddha positioned on a small island in the middle of the lake. He read later that the sculpting of the granite statue and its subsequent placement resulted from the Buddha Purnima project in 1985. The monument was finally produced and erected on April 12, 1992. The image of the Buddha produced a deja vu effect, reminding Winters of an image he had seen in western news footage. He was certain it was something back in the 2013 to 2014 timeframe, but he just couldn't put his finger on it. The Buddha was standing erect with a right hand held aloft as though swearing an oath. *The same but different,* he thought. He finally stopped gazing at the statue, realizing it would probably come to him later, and continued his short survey of the lake.

An hour later he returned to the dock, moored his boat, and locked it up. Shortly after he returned to the residence, it was time to get online and review the correspondence from Lyman relaying Bleckhaus' instructions.

# CHAPTER 12

On Tuesday afternoon, Dawson picked up the gear he had requested for Winger and Romero at NSA headquarters. The devices were ready, and the technician walked Dawson through their operation in about thirty minutes.

Tina Gosbee was a dowdy forty-something woman who looked as though she'd be more at home on a manufacturing floor than in an office. The labs where devices like the ones Dawson requested were probably the closest she could come to a practical application of her two engineering degrees at NSA. Gosbee stood five feet two inches tall, with close-cropped hair the color of old rust, and no discernible signs of makeup. Her bloodshot eyes squinted at Dawson through contact lenses.

"How rugged are they?" Dawson asked, as they reviewed the equipment.

"We broadened our validation of the ambient temperature ranges from the testing done on the Salacia device," Gosbee said. "These are confirmed to work effectively to temperatures down around twenty degrees Fahrenheit, so they should have no trouble with the mountains where they'll be deployed this time of year. If your team was going over in January or February, I'd want to have another look at them, but I'm sure they'll work fine for you on this outing."

"What are the power requirements?" Dawson asked.

"It depends on use, of course," Gosbee responded. "The laser will drain battery power in less than ten minutes if operated continuously. But most of this equipment is used in bursts, and so I would say—knowing a little about the mission parameters from Daniel's description—you probably have several days' worth of battery life before you need a recharge. I could send extra batteries with you but it sounds like weight and space are limited."

"Right," Dawson replied. "Given the choice between an extra battery and an extra magazine of ammunition, I think these guys would prefer the ammo."

"I understand," Gosbee said. "And over here," she swept her arm toward another table along the wall behind her, "is the equipment you requested for your own use." On the table were two miniature portable lasers and several surveillance devices designed to be easily concealed along with signal boosters. "In this case, I did include an auxiliary battery pack for each of the lasers." There were also a few clip-on sensors for monitoring both air quality and radiation levels. Gosbee carefully loaded all his equipment into a small bag for him and handed it over.

"Perfect," Dawson smiled.

"Is there anything else you'll need?" Gosbee asked.

"No," he responded, throwing one backpack over each shoulder. "I think this is everything. Wow," he continued, hefting the packs, "these are lighter than I expected. Thanks, Tina; it was nice meeting you."

"You're welcome," Gosbee replied. She walked with him to the elevator and pressed the button for him. "Hope it all works out. Return the equipment if you can, please."

"We'll try, but …"

"Yes," she smiled, "I get it. In the worst case, of course, just …"

"I know," Dawson said, "put it in the backpack and trigger the self-destruct."

"Exactly," Gosbee said as the elevator door was closing between them. "Good luck to you and your team, Sir."

By four p.m., Dawson was huddled around his desk at the Foundation with Winger and Romero. He walked through the functionality of the two devices and reviewed the overall game plan.

"The fact is, I have only a rough idea about the timing for you guys," Dawson said. "I don't know how long it will take for you to rendezvous with Potter and his team, or precisely how long it will take you to get back to the compound outside of Mezhgorye. Then, after you're on station there, I don't know exactly how long it will take you to get finished with your work; though that is probably the clearest of the timeframes."

"You'll know as things unfold, though," Romero pointed out.

"Right, Chief," Dawson replied. "I'd like updates whenever it's safe and reasonable for you to provide them, and that will help with our coordination. I'm also going to lay in a contingency plan in case things go truly sideways, but it's very, very ugly and I'd sure like to avoid using it if we can."

"All right, Boss; we'll try to stay out of trouble," Winger replied, "but you know how it goes. This ain't gonna be easy."

"Right," Dawson said, "our stuff never is."

"One thing I need to understand better," Winger continued, "is our priorities. I know you want us to get images and samples from the device through the spectrum analyzer, and take readings from the electromagnetic field detector, and get geometric dimensions on unique design elements. But we'll be working under some time constraints here. What are the most important things to get if we run out of time?"

"It's a great question, Billy," Dawson admitted, "and I wish I had an answer for you. I stopped in to talk with Dr. Brystol a little about it, and frankly this is an area where the US—or at least the Foundation—is so far behind these guys, we really don't have any idea what we're looking for. He was still wrestling equations on a blackboard. The electrical arcing we saw is significant, but we still don't know how they have attacked this problem. You understand the equipment we saw levitating over there as well as anyone I know; the tank for sure. I'd start with whatever you see that doesn't belong there. I'm guessing everything contributing to the taller side plates at the base of the vehicle, between and just above the tracks, is where we ought to be focusing."

"Yeah, I figured as much," Winger replied.

"Boss, it seems to me the video and still images will be pretty quick to capture, and probably oughta be first," Romero opined. "Even without precise measurements, they would provide a kind of high-level picture of the mechanism. If we start there, then move on to closer examination of what look like critical components, then the EMF scan, and lastly do metallurgical data collection—if we still have time—I think we'd be likely to get the most important stuff first."

"Sounds like a plan to me, Chief," Dawson replied. "I wouldn't be surprised if you end up having to wing it to some extent, though, based on what you find when you get inside. I wish we could send some true technicians in with you, but it's just too dangerous and frankly I'm not even sure what specific skills I'd be looking for. We put a team into Iran several years back to take a look at their enrichment program, and something called superplastic forming was determined to be a critical technology. While the technology itself wasn't new, it was pretty rare and not a lot of people knew what they were looking for. So if you put two or three technologies like those together, and maybe throw in one or two no one has even seen before, the group of subject matter experts required makes an insertion team untenable. The best we can do is put a couple of experienced operators in there and try to get the information out. So it falls to you."

"Got it, Boss," Winger said. "But if all goes as planned, and you get the designer, maybe what we are able to gather won't be as important."

"Let's hope so," Dawson agreed. "But your end of this is tricky enough. I'd hate to rely on that all working out. As you said earlier, we have a lot of moving parts."

# CHAPTER 13

Bi-shou's mobile phone buzzed about three p.m. Thursday, and she was surprised to find that when she said, "Hello," she was greeted by a voice speaking Mandarin. "Bi-shou," the caller said, "my name is Hu Li. I work for a former associate of yours, Mr. Teng-hui. I would like to meet with you and discuss some business matters of mutual interest."

"I doubt there are matters of mutual interest remaining between myself and your employer," Bi-shou responded, but she was intrigued. She realized this was almost certainly connected to the recent surveillance on Winger and herself. To be approached in such a casual manner was a bit unsettling.

"I assure you there are," the caller continued, "and I will not take much of your time. Would you be willing to meet with me here at the embassy?"

Bi-shou smiled as she said, "No, I have no intention of walking into the embassy, Hu Li. If you would like to speak with me, we need to find a nice public place for our conversation."

"Very well, then. Where would you prefer to meet?"

"I will meet you in the lobby of the Ritz-Carlton at the Pentagon City Mall," she replied. "There are a number of places within a few steps which offer privacy in the area."

"Yes, I know it well," Hu Li said. "Would six p.m. be acceptable?"

"Yes, I will see you there," she replied, and ended the call. Bi-shou's instincts told her the meeting could be trouble and she needed to prepare. Having less than three hours, she wasted no time. She dressed quickly for the occasion and left immediately. Two blocks from her condo, Bi-shou walked into a small storefront called "Chinese Dragon Grocery." She lingered near the fresh meat and seafood counter at the rear of the store until she caught the eye of the proprietor. He nodded to her discreetly. Glancing around to ensure no one was observing, she slipped behind a display in the back of the store, and pushed through the gray rubber swinging doors into the stockroom.

In a back corner of the stockroom, a metal pedestrian door presented the only entry into a small, unmarked cinder block room about the size of a walk-in closet. This room served as Bi-shou's local ordnance and operations gear storage, and because it did not appear on any lease registered to Bi-shou, it hadn't been seized along with her other assets by the federal government when she was arrested a couple of years earlier. Alongside the door was a keypad, into which she punched an eight-digit code. Inside the cinder block room was a series of metal cabinets lining one wall and a narrow shelf along the opposite wall. Fluorescent overhead lights were activated automatically by a motion detector when she entered the room.

She used a key to unlock two of the eight metal cabinets and withdrew two items. The first was a black case designed to resemble a standard clamshell case for reading glasses. It contained four single-use needleless syringes called Lorentz-force actuators. She also retrieved a small .22 caliber automatic pistol with an elongated barrel containing a built-in silencer. The pistol was thin to enable concealment and worked well in a purse or shoulder holster. For the meeting with Hu Li, she decided to use a stylish handbag with padded compartments designed to conceal both items. With her weapons in place, Bi-shou left the store and caught the Metro to Pentagon City Mall.

Bi-shou arrived at the Ritz-Carlton a few minutes early and entered the hotel from the mall. Walking along the corridors of the storied building, as always she invoked the appreciative smiles of the hotel patrons, especially the males. She passed through the main lobby area and walked to the bar. By six p.m., the place was awash in business travelers, high-ranking military visitors, and local celebrities. She ordered a sparkling water with lemon and found a seat at a small table near a side entryway opening onto another corridor. She knew from previous visits that this corner of the room was not covered by in-house surveillance. About ninety seconds later, a very well-dressed Chinese man in his early forties approached and bowed slightly, then extended his hand.

"Bi-shou," he said, "I am Hu Li. It is good to meet you in person." Bi-shou took his hand and noted his grip wasn't particularly strong. His hand seemed cool and a bit clammy. *Perhaps he had been holding his drink in that hand,* she thought. She waved him to the seat across from her.

"How can I help you, Hu Li?" she asked noncommittally.

Hu Li settled in and crossed his legs, and offered his best Cheshire cat smile. "As I mentioned earlier," he replied, "I work for Teng-hui." He slid a gold-embossed business card across the table until it rested near her glass.

"Have you worked for Teng-hui very long?" Bi-shou asked, glancing only briefly at the card.

"I have been in this assignment for about six months now," he replied, "and before this I was in Beijing. But I have also held a number of other international positions, including postings in London and Moscow."

"I see," she said, her gaze gliding over the room. "Tell me, Hu Li, does Teng-hui know you have asked to meet with me here today?"

Bi-shou could see tiny beads of perspiration had begun to appear above his small, round eyeglasses. Hu Li brushed aside her question. "We would like you to return to the service of your country, Bi-shou," he said softly. "If you do, then all will be forgiven." He swirled a Macallan on the rocks in his glass.

"And if I do not?"

"Then almost certainly, misfortune will befall you. I believe you think the Americans will protect you, but they will not. And your new friend Mr. Winger will likely suffer misfortune as well. You could be very helpful, Bi-shou. You could make a difference, and not just be another greedy westerner who puts her own interests above the needs of her country. Or you could be washed away with the rest of this decaying society, when China crushes it underfoot. We already own nearly two trillion dollars of US debt. Eventually, the United States will become just another second-class power, like the countries of Europe. Then we will own whatever we want of this country. Do you not wish to be on the winning side, Bi-shou?"

"I do not wish to be on any side at all," she replied demurely. "But what is it you really want from me, Hu Li? Why do you have me followed by this man Burke? It would be much more helpful if you would simply tell me what you want. China—which you keep referring to as 'my country'—has tried to kill me repeatedly because I refused to return to their service. Surely you must realize that simply threatening me with a 'misfortune' will not be helpful."

"I do not threaten you, of course. You and Mr. Winger seem to become involved in matters which could be quite hazardous. Without the support of your country, this is very dangerous. But we could offer you support and protection, and an opportunity to do things which are vital to China. The Americans would not even need to know you are helping us, of course. If you would prefer, your friend Mr. Winger would not even need to know. We can be very generous as well."

Hu Li leaned back a bit, reflecting a self-gratified expression. "We are not interested in Mr. Winger, in any case," he said. "We are interested in other operatives, closer to the technical work than the operations, who are following more important matters. But you are resourceful, Bi-shou, and we believe you can assist us, using your new-found relationships, in contacting the individuals we need to reach."

Looking him squarely and dispassionately in the eye, Bi-shou asked, "Who are you asking me to deliver up?"

"We need one of the NSA's lead technical people. I can say no more until you have agreed to join us again."

Based on the coffee shop conversation with Winters a few days earlier, Bi-shou suspected it was him the MSS was after. Bi-shou sighed lightly, and then her smile disappeared. She leaned in slightly, seeming to think about this while reaching for her purse. She pulled her mobile phone from her purse, checked the time on it, and opened up her photo application. She thumbed through the photos, but rather than selecting one, she left the thumbnail image page on the screen.

Then she spoke again. "Hu Li, as you are aware, I am quite busy these days. I believe you must be very busy as well. I have asked you to come to the point and tell me precisely what you want from me twice, and you continue to insist I should return to the MSS both times rather than tell me precisely what it is you want me to do for you. It is really quite frustrating. But I think I have something here you would be interested in. May I show you?"

"Of course," he said, puzzlement sweeping across his face. "What is it?"

Bi-shou stood and walked nonchalantly around the table, placing her phone on the tabletop in front of him. Leaning down so that her back and hair masked her movements, Bi-shou's proximity and fragrance were disarming to Hu Li. She said, "Open up the first image in the third row." As Hu Li reached toward the phone to touch the image, she whispered, "Yes, that one," while surreptitiously discharging the hypo hidden in her hand against his neck. The content of the Lorentz-force injection, sprayed through the skin and into the carotid artery in microscopic droplets by the hypo, contained a debilitating combination of drugs often classified as "predator drugs" by the media. Chemical agents in this category include flunitrazepam—Rohypnol—and gamma-hydroxybutyrate, but the combination used by Bi-shou was far less likely to be detected in the bloodstream. When Hu Li was found following his death, which would come after a few minutes as his respiratory system shut down, it would look as though his heart had merely stopped. A more accurate explanation would be that he had simply stopped breathing.

Anyone glancing over at them along the wall would simply see the back of a woman showing something to a man on her mobile phone. While she was still in the same position, Bi-shou gently slipped Hu Li's small, round eyeglasses from his face and folded them gently into her hand along with the used hypo. Then after a moment, she retrieved her phone and returned to her seat across the table. Hu Li continued to sit, staring down at the tabletop between them and completely immobile. Only a small patch of slightly reddened skin just at the line of his collar indicated the hypo had been used. While he was still alive and conscious, Bi-shou spoke softly to him with a smile as she retrieved her purse and her glass, "I will remember our conversation today, Hu Li. But it seems misfortune has overtaken you first."

She moved across the room and left her glass on the bar, where she knew the bartender would remove it and toss it into the bin for washing along with the other glasses and plates that evening. If the authorities detected something unusual when Hu Li was found, and one of them was industrious enough to look for fingerprints, there would be no trace of Bi-shou.

On the way back to her apartment, Bi-shou stopped at one of the local print shops and used a public computer to produce a short message for Teng-hui, along with a mailing label. Using a combination of fresh wipes and plastic gloves from her purse, she assured Hu Li's eyeglasses were free of fingerprints and prepared a small mailing box. She enclosed Hu Li's glasses and a note which read: "I trust one warning will be enough." She mailed the package from a small post office a block away, then turned for the Metro station, and home.

Just as she entered her apartment, Bi-shou received a message from Gerard which read: "Your Irish friend is back." Suddenly, Bi-shou's mind was racing. *Did he see me with Hu Li?* she thought. Quickly, she typed a reply: "Since when?"

The reply took about fifteen seconds. "He was waiting across the street when you returned a few minutes ago."

*All right,* she thought, *then he doesn't know about Hu Li.* She shot a text back to Gerard: "Understood. Where is he now?"

"Sitting in his rental car across the street near the corner at West Mound."

"Got it. Thanks," Bi-shou replied. "I will take it from here."

There was no response. Bi-shou knew Gerard must be seething at the notion she was being expected to protect her. Gerard's mistrust of Bi-shou was almost palpable. But her professionalism and deference to Dawson's judgment was keeping her in line, and probably the only thing keeping Bi-shou and Gerard from mortal combat. She had tried to mend fences at one point, but—although Gerard had understood her intent—it had no apparent effect.

In fact, Gerard was angrier at Burke than anyone else. She had warned him off in a meaningful way; he'd barely avoided a trip to the emergency room. Yet he was back, and while he was doing nothing threatening, he was obviously still surveilling Dawson's team.

Bi-shou changed into more casual clothes, piled her hair up onto her head and pinned it in place, then slid a fresh hypo into an outside pocket and her pistol into an inside pocket of a loose leather jacket. After donning the jacket and a plain black watch cap over her hair, she took the back stairs out of her building and emerged into an alleyway at the rear. Moving along the alley parallel to the street, she walked two blocks before returning to the street in front of her building and crossing at the light. It was eight p.m., and an overcast sky produced an early dusk. Bi-shou was swallowed up in a clotty flow of faceless city dwellers passing through patches of storefront lighting, neon signage, and shadows along the sidewalks.

She spotted Burke sitting in his car, staring at the entrance to her building, and listening to something through earbuds; probably music, she guessed from his expression. She stopped into a convenience store along the way and purchased a large carbonated drink from their fountain drink bar. She didn't bother with a straw. Then, she was back out on the sidewalk and moving toward Burke's car from the rear. She poked a small hole in the Styrofoam cup near its base with a disposable ink pen, creating a tiny stream of soda emanating from the container. She kept her finger over the hole until she passed by the vehicle, where she set the cup gently on its roof so the stream would begin to run down over the car's windshield. She continued on for a half block, then turned into a store's entryway briefly and doubled back.

When Bi-shou had positioned herself a few yards behind the vehicle, she turned her back toward it and waited for a lapse in pedestrian traffic along the sidewalk. As soon as one appeared, she tossed the pen into the air so it would land on the roof of Burke's car. She turned and stood facing away from the car as though talking on her mobile phone. In her peripheral vision, she could see the ploy was working. She gripped her second single-use Lorentz-force syringe with her free hand inside her jacket pocket.

Burke had heard the pen hit the roof of the car, even through the music he was listening to. He looked toward the sidewalk and was puzzled to see a stream of liquid pouring down the windshield. He pulled the earbuds from his ears and tossed them into the seat next to him along with the iPhone to which they were attached. Then he emerged from the vehicle to see the soft drink container, and walked around the back of the car to remove it. As soon as his back was turned toward Bi-shou, she silently closed the distance between them and pressed the hypo to the back of his neck, just below the skull.

Burke went immediately limp, and Bi-shou quickly turned to bring his arm around and over her shoulder. She opened the car door on the passenger side of the vehicle after half carrying him the remaining two steps to drop him into the front seat. Standing again, she checked to determine whether they had been observed. As she hoped, there were no other pedestrians nearby. Seeing no one paying attention, she walked around to the other side of the vehicle and slipped into the driver's seat. The keys were still in the ignition. She reached across Burke and pulled the seatbelt into position to secure him and then—less than five minutes after making the small hole in the soda cup—she drove away.

Bi-shou headed northwest toward Frederick, Maryland, after punching in a number on her mobile phone. After three rings, a gruff voice answered: "Yn."

"Hello, Mr. Yn," Bi-shou replied. "This is Lotus."

"Ah, Lotus! I have not spoken with you in many months. How can I be of assistance?" All gruffness was gone now; only a little surprise lingered where the annoyance had been.

"I am delivering a package for you. I am on my way now and will be there in about an hour."

"I will be ready," the voice said. "Just one item?"

"Yes, just one," she replied. "About eighty kilos. See you soon."

In the passenger seat, Bi-shou sensed the tension and inner struggle as Burke tried to will his muscles to move, and fought against the darkness engulfing him as his respiration slowed with each passing mile. She knew it would be only minutes for him now.

"You know, Mr. Burke, all of this could have been avoided. You were warned twice—with increasing emphasis—to leave me alone. People who pursue me never find it productive in the end. Well, in some ways I suppose Ben Dawson did, but he was the exception. I digress though, and you do not have much time left. So I will just say you should be disappointed in yourself. As a professional, you have demonstrated very limited skills. And now, that lack of professionalism has cost you your life. A pity, really. You are another among many examples of what Charles Darwin would have called 'the process of natural selection,' I suppose. Do you like music? Perhaps I can find some music on the radio to soothe you as you drift away." She hit "Seek" on the XM radio until she found a classical music station, and Burke stopped breathing somewhere in the middle of the Blue Danube Waltz.

When she had traveled about halfway to Frederick, Bi-shou came to a familiar turnoff with a sign which read: "Gaithersburg Waste-to-Energy Project." This particular center was funded largely through a US federal government grant originating around the same time, and through the same mechanism as the infamous Solyndra project. Unfortunately, like most of the "green programs" initiated by the Obama administration, Solyndra collapsed, leaving taxpayers liable for $535 million in federal guarantees. This program, however, looked as though it might at least break even after several years if it could be scaled properly. It focused on generating electricity from the burning of biomass through a process called co-firing. Co-firing in biomass power stations was considered an attractive option. It consumed waste in the form of biomass mixed with ground coal as fuel for the boiler. The combination of biomass and coal was heated to power a steam-based turbine which, in turn, produced electrical current.

While the bulk of the biomass used at this site was comprised of agricultural waste, the MSS had arranged through a series of bribes to make unofficial use of the facility when it needed to dispose of inconvenient waste matter. A Chinese national named Morris Ng with MSS connections had been taken on as night shift superintendent at the facility, which made things even more convenient. When she left the MSS, Bi-shou continued to make occasional use of the facility as an independent contractor. She simply continued to use Lotus—her old code name—and paid cash for the service. The going rate was five thousand dollars per "item," and the "items" involved were usually dead bodies. Tonight was no exception. Before morning, Burke would be ground up like hamburger, mixed with granules of coal, and incinerated. The Washington, DC area would benefit from a tiny addition to the electrical grid and Bi-shou would no longer have the problematic Mr. Burke to deal with.

When Bi-shou had emptied Burke's pockets, she drove back into town. She removed his belongings from the hotel room and deposited them in a nearby dumpster, returned the rental car, and took the Metro back to her condo. In the morning, she would return the pistol and the two unused hypos with the remaining sedative to her personal armory at the Chinese Dragon Grocery.

Bi-shou instinctively decided to share her actions related to Burke with no one. No one else had a need to know, and based on her lengthy experience with assassinations, everyone who knew represented a liability.

In the meantime, she was back home again by eleven, which was just as well. She was awakened early the next morning by a text message from Dawson. The next few days were going to be busy ones. There was a great deal of preparation to do before their trip.

# CHAPTER 14

Bleckhaus' message was received and rerouted to Dawson on Thursday morning. It was everything Dawson had hoped it would be; it spelled out the time and location of the auction, and instructed the participants to arrive prepared to take possession of "all intellectual property, including electronic media as well as personnel," and to "be prepared to perform funds transfers commensurate with negotiated terms." The auction was to be held at the Aria Hotel Prague one week hence—on Friday evening at ten p.m. Bidders were instructed to take up residence in the hotel and inform the front desk they were participating in the International Agricultural Association Conference. They would be provided with further instructions related to the meeting time and room at the time of their check-in. Participants were expected to be checked into the hotel by midnight the prior evening. In the meantime, Bleckhaus required the names of participants be sent to him immediately, and stated no more than two participants from each bidding organization would be permitted in the room.

Dawson had already set Mickey Wahl to work on passports, visas, and drivers' licenses identifying Bi-shou as Sheryl Wen, Dawson as William Lee, Winger as Steven Elliott, Gerard as Linda Kaye, and Romero as Lloyd Arnold. All of the passports and other identification documents were Canadian. When Dawson responded—on behalf of Bi-shou—to Bleckhaus' request for attendee names, the only name he provided was Sheryl Wen.

Upon learning of the location from Wahl, Dawson replied: "No, that's not where the auction will occur, but it will be close by. I'm guessing they will transport participants to a nearby facility. The hotel is too public and well known. I think they even use it as a movie location from time to time. I need to get over there immediately and see whether I can figure out where this will really be going down. Mickey, will you poke around and see what likely spots would be within a ten-mile radius, please? I'm thinking this will be a building with multiple high-speed Internet connections set up within the last thirty days. They will likely have secure networks and isolation from surrounding buildings. Based on what we've seen, they'll also be using a lot of electricity which probably means generators since I don't think the power grid would handle substantial spikes well. And if they are doing a demonstration there, it will need to have high-bay space in at least part of the building. A warehouse, a large old retail store, something like that. An airplane hangar would have been ideal but the area is too populated. The Aria Hotel is right downtown in the Mala Strana quarter of the city; you could almost hit the Charles Bridge with a well-thrown baseball from there."

"Yes, Sir," Wahl replied, "I'll get right on it. Should have something for you by the end of the day."

"Thanks," Dawson said, and headed for the door. He had almost made it to his car when his phone buzzed. He looked at the message and turned around, retracing his steps.

"Sorry, Ben," Wahl said as Dawson reentered his work area. "It didn't take nearly as long as I expected. I just reviewed the databases associated with electrical power and Internet service connections in the last thirty days, and this newly leased distribution warehouse popped up. Looks like it was leased about six weeks ago, and all the infrastructure service permits have been flowing like water since then. The lease runs to a blind, and one of the names on the other side of the blind is Werner von Janowski. Janowski, you may remember, is one of the names on the frequent caller list of ..."

"Professor Bleckhaus," Dawson finished the sentence for Wahl. "Yes, I remember that name from the network diagram you and Daniel were showing me a few days ago. Nice work!"

"We aim to please, Sir," Wahl beamed, "but the truth is you did most of the work for me when you told me exactly what to look for."

"So where is this place, Mickey?"

"East of the downtown area, out here near the railroad tracks," Wahl replied. "Less than ten miles, but far enough away from the heart of the city to allow for some privacy." He pulled up the street view from an online image. "It's a high-bay facility with some kind of multi-story automated storage system down in one end of the building, but a lot of open space at the other end, near the shipping/receiving doors. Looks like that part of the structure is at least fifty feet high inside."

"That's got to be it, Mickey. What would the driving time be between the hotel and this site?"

"Well, Sir, it depends on traffic, of course. But my online mapping software estimates it at around fifteen minutes."

"Got it," Dawson replied. "Looks like I need some travel plans. Please let Daniel know what we know now, and see what you can do to hack into comms and data flows at the site. Keep me apprised. I need to get moving." He headed toward the door.

On his way, Dawson detoured on his route to stop by Charles Jennings' office. Jennings was out, but his administrative assistant, Gloria Treadway, had everything well in hand. Treadway was an African American woman in her early fifties. Intelligent and insightful, she always seemed to be one step ahead of Jennings and sometimes understood Dawson's cryptic communications better than her boss did; requiring her to act as a pseudo-translator. Dawson was on a very short list of people for whom Treadway almost always had a ready smile, and today was no exception.

"Hello stranger," Treadway said as she looked up from her computer monitor. "An unexpected pleasure." Then she shifted her gaze to the backpacks and duffle bag and said: "I see you're traveling again."

"Hi, Gloria," Dawson smiled back at her. "Yes, you know me; I like to be a *moving* target."

Treadway arched her eyebrows and replied: "I'm looking forward to the day you just stop being *any kind* of target and settle down, Ben. You're getting a little old for this globe-trotting thing, aren't you?"

"If you don't tell anyone, I won't," Dawson said with a wink.

"Have you got time for a cup of tea?" Treadway asked. "I just replenished our supply of Splenda."

"Thanks," Dawson replied, "but you are right; I'm pressed for time. I just need a favor."

"Of course," Treadway replied, "just name it."

"I need you to reach out to Vladimír Kolář in Prague. I'd like him to meet me in our favorite coffee shop around eight a.m. next Thursday."

\* \* \* \*

On Friday, Winger and Romero landed in Ankara and took a cab to the Hilton where they were met by Rick Potter. Potter had arrived the previous day. Since they had never met before, there were a few minutes of self-introduction and small talk over breakfast at a corner table in the hotel restaurant. Then they got down to business.

"I'm sure this kind of work is familiar territory for you gentlemen," Potter said. "But just to be clear, the crew I am assembling is pretty volatile. Many of them have not met one another before, and they are not naturally trusting types, if you see what I mean. There are four men who have been working in the Ukraine, six more from Karachay, and the rest are from Chechnya and Dagestan. Twenty operatives besides myself."

"That's a lot of men," Romero remarked. "Gonna be hard to move a group of twenty operators across country unobserved."

Winger nodded in agreement, saying: "This helps us with security once we're there, though. I wouldn't want it to be any larger. Since you and I have been there before, we probably ought to go in as two groups with one of us leading each group. That way, if something happens to one team the other still knows how to get to the target."

"The Agency has been doing some surveillance in the area," Potter said. "It looks as though there are pretty regular deliveries of some kind made by commercial vehicles running into Mezhgorye from Magnitogorsk, an industrial city to the southeast. One of my operators is originally from the area, and I think we can use that to move operatives and weapons into near proximity."

"It would get you pretty close, all right," Winger replied. "It'd only be a day or two through the woods from the town. I've heard something about Magnitogorsk before. Big iron producing area, isn't it?"

Potter nodded. "It was named for the Magnitnaya Mountain which is almost pure iron, a real geological anomaly. It's also the second largest city in Russia that does not serve as an administrative center for either a federal subject or an administrative division, which is useful for us; there are fewer military and government personnel. The largest iron and steel works in the country, Magnitogorsk Iron and Steel Works, is located here. About once a month, one or two trucks run between Mezhgorye from Magnitogorsk. They appear to be more heavily loaded when they travel south to Magnitogorsk, so it looks like they're moving something heavy in that direction, then dead-heading it back north again."

"Doesn't make much sense, does it?" Romero asked through a frown. "What would they be carrying from Mezhgorye—basically the middle of no-where—down south to a big steel-producing town?"

Potter shrugged, and rubbed at a couple of days' growth of beard along his chin. "The boys at Langley are still scratching their heads over it, too," he replied. "But I'm pretty sure the truck driver will be happy to look the other way while I load my team and their gear into the back of his truck for the ride up north. I'm guessing a thousand dollars' worth of rubles will do the job."

"So we rendezvous just outside of Mezhgorye then," Winger said. "Chief and I will head in from here and set up just outside the northwest edge of town. You got a satphone?"

Potter nodded in the affirmative and they exchanged numbers.

"OK then," Winger said, "we'll use those when we can, and worst case, we'll contact you through your regional HQ, wherever they're routing signals these days."

"Roger," Potter replied. "I'm thinking that if my end goes well, we'll be up your way about midnight on Monday. Will that work?"

"It should," Winger said. "There's just a lot we don't know here, which always makes me feel a little hinky."

"I know what you mean," Potter replied. "Seat-of-the-pants is no way to run an operation, but given the importance and urgency, I guess we really have no choice."

\* \* \* \*

Several hours later, with Potter well on his way back toward Moscow, Winger and Romero found Grigol Orlov in a local pub, just finishing up his coulibiac and washing it down with Efes Pilsen beer. He greeted them like an old friend, and moved from the bar to a table, ordering beers for Winger and Romero as well.

"Are you comrades ready to go for a ride with me again," Orlov smiled. "And where is your friend, Dawson? I like him. He has сердце, what you say—'heart!'"

"Yes, Ben has heart," Winger replied, wondering how much alcohol Orlov had already consumed that day. "But he isn't with us this time. It's just the Chief and me, so it's two men and our gear. No problem, right?"

"Sure, sure. No problem; do not worry, comrades," he said, smiling. "I am at your disposal. I am at the Mövenpick Hotel, but I can be ready to leave within an hour. You are going back to where I found you before?"

"Yes, that's right."

"OK. This is no problem. You want to go now or in the morning?"

Winger told Orlov he and Romero were going to get some sleep, suggesting Orlov do the same. "We'll meet you at the plane in the morning. Will 0600 work for you?"

"Of course, comrade! I will be there, ready to go. You remember where the airfield is?"

"Yes," Winger replied.

"Same aircraft?" Romero asked.

"I have only one," Orlov shrugged.

Winger smiled and clapped Orlov on the back as he rose from his seat, saying: "We'll see you there."

After they had emerged from the bar, Winger gestured for Romero to step into a doorway along the street and said in a low voice: "You mind doing a little surveillance before we get some shut-eye tonight, Chief?"

"What do you need, Boss?"

"I just want to be sure our friend in there doesn't have a tail of some kind. Something just doesn't seem right," Winger replied. "There's nobody else in the bar right now who looks like a ringer to me, but I'd just like to make sure he gets back to his room tonight in one piece."

"Roger that," Romero said. "You want me to tail him and make sure he's OK?"

"Yeah," Winger said. "I don't think he's gonna be in there much longer—he'll probably finish his drink and head to his hotel. I would just feel better if we knew he wasn't being watched."

"Consider it done."

"Thanks, Chief," Winger said, turning to head down the street. "I have a couple of errands to do. See you back at the hotel."

Winger found a taxi, and directed the driver toward the local airfield.

In the meantime, Romero found a likely spot near the bus stop just down the sidewalk, where throngs of people formed a teeming river of humanity pouring into and out of the buses lining the streets. He blended into the crowd and watched the door of the bar where, as Winger had predicted, Orlov emerged about ten minutes later.

Orlov turned in Romero's direction, heading toward the bus stop. Romero repositioned himself by backing into a doorway of one of the buildings and continued watching. Just as Orlov was about to step up onto one of the buses, Romero saw a young woman with a backpack, knit cap, and earbuds walk past him and drop something on the sidewalk as she cut through the queue of people getting onto the bus. The backpack was adorned with a patch, reading: "Tobb University of Economics and Technology." The woman was dressed as a college student, with auburn hair streaked with blond appearing in spots beneath her knit cap. But the glimpse Romero caught of her face seemed older. She knelt for just a moment to retrieve the item from the curb, and then moved hastily on down the sidewalk—disappearing into the crowd of pedestrians as rapidly as she had appeared.

But Romero saw what others hadn't noticed. As she returned to an upright position, the woman had pinched the hem of Orlov's coat momentarily with her right hand. When she moved on, there was a black button about the diameter of a pencil eraser attached there. Orlov had been tagged with a homing beacon.

Romero moved quickly, and barely made it into the bus with Orlov. The bus was crowded, and it took a couple of minutes for Romero to work himself into a position where he could speak to the Russian, who was hanging onto an overhead rail as the bus moved along. He leaned in and spoke quietly into

Orlov's ear, then moved on toward the back of the bus. As he did, another passenger near the back of the bus peered into his mobile phone as though selecting new music. In fact, he was surreptitiously snapping a photo of Romero and Orlov. Moments later, the photo was attached to a text message and sent off to the young woman who had attached the beacon to Orlov's coat a few minutes earlier. The woman stared at the photo for a few seconds, concluded she didn't know the operative in the picture, and forwarded the details in an encrypted email to her handler at the Russian Federal Security Service.

At the next stop, earlier than he would normally have done so, Orlov disembarked from the bus. He strolled along Durak Street, and eventually found what he was looking for—a homeless man cowering in an out-of-the-wind corner along the back of an aging restaurant. He shocked the man by giving him his coat. Then he walked back to the bus stop, where he resumed his journey with one more stop along the way at a local store to replace his recently donated garment. Romero continued to watch Orlov from a distance throughout the remainder of the journey, breaking off only when he observed Orlov entering the elevator at the Mövenpick. Then he headed back to his own hotel. Romero had detected no other tail on Orlov. It was another hour after settling into his own room at the Hilton before Winger knocked on his door.

"Just got back," Winger said when Romero had waved him to a chair. "I went to the airfield and poked around the aircraft to see whether there was any kind of locator or bomb or anything like that. I didn't find anything except Orlov's pistol—in a hidden compartment next to his seat—but I think we'd better check it again in the morning."

When Romero recounted the events of his evening, Winger pursed his lips and said: "So somebody is suspicious of Orlov, and it's somebody who knows he is in Ankara."

"It would have to be someone who knew he'd be here. Either someone he told or someone with access to his flight plans," Romero replied.

"Agreed," Winger replied through a frown. "He's pretty chatty with people he trusts, I guess, but the guy's basically a recluse. He lives in a cabin in the middle of Siberia most of the time; he has no family left up there. So I'm betting it's someone who can get to the flight plans he files."

"Well then, it's likely to be either the Russians or else …"

"Or else somebody on our side, and since he came to us through the Agency, that would mean somebody at CIA."

"Seems like it," Romero agreed. "But why try to tag him right now?"

"No way to know for sure, my friend," Winger said as he rose to leave. "Either they were hedging their bets on surveilling him while he is here in Ankara, or the beacon was designed to let them reacquire him when he gets on the ground to drop us off. We may never know. I'll leave the boss an update tonight before I turn in. See you for breakfast around 0500?"

"I'll be downstairs packed up and ready to go," Romero replied. He saw Winger out, and continued to turn it over in his mind until he finally drifted off to sleep about an hour later.

# CHAPTER 15

Before dawn on Saturday, Winger and Romero each rose even before the alarm clocks on their cell phones sounded. Both men had developed internal "alarm clocks" of their own, but liked the backup provided by their phones. Not much was available in terms of breakfast food at five a.m. in the area. But the night before, Winger had come across a 24-hour market offering baked goods as well as fresh fruits and light grocery items between the hotel and the airstrip, and it worked nicely for them.

They arrived at the airfield just after dawn, and Orlov was about ten minutes behind them. They stowed their gear in the back of the aircraft, and then—as Winger and Romero had discussed—made another quick visual check of the plane inside and out. Orlov seemed a bit puzzled at first, but humored the men. As they were about to finish up, though, using small flashlights to explore all of the dark crevices along the surfaces, Romero spotted something.

"Grigol, could you take a look at this?" Romero called down quietly to the Russian pilot.

Orlov and Winger both walked around to the port side of the aircraft and stood, one after another, on the small wooden stool alongside the plane Romero had been perched on.

"This is not mine," Orlov said angrily. "I have no idea how this is on my plane!"

"I believe you," Winger said. "I checked the aircraft out last night, and …" he grunted lightly as he stepped up onto the stool, "… this was definitely not here. It looks like a small transponder antenna. The transponder itself is somewhere else on the aircraft, of course. Grigol, are there any panels on the exterior of the fuselage that are easy to remove and replace quickly?"

Orlov thought for a few seconds and then said: "If I was hiding a homing device on this aircraft, I would put it in what you would call the tail boom," he said. "There are two panels there—one on each side—which are attached only with slotted screws to provide openings for maintenance and repairs." It took less than five minutes for Winger and Romero to remove the two covers and find the transponder. It took another five to remove it and toss it aside. With both the antenna and transponder discarded, the three men boarded and started the aircraft. Within twenty minutes they were taxiing down the airstrip. Only when they were airborne did a figure emerge from the shadows, where she had been observing the three men and silently snapping photos. A few minutes later, the same woman who had attached the beacon to Orlov's coat the night before was sending the images off from her smartphone.

Contrary to the dazzling performance reflected in so many American television dramas, facial recognition software is limited in capability. Beyond those limitations, archives that may be queried vary from agency to agency. Finally, even when an American operative is spotted in an area of interest, unless there is an alert similar to the American BOLO—be on the lookout—not much is done with the information. As a result, under most circumstances the observation of Billy Winger in Ankara would be of little interest to Russian intelligence.

However, as it happened on that day, an old adversary of Winger's was working the surveillance desk which had Orlov on its target list. As a result, suspicious activity associated with Orlov was being funneled across his desk, and—although the software hadn't recognized Winger—Yuri Dressen certainly did.

Now in his late fifties, Dressen was no longer an active field operator, but still worked an international counterintelligence post at the Federal Security Service in Moscow. He and Winger had crossed swords more than once when he was a younger man, and Winger had killed one of Dressen's closest colleagues in a gunfight in 1999.

When Winger's face appeared in the Orlov update report from Ankara, Dressen stiffened and said: "William Winger. So we meet again." He reached for the phone and called a friend who was closer to the heart of the action in Yasenevo. "I am working on an inquiry for Chief of the Soviet Operations and Technology Directorate, Vadim Shelepin," he said. This was a stretch, but Dressen was willing to risk a mild rebuke should someone try to verify his authority. "I need everything related to current activity on an American operative, William Winger, just as soon as you can provide it."

\*   \*   \*   \*

On Saturday evening, the phone on Yuri Dressen's desk rang. It was the operative he had spoken to in Yasenevo, informing him of an encrypted file he was sending. The file contained the information he requested on William Winger.

Dressen logged in to his email on the Federal Security Service's restricted network and downloaded the file. Information contained in the file from the "old days" was much thinner than he expected. Clearly, no one at the Service understood the impact of the loss of his former colleague, whose death at the hands of Winger was relegated to a single line in the report. Winger was still active and operating now somewhere near Russia—perhaps even in Russia itself. And now he was associated with Orlov, a man suspected of smuggling and who knew what else.

The file stated Winger had been doing independent security work for several years, apparently loosely associated with the American National Security Agency, and working on projects at the Brystol Foundation. Dressen knew a little about the Brystol Foundation; an American R&D company that worked mostly on US Department of Defense research and development projects. What would Winger do for such a company? And whatever it was, would it represent some kind of threat to mother Russia? The biggest R&D projects Dressen knew about were basically computer hacking of one form or another. Most substantial weapons technology research was now outsourced because of Russia's precipitous financial condition.

Basically, Russia bought or stole what others developed these days, with the possible exception of the Sukhoi PAK FA, which the Americans referred to as the T-50 fighter. Russia had placed a substantial financial bet on including stealth technology, new construction materials and coatings, and artificial intelligence. They were attempting to elevate Russia's military aircraft to a qualitatively new technological level, eclipsing the products of Boeing, Lockheed Martin, and Northrop Grumman in the United States. But almost immediately, international buyers who were planning to purchase the aircraft from Russia began to see critical reports on the product. Industry analysts described the platform as unreliable, with inadequate radar, and stealth features that were badly engineered. Russia's ability to make big investments like this with an uncertain payoff was diminishing. Although no one in the Russian government dared admit it, Dressen knew the situation was dire.

And then it dawned on him: *Could it be Shelepin was running a secret project? If he was, could the Americans possibly know? Could Winger be trying to sneak into Russia using Orlov and uncover it somehow?* The odds against it seemed astronomical. Even Dressen had no idea what Shelepin was doing these days. He only knew there was a top secret intelligence facility somewhere in Siberia, and they were going through a significant amount of money and scientific intellect. If the rumors were correct—and there were very few rumors—the talent involved was mostly physicists. There were only the hushed whispers of a few men, well past their appropriate intake of vodka, who had lost all of their discretion and most of their credibility. Those people typically disappeared shortly after starting such rumors, and Dressen had no intention of following in their footsteps.

How would Shelepin react if he suggested an American agent might be stalking his project, especially when Dressen knew so little about it? At this point, they knew nothing of Winger's purpose or destination. They only knew he was traveling with another man there in Turkey, they were with Orlov, and they were concealing their activities. He weighed the matter carefully for nearly an hour, and then made his decision. He would inform Shelepin. He would rather be perceived as too careful than derelict in his duty.

His next call was to a colleague at the Federal Border Guard Service of Russia. He reported that Shelepin was keenly interested in a low-end criminal named Grigol Orlov, and was inquiring about whether the Border Guard had any records of smuggling by Orlov. His friend reported there were no indications of such activity on Orlov's part. Several low-level bureaucrats and one mid-level Russian official had actually used Orlov's services for transport during hunting and fishing trips. As a result, the Guard had records of his pilot's license, aircraft identification number, and so on. It all looked to be in order.

"I understand Orlov is flying into Russia from Ankara today," Dressen said. "Do you have flight plans for him?"

"No, comrade," was his friend's reply after a moment of checking, "but sadly that does not mean very much. If the plans were filed in Ankara they would take some time—perhaps days—to catch up, and sometimes they do not come through to us at all. Especially in Siberia, these things are very uncertain."

Dressen thought about this for so long that his friend said, "Are you still there, Yuri?"

"Oh, yes, forgive me. I was thinking," Dressen replied. "I wonder, does the Guard have any aircraft patrolling the area where a small aircraft originating in Ankara would likely cross into Siberia?"

"We have a few assets there," his friend said, "but it would be what the Americans call a needle in a stack of hay. Most of our assets are maritime vessels, and our people are also watching the sea lanes. But the aircraft he is flying, an old Chernov Che-25, does not even have a modern transponder."

"Yes, you are right," he said. "But if there is someone patrolling along the border, please pass along the identification number of Orlov's aircraft anyway. I know the odds are against us, but one never knows. Someone may see something."

"Yes, of course," his friend replied. "I will order anyone who stops him to detain him and notify you. And I will send you his official address, in case you wish to send out a ground team. He lives up in the mountains—not very hospitable terrain, Yuri. But it is there where you are most likely to find him first."

Dressen thanked him and signed off.

\* \* \* \*

Orlov, Winger, and Romero were skirting mountaintops and, as they had done on their way out of Siberia the first time, hopping from lake to lake as they moved toward Mezhgorye. About midpoint on their journey, Orlov set down for the night on a river at Chyorny Yar. It was raining and windy, and Orlov's aircraft had been bounced around quite a bit; the travel time was almost twice what he had expected. Chyorny Yar was large enough for decent hotels and restaurants, and they were losing daylight, so it seemed a reasonable plan. Orlov knew he could dock his plane on the river there, and it would likely go unmolested during the night.

They landed at dusk, and the rain cleared enough for them to get safely down and taxi to shore with little trouble. Finding an abandoned pier at the city's edge, they tied up and locked the aircraft, leaving it rocking gently on the waves. The twinkling lights of the nearest buildings appeared to be about a quarter mile away. All three of the men were relieved to get out of the plane for a while.

They set off to walk into the city. Not far past the end of the dock, however, Orlov felt chilled and asked Winger and Romero to wait while he trotted back to the aircraft to grab his jacket. Just as he arrived at the aircraft, a small Russian Border Guard patrol boat that had been moving slowly upriver swung in toward shore. The boat fixed a spotlight on the Chernov's tail number, and then on Orlov as it approached. Over a bullhorn, one of the two crew members aboard the patrol boat called out to Orlov, commanding him to stay where he was.

"This isn't good," Winger said to Romero, and the two men walked a little distance down the shoreline, getting away from the pier. "We're going to have to flank them somehow and try to get them contained before they call for backup."

"I don't think a gunfight is a good idea, Boss," Romero said. "We're too close to the city."

"You're probably right, Chief," Winger replied. "If I distract them once they get up by Orlov, do you think you can scramble up the end of the pier where those pilings are and get the drop on 'em?"

"Looks like about the only thing to do, at this point," Romero said. "We're lucky we were already up here when these guys rolled in."

"Yeah, you got that right," Winger replied. "OK, let's give it a try. You wander downstream before you cut back over to the shoreline, so you're hidden by the aircraft a little as you approach. I'll give you a couple of minutes and then start the show."

Understanding seconds mattered, Romero walked briskly away into the dusk as Winger removed his jacket, turning it inside out. He pulled one side of his shirt loose from his pants, pulled the inside-out jacket back on, and lurched toward the pier. Winger sang the only song he knew in Russian as loudly and sloppily as he could. He staggered occasionally, falling to the ground at one point, and regaining his stance by pulling himself up by the railing along the pier. Finally, when he could see one of the two patrol boat crew members had docked their boat and the other was clambering ashore, he staggered the last few steps until he was just a few yards from Orlov. Pretending to be oblivious to everything around him, Winger unzipped his fly, and continued singing loudly as he began to urinate over the edge of the pier.

Winger could hear the shouts of the nearest Border Guard patrolman as he attempted to get Winger to move on, but Winger ignored them. Attempting to sing even louder, he turned to face them. His urine was still splashing freely in a stream that wavered heavily in an arc approaching the first patrolman. At this point, Winger was reaching a crescendo, raising his arms high in the air, and singing at the top of his voice. The patrolmen were no longer amused now that this large, drunken man was seemingly prepared to urinate on uniformed officers of the Guard, and they both focused their attention momentarily on Winger.

At that point, Romero slipped over the edge of the pier and headed for the patrolman closest to him. He was only eight or nine feet away, and closed the distance in seconds. Reaching around him, Romero used his KA-BAR knife to slit the man's throat, then gently lowered his body to the pier. The patrolman closer to Winger, standing just abreast of Orlov, heard none of this. But he was beginning to reach for his sidearm anyway, apparently to punctuate his shouted warnings to Winger. It was enough. Orlov lurched forward to hold the patrolman's gun hand down as Romero grabbed him from behind, ending his life in a manner similar to the first man.

Winger finished urinating over the side of the pier, redressed, and returned to the group. Romero and Orlov were already stowing the two bodies on the patrol boat, and covering them with a tarp.

"I don't think they had time to call in for backup, Boss," Romero said, "but I still think we'd probably better find another spot to refuel and eat, don't you?"

"Da," Orlov agreed. "The Border Guard must be looking for my aircraft."

Winger concurred. "You're probably right, Grigol. Let's put some distance between us and this place. Even thirty minutes would be enough, I think."

"I know another place," Orlov said. "Let us go before there is no light left at all."

Within ten minutes, the trio was airborne again, headed to another spot Orlov knew was a bit more off the beaten path. Once they were aloft, thinking about what had transpired, Winger said: "Grigol, I think we have to assume someone has identified us, and they are now watching for us. It would be dangerous, I think, to land at your place as we had planned. Is there another place to land, not far from Mezhgorye, but not so close it would attract the attention of our friends on the ground?"

"Yes, I have another place," Orlov replied. "It is more difficult, but it can be done. Since the weather is clearing now, I think we should be there before noon tomorrow, even after we stop for a while tonight for rest."

"Great," Winger replied. "Thanks, Grigol. Just keep us as close to the tree line as you can so we don't have any more visibility on radar than we have to."

As it turned out, the landing strip was very short, even for Orlov's comparatively small aircraft, but it had two advantages; it was surrounded by thick trees, and it was actually closer to Winger's rendezvous point with Potter. Especially with pursuers now on the hunt, Winger knew he needed every edge he could get.

# CHAPTER 16

Bi-shou left her true identification papers at the Chinese Dragon and transformed herself into Sheryl Wen before crossing into Canada by automobile. At the Toronto airport, she saw Dawson traveling as William Lee and Gerard who was traveling as Linda Kaye. In the guise of independent passengers who were ostensibly strangers, the three didn't interact during the trip, and separately arranged for transportation to their hotels in Prague.

* * * *

By the time they landed on Monday afternoon, Winger and Romero had less than a day to make it to the intended rendezvous point with Potter. While a few hours probably wouldn't matter a lot, it was dangerous for Potter and his team to loiter anywhere for too long. On the other hand, trying to move too quickly on foot through the Siberian terrain was just as dangerous, even for experienced operators like Winger and Romero.

They said farewell to Orlov and got under way. The portable GPS unit built into Winger's watch led him and Romero through a narrow pass between Orlov's landing strip and a steep, rocky hill, then on toward the rendezvous location. It was a fairly arduous trek. Like their earlier visit, Winger and Romero were careful to watch for signs that their path might be planted with surveillance equipment, further slowing their approach. Even so, they arrived in just over four hours.

Potter and his team were there, and Potter walked out from his camp to meet them. His team was comprised of nineteen men and one woman, all of whom were battle-hardened veterans of various conflicts with the Russian armed forces. A few of them were in their thirties but the others ranged in age from their forties to their fifties. All appeared to be physically fit and seemed comfortable with their AK-47 rifles. They wore backpacks and carried sidearms. Potter also carried a field duffle with C-4, ammunition, and some other ordnance. Four of them spoke English well and the others understood some basic English phrases. Between that and Winger's knowledge of Russian, the situation seemed workable to Winger and Potter.

The group split into two teams. The first team was led by Romero and the second team was led by Potter. Winger and Potter's lead man, a serious-looking young fighter called Mikhail, performed advance scouting work. The teams started out about an hour apart. If Winger's calculations were correct, they would arrive sometime on Wednesday at the hunting lodge where he, Dawson, and Romero had set up surveillance the last time they visited Mezhgorye.

\*  \*  \*  \*

On Tuesday morning, Vadim Shelepin's mobile phone buzzed. Shelepin was being chauffeured through Prague. His black limo was followed by a single chase car containing his four-man personal security detail. He was headed toward the auction site to look over the facility as final preparations were underway. The buzz was an incoming email from his executive assistant. Shelepin checked it immediately, and then directed his driver to change course, turning instead toward the Russian embassy. "Pod Kastany One, driver. Right away," he barked.

The driver knew that address and corrected course immediately, speaking briefly into his mobile phone to the driver of their security detail in the chase car as he drove.

At the embassy, Shelepin moved briskly through the security checkpoints and into the office for visiting dignitaries, brushing aside the deferential offers of assistance from various members of the embassy staff as he moved through the building. With the door closed firmly behind him and his lead security operator posted just outside, Shelepin punched the number of his own office from the secure line in the room. His administrative assistant picked up immediately.

"Sir, I have a report from the one of our people, Captain Yuri Dressen, who is working a counterespionage desk up at Yasenevo. He reported the movement of an American operative in northern Europe, with suspected travel plans around or into Siberia. The operative's name is William Winger."

"Why does this strike you as urgent?" Shelepin growled. "You know I am extremely busy."

"Yes, Sir," the assistant replied, seemingly undeterred, "but Winger is a former clandestine operator associated with the Central Intelligence Agency, a former American Special Operations staff member of the United States Army, and has been on the watch list here in the Russian intelligence community for years. More importantly, Winger is now believed to be working for the US National Security Agency and supporting special projects for a black operations research contractor called the Brystol Foundation."

Shelepin thought about this. "Where was he seen, and by whom?"

His assistant read out the pertinent details, and Shelepin continued to think about what he was hearing. "So this Winger is traveling with one other man and a tour operator—someone named Orlov—last seen in Turkey, and Captain Dressen says this is a matter of urgency for me?"

"Yes, Sir," the assistance replied evenly, "and he could be correct. Winger was responsible for the loss of one of Dressen's friends several years ago in a matter you may recall—we called it 'Leopold' in those days."

Shelepin remembered the incident all too well. A breathtaking advance in methods for uranium enrichment had nearly been obtained from some rogue Pakistani scientists, and at the last minute, the CIA had become involved. Months of undercover operations were blown, they lost three of their best agents, and they lost an opportunity to advance the Russian nuclear program by several years. If he surmised correctly, that debacle was likely the reason Captain Dressen fell off the fast track in Russian intelligence, landing him on a counterespionage desk. *He was fortunate with that fate,* Shelepin thought.

"And you suspect there may be a connection between Winger and my on-going work?"

"I cannot say, Sir," the assistant now demurred, not wanting to be chasing ghosts. He could tell it was a delicate time in Shelepin's work, and had no desire to be raising false alarms. But the alternative of failing to call a potential threat to Shelepin's attention could be far worse. "But it is very coincidental timing."

Shelepin had already moved both the core demonstration technology and Antonov to Prague, so he perceived no immediate threat from one or two American operatives buzzing around the Siberian wilderness with a hunting guide. If it was the new anti-gravity technology they were after, there was a great deal of the intellectual property still at the facility in Mezhgorye. But there was little likelihood one or two operatives would be able to break into an armed facility, remote though it was, and spirit the information away.

Then an idea occurred to him; perhaps he could use this event to cover the loss of the technology resulting from his surreptitious auction. It would be extremely convenient. Sell the technology to the highest bidder, blame the loss on American spies, and perhaps even capture or—better still—kill the spies in the process. Even if this man Winger was simply doing some fishing or hunting, Shelepin felt he could probably make use of him for that purpose. *Yes, this has real possibilities,* he thought.

"Very well," he replied to his assistant, "you say there is now an alert for this American agent issued through the Border Guard?"

"Only for the tour guide Orlov, Sir," the assistant replied, "and it is now designated as a low priority. Dressen has no knowledge of your work, of course, and reasoned you might not want to draw unnecessary attention."

*Dressen sounds like a wise man,* Shelepin thought. "Very well," he replied. "Thank Captain Dressen for his discretion, and tell him I expect it to continue. I want him to quietly but aggressively pursue the Americans on my behalf, and let you know as soon as he has found them. I want to bring Winger and this other man into custody as soon as possible."

"Yes, Sir," the assistant replied.

"And no leaks. I want this completely off the radar. Make sure that is understood."

"It will be done, Sir," the assistant replied again.

Fifteen minutes later, Shelepin was back in his limo and headed to the auction site.

When he arrived, Shelepin found the building was coming along nicely. As long as there was no interest in a sustainable facility, it was relatively easy to cover the decaying walls and crumbling floors with curtains and rolls of carpeting. Portable lighting was positioned in appropriate ways to lead the eye only to the areas desired, abandoning the balance of the structure to indiscernible gulfs of darkness. It left the impression of an ancient castle, dressed up for a Christmas ball.

The display area had been outfitted with an elevated lectern and microphone. Three demonstration areas were erected in an arc surrounding the lectern, facing the offices where bidders would be housed during the auction. It was impressive, backed by heavy blue draperies that disappeared into the darkness some thirty feet above the floor.

The offices themselves were being outfitted with rented furniture to suit their intended occupants; bars were being set in place, speakers wired, and computer terminals positioned in one corner of each room for purposes of conducting the actual bidding. Flat screen displays were mounted in the offices, enabling bidders to shift their virtual vantage point to multiple cameras, even as they observed the events in real time below them on the display floor. There would be two technicians in each office, along with the bidder or bidders. Each party was allowed up to two participants. One technician assured all of the electronics were working properly and that bidders would be able to understand how to use them. The other technician would be there for processing wire transfers and assuring the fidelity of the bids.

A security person would be posted outside each office. Individual bidders would be met by Shelepin's people and driven separately to the venue on a strict schedule, with limo windows heavily darkened. Arrivals would be spaced at intervals which kept bidders from seeing one another, and had everyone in their bidding chambers at least ten minutes before the event began. Shelepin could see it was all coming together nicely. By Friday morning, they should be down to dry running the presentation and stocking the liquor cabinets.

\* \* \* \*

After arriving in Prague on Wednesday, Bi-shou checked into the Aria Hotel. Dawson and Gerard were booked into the Four Seasons, carefully minimizing their exposure to anyone who might be watching the Aria, or watching Bi-shou.

As Bi-shou checked in, the desk clerk inquired as to the reason for her visit in Prague. After saying she was in town to participate in the International Agricultural Association Conference, the desk clerk smiled and said: "Oh yes, of course. We have you listed as a conference attendee." He slid an envelope across the desk to her and said: "I think you will find this information about the conference helpful."

"Thank you," Bi-shou replied. "Tell me, have any of the other participants arrived yet?"

The clerk's smile froze in place as he stated resolutely: "I cannot say, Ms. Wen. I do not have the participant list. I only see that individuals are attendees when they arrive and check in."

"Oh, I see," she responded coyly, "then I am the first to arrive?"

"I only just came on duty recently, so I really could not say," the intrepid clerk replied. "Will there be anything else?" He was beckoning to the bellman as he spoke. Clearly, he had already determined there *was* nothing else, and Bi-shou was escorted to her room.

When she had settled in, Bi-shou opened the envelope provided to her by the clerk. She found a message typed on a single sheet of paper with an official-looking logo which merely instructed her to be prepared to depart for the conference from the lobby at nine p.m. Friday. Transportation would be provided. Since it was Wednesday, Dawson and Gerard had roughly a day and a half to get whatever preparations they wanted in place. She photographed the document and placed it in the drafts folder of her Gmail account. As she headed downstairs to arrange her dinner, Bi-shou wondered what Billy Winger was doing.

\* \* \* \*

At the Four Seasons Hotel, Dawson and Gerard checked in separately. Gerard waited discreetly while Dawson checked in first, then approached only as Dawson moved toward the elevators. He entered the elevator, and as he punched the button for the sixth floor, another passenger slipped in beside him carrying a large duffle. The man was a nondescript middle-aged man. He looked to Dawson to be in his early forties, wearing business casual attire and wireframe glasses. When the door closed, the man turned to Dawson and stuck out his hand. "Ben Dawson?" he asked.

"That's right," Dawson said. He'd been expecting something like this.

"Todd Connelly," the man said. "I have your equipment. It came in as diplomatic material with a courier this afternoon. I'll take it to your room for you, if you'd like."

The elevator had stopped and it was time to exit. "That would be great," Dawson replied. "Thanks."

The men walked down the hall, rounded a corner, and Dawson set his own bags down on the floor just outside the door of room 603. "Thanks, Connelly," Dawson said again, "this is me." He nodded to the room. "I'll take it from here."

Connelly set the duffel down. "All right," he replied. "Good luck, and enjoy your time in Prague." He wheeled and turned back toward the elevators. Dawson took his time, and only when Connelly was out of sight around the corner did he lift his bags and reposition them across the hall. Dawson was actually in room 604, but he saw no reason to make his room number known to Connelly, though he had no reason to mistrust the man. *Old habits,* he thought. *Well, they've kept me alive for quite a while now.*

Gerard came by Dawson's room about thirty minutes later and they unpacked the equipment. Gerard took half the equipment back to her room and prepared for the next day's excursion. Each of them ordered room service and by midnight Dawson and Gerard were both asleep.

# CHAPTER 17

Early Thursday morning, Dawson and Gerard met just outside the hotel and walked to a nearby coffee shop. They each wore a medium-size backpack and were dressed casually in cargo jeans and rugged shoes. As soon as they had placed their order, Dawson nodded in the direction of a corner table where a spindly man was seated alone, sipping coffee and reading the local paper. Dawson approached the man, and smiling, stuck out his hand. "Vladimír Kolář, it is good to see you again," he said.

The man looked up, smiled, and put down his paper. "And you, my friend," he said. "It has been too many years. But you are looking well."

Kolář, now in his seventies, still had the bright eyes and supple movements of a younger man. Dawson introduced Gerard and they sat down across from him. Dawson explained to Gerard that Kolář was an old friend, and he was renowned for his familiarity with the Prague underground. In fact, Kolář had been a useful local intelligence source for both the CIA and NSA for decades.

"Underground?" Gerard asked.

Kolář smiled. "Yes, my young friend, but probably not in the exact sense you are thinking of. Underground places interested me even as a boy, which is why I went to study at the School of Mining and Geology. In my second year, in 1965, I joined the Prague Speleological Club with pupils of Prague's primary schools. I started exploring caves with fellow cavers and later became very intrigued by the Petřín tunnels. There are more than 4,000 kilometers of sewers under the city. Much of Prague's historical sewer system, the part constructed before World War II, remained intact even after the new sewer system was built. I worked on the Metro for twenty-six years in the safety system control center, and I know it all."

"I had no idea there was such an elaborate underground in Prague," Gerard replied. "It sounds mysterious."

"It is certainly unusual," Dawson interjected. "Tell me, Vladimír, is the restaurant in the cave where we dined the last time I was here still open?"

"The Black Sun? Oh, yes, and many others like it," he said. "There's Seven Swabians, Peklo, Czech Master's; quite a lot of them these days."

Looking back again at Gerard, he continued: "Yes, and parts of it are quite mysterious. For example, there are underground hospitals like the Thomayer University Hospital, Na Bulovce Hospital, and also the former underground hospital at Charles Square." The old man chuckled. "But that is now in very bad condition because it has been used as a vegetable store over recent years. In Prague, there are also many church facilities such as crypts underground, some of which contain a lot of mummies, and that is particularly interesting to tourists. There is also an extensive burial place in the Church of the Most Holy Trinity—Kostel Nejsvětější Trojice—on Spálená Street."

"Fascinating," Gerard replied, and then looked at Dawson. "But I presume we are interested in these for our own purposes?"

"Yes," Dawson replied. "Vladimír has agreed to escort us to the area we are focused on this morning. I'm pretty sure we'll find it useful."

After a bagel and hot tea, they hailed a taxi and traveled to a street corner about two blocks from the building they believed to be the auction site. They followed Kolář down a dank, close alleyway to a rusting iron gate. The gate controlled access to an unmarked opening in a narrow stone wall. Kolář produced a large iron key and pulled a bulbous electrical lantern from the pocket of his overcoat. Once inside the gate, he locked it again while Dawson and Gerard retrieved flashlights from their own backpacks, then pulled on tight gloves. Gerard pulled her fiery auburn hair back into a ponytail and fixed it there.

Humming quietly to himself, Kolář moved off down the cave, at first strewn with trash, but rapidly giving way to largely undisturbed passageways of stone and mud, damp and pungent and seemingly endless. They walked on at a steady pace for about twenty minutes, and finally Kolář slowed and began to probe one of the openings stemming from the main passageway. The only distinctive feature marking that particular opening was a small and nearly unreadable sign scratched in the stone which read: "Malá Strana."

There, they turned and walked almost ten minutes further. At that point there was a larger room with two doorways positioned on their right, about three feet above the surface on which they stood. Both of them looked as though they were solid and ancient oak. The first door was positioned above crumbling stone stairs, and there were no stairs at all below the second one. They were fixed with massive, roughly fashioned iron hinges that looked as though they were centuries old. Kolář whispered: "This is the one."

Dawson and Gerard unshouldered their backpacks. First they donned lightweight coveralls with small badges that signaled their wearers in the event of methane, carbon monoxide, and other deadly gasses in significant concentration. Then Gerard brought out a device similar in size and shape to a cell phone, with earphones attached. Another lead from the device ended in what looked like an elongated push pin. She pressed the pointed end of the lead into the wood of the door, and then they all stood silently as Gerard tuned the device. She listened carefully through the earphones, then removed them and said, "all clear."

As Gerard returned the device to her backpack, Dawson removed the cover from a short, stubby metal cylinder and pulled on some small darkened goggles. He positioned his flashlight on the ground where it shone onto the latch that locked the door in place, and nudged the goggles into position. As he did so, Gerard and Kolář turned their backs. Then Dawson engaged the industrial-strength laser and cut his way through the lock. After returning the laser to his backpack, Dawson retrieved a small pry bar. He went to work around the edges of the door closest to the lock, and after about five minutes, had the door open by a few inches. While Kolář held the lantern, Dawson and Gerard moved, getting into positions where they could use the strength of their legs to greatest advantage. Another five minutes of exertion allowed Dawson and Gerard to widen the opening enough to squeeze through.

The next passageway was partially obstructed by dirt and debris, washed loose over the years. Another forage in the backpacks produced camping shovels. Gerard and Dawson moved enough of the obstruction to clamber over the remainder of the pile. The end of the passage was another heavy wooden door. Gerard repeated her exercise with the listening device, taking longer this time. When she removed the earbuds, she whispered to Dawson and Kolář: "I can hear people talking and moving around but they seem to be a long way off, maybe even in another room. I think we can go ahead and try to work the mechanism—see if we can gain access—but we'll need to be careful."

Both men nodded. The air was now stuffy and foul. Not the smell of sewage, but decay and wet soil. All three of them were glossy with perspiration, and mud stuck to their shoes in heavy clumps as they worked. Dawson checked the gas indicator on his badge, and then brought the compact laser to bear again on the ancient iron mechanisms securing the door. When it seemed he had worked his way through them, he stepped back and waited as Gerard listened again at the door.

This time they waited silently for almost three minutes before Gerard withdrew the device and said, "It's no louder. I still hear a few muffled and distant voices, and some mechanical sounds—machinery of some kind—but I sense no alarm."

With that, Dawson and Gerard went to work again with their small pry bars and shovels. After nearly an hour, Dawson was thinking they might have to return later with small winches or larger pry bars. He and Gerard were both getting tired and cold, and Kolář appeared to be uncomfortable as well. He looked as though the cold and damp was creeping into his thin, aged frame.

Just as Dawson was about to admit failure for the morning and recommend a return engagement in the afternoon, he felt the edge of the door give a fraction of an inch. It made a wet scuffing sound; rotting wood moving heavily across the stone threshold. Again they paused, and Gerard listened. Again she signaled Dawson to continue. Less than thirty minutes later, the door was ajar and they could see dimly inside the underground chamber below the distribution warehouse Wahl had discovered some days earlier.

A quick examination around the edges of the door revealed no alarms or tripwires. Scanning the tiny chamber with his small flashlight, Dawson could see no sign of surveillance cameras. In fact, it looked as though no one had even entered the room for many years. The air was fresher, and the three weary spies inhaled it gratefully as it streamed into the cavern. Working the door as quietly as they could, Dawson and Gerard managed to get it open enough for one person at a time to squeeze through.

Once inside, they found a place for Kolář to sit, and Dawson instructed him to stay put while he and Gerard explored the facility. Dawson and Gerard removed their coveralls, hoping that if they were spotted it would not be obvious how they had gained entrance. Initially, based on the muted sounds and limited light filtering into the underground through cracks in the floor, Dawson thought the entire underground level was unoccupied. But as he and Gerard picked their way carefully through the chambers, they discovered a large room near a freight elevator on the far side of the building. It was being used as a storage and equipment staging site. The building was enormous, and the floor of the underground chambers was a debris field comprised of old office furniture, packing materials, and loose bricks. It appeared the rickety freight elevator had been restored to a usable condition. In the storage room, Dawson and Gerard found lighting equipment, rolls of electrical cabling, portable screens, and some sound equipment; components one might expect to find in the control room at a theatre. Just outside the room on the opposite side of the freight elevator was an open stairway leading to the ground level. It was unguarded, and again Dawson found no alarms or surveillance cameras.

Dawson and Gerard crept forward, climbing the stairs cautiously. Dawson's flashlight was at its narrowest and dimmest setting, and Gerard had hers stowed in the pocket of her cargo jeans. Both of them still wore their backpacks and carried 9mm pistols. The stairs turned ninety degrees across a large landing at midpoint, then continued on to the ground floor. No sentries were posted at the top of the stairway. At the landing, there was sufficient ambient light from the ground floor to allow Dawson to stow his flashlight as well. When they reached the top of the steps, they peered tentatively into the enormous ground floor of the structure.

It was a beehive of activity, and the transformation of the old warehouse was already amazing. At the far end of the building, most distant from the receiving and shipping docks, was a mezzanine-style row of what must have been offices overlooking the main floor. The windows had been removed, so there remained a half-dozen rooms with unrestricted views of the auction. Large spotlights had been erected over them which were directed downward about twenty feet above the floor. Another row was positioned parallel to the floor of the facility and about forty feet above the ground. It looked as though there was a stairway formed from iron grating opening into each end of a narrow hall just behind the offices, undoubtedly to provide access to the offices through individual doorways off the hall.

Dawson whispered briefly in Gerard's ear. Even though they were both dirty and covered with perspiration, Dawson caught a tiny wisp of her fragrance, Sand & Sable, from the skin behind her ear as he whispered, and he drew in a deep breath as he finished. She nodded, smiling to herself because she had noticed, and stepped back. She retrieved a small video camera from her backpack as Dawson watched their surroundings, set it on low-light, and engaged it. She followed Dawson as he slipped around the edge of the stairway and made his way to the deepest shadows along the wall, then through them toward the area where men were working feverishly to set up the auction site.

Because there was so much activity underway, and because the warehouse was so large, Dawson and Gerard remained fairly obscure and completely unnoticed. There were armed sentries just inside the main doors and at the shipping and receiving dock area. But there did not appear to be any security people working inside the facility itself. It looked to Dawson as though there were about two dozen people erecting the main display area, installing power cables, and organizing the preparation zone just behind ten-foot-tall portable screens. A wall of screens stood about fifteen feet behind the main display area, so the offices were primarily overlooking the display but also able to see the preparation zone in the distance. The main control center for lights and sound was a large office cubicle erected hastily behind the last portable screen, out of sight of the mezzanine offices in one corner of the preparation zone.

The workers appeared to know exactly what to do, but there were a few commands barked out from time to time by a burly-looking man near the center of the display areas. He was bent over a blueprint laid out on a portable table, and all of the orders were spoken in Russian. Occasionally the man would respond to a question or statement made through a portable radio, and he would usually stiffen up and look briefly over one shoulder at the mezzanine area when he replied. There was clearly work going on in those offices as well, and over the course of an hour or so, florescent lights flickered to life in each of them.

Dawson and Gerard moved around more than half of the perimeter, videotaping and skirting carefully around the security guards at the front door. During their excursion, one bank of six mercury vapor lights slowly came online over the main display area. These were suspended from metal roof trusses, about fifty feet above the floor. Mercury vapor lights have a very slow start-up sequence, and cast the area in an unhealthy-looking orangish yellow pallor. They were very common factory lighting devices between the 1950s and 1960s because they produced a great deal of light at very low cost, and the lighting elements were quite durable. As the glow from these lights intensified, it ate away at the deep shadows concealing Dawson and Gerard. Within about thirty minutes of their ignition, the lighting had become reasonably bright and Dawson knew they would have to retreat soon.

The workers wore no uniforms; they were all dressed in various forms of casual clothing and work boots. Some wore work gloves and a couple of them operating power saws and drills had donned goggles. But as nearly as Dawson could see, there was nothing about their clothing that really distinguished them from the Russian workers. After considering this for a minute, Dawson decided he would take a chance. He softly whispered again into Gerard's ear. This time, as he explained his plan, he sensed her face tightening into a frown; she didn't like this at all, but he knew she would comply and cover him to the extent she could.

Dawson and Gerard had watched laborers carrying rolls of electrical cabling, curtains, and other materials up the iron stairs for some time, supplying workers in the mezzanine with materials they were using to fit out the offices. Just to confirm his suspicions about the purpose of these offices, Dawson wanted a closer look. When there was a pause in the action, Dawson left his backpack with Gerard and emerged from the shadows. He strode to a pile of materials near the bottom on the stairs and grabbed a spool of electrical cable. He carried the spool up the stairs and walked slowly down the hallway, looking as long as he dared into each room off the narrow hallway as he went.

In four of the rooms there were comfortable chairs installed in front of the windows, with narrow tables in front of them. Electrical wiring had been run to speakers beside the chairs and to microphones positioned on the tables. Every room was also fitted out with a small bar and ice dispenser. On each table there was a pair of binoculars, and at the end of each table was a folding chair and what looked to Dawson to be an Ethernet hookup for a laptop computer. There were workers in the first three offices so he continued on. When he passed the fourth room, he could see there was no one in it. He stepped inside, pulled the small camera from his cargo jeans, and slowly swept the room with it. Then he stepped forward and, staying behind the wall alongside the window, used the camera to pan the display area below and its surroundings. Then he slipped it back into his pocket and returned to the hallway.

The fifth room, which was also unoccupied, was set up differently. The glass was still in the window overlooking the main floor. There were two benches in front of a long, low cooling unit. Dawson had seen units like these a number of times. In mobile data centers, they were used to cool computer servers. This was unmistakably the control center for the auction activities to come. Dawson moved as rapidly as he could without raising suspicion, returning to Gerard on the main floor. He sat the spool of cable down on the floor and foraged in his backpack again.

Whispering, Dawson explained, "I found the control room. I need to get a bug in there."

Gerard replied, "Ben, it's getting lighter in here. I think we've got less than ten minutes to get back to the stairway."

Dawson nodded his head briefly and said: "I know." Then, pulling a small case from his backpack, he was off again. This time he left the spool, which was too bulky to manage well, and grabbed a bolt of navy blue cloth to take with him. The cloth was being used to construct curtains against the walls of the offices. This made sense to Dawson; faster than painting, the curtains would add sound-deadening qualities, and in the dim lighting of the ware-house, would make the dingy office spaces seem almost elegant. The floors of the offices had been covered with thick rugs as well. Dawson crossed under-neath the mezzanine, nodded silently to another worker who was walking in the opposite direction, and didn't respond to his mumbled Russian greeting. Dawson didn't know any Russian, and right about then he was wishing Billy Winger was there. Winger knew enough Russian to get by. Forced into a con-versation, Dawson would be completely helpless.

When he reached the control center again, Dawson wasted no time. He threw the cloth aside, ripped open the small case, and yanked out two dime-sized wireless audio-video surveillance cameras as well as an electronic signal booster. He placed them as quickly and strategically as he could, snapped the case closed, and grabbed the cloth again. Just as he turned to leave the office, a man's back appeared in it. Dawson stepped back and watched helplessly as the man grunted and continued walking backward through the door, carrying one end of a long computer server rack. Dawson simply stepped back and allowed the two men to pass. Fortunately, they were devoted single-mindedly to their task, and barely recognized there was another person in the room. As soon as they got inside with their cargo, Dawson slipped behind the second man and raced down the stairs. Rejoining Gerard, he dropped the cloth atop the spool of cable, and the two began to thread their way back again toward the stairs. If the light erased their cover completely before they could enter the stairwell, Dawson knew their odds of escape would drop to nearly zero.

It took nearly twenty minutes for Dawson and Gerard to make their way back to the top of the stairs near the freight elevator. About fifty feet from the stairway entrance, they were both startled to see bright light dawning from the direction of the receiving docks, and a jarring clatter of activity. Light was flooding in from the opening of the dock's outer doors, blocked only slightly by an air curtain of grungy plastic strips suspended over the opening.

Realizing they had mere seconds, Gerard followed Dawson's lead as he hastily removed his backpack and carried it in his arms as though it was cargo to the stairway. He reasoned that if it looked as though he was simply carrying supplies down to the storage room, he wouldn't seem out of place. It worked; Dawson and Gerard made it into the stairway and almost to the landing before footsteps and the sound of motors—*diesel powered forklifts,* Dawson surmised—began to emanate from the front of the stairway where they had just been. *It's a miracle,* Dawson thought. Although it was pulled back into a ponytail, Gerard's beautiful auburn hair was far too red to resemble any of the Russian workers Dawson had seen. Even in cargo pants and a denim shirt, her profile was undeniably feminine. Anyone who paid even a modicum attention to them would have spotted the incongruities almost immediately.

When Dawson and Gerard returned to the tunnel's entry point, they were alarmed to find Kolář missing from the position where they had left him. But a few seconds of panning the room with their flashlights revealed the old man leaning back into a dark corner, softly snoring on a pillow fashioned from their coveralls. Dawson continued to look backward along their path of escape from the warehouse while Gerard gently awakened Kolář, and one by one, they squeezed through the barely-open doorway to the underground caverns.

As soon as they emerged into daylight, Dawson retrieved his phone and placed an email in his Gmail account drafts folder, with the file name "Wahl" and the current date. The message cryptically informed Wahl their target location was correct and surveillance devices had been placed there. Then he sent a text message to Wahl telling him to check his incoming mail.

* * * *

Bi-shou spent Thursday morning performing a number of errands. She took a cab to the local car rental office, where she rented a mid-size van with room for five people and cargo. Then she drove to the train station and picked up express tickets secured by Gloria Treadway under their assumed names for Dawson, Gerard, and Bi-shou, as well as one ticket for an additional passenger, Andrei Aksyonov. Treadway had arranged for the train tickets through John Deering's office at the CIA, since the involvement of Potter's team made this a joint operation. Similarly, Treadway arranged for flight reservations under those names leaving Dresden, Germany a day later than the train, in case there was a need to drive some distance from Prague in order to avoid potential pursuers.

In the lining of her travel bag, Bi-shou carried identification papers—a Canadian passport, a MasterCard, and a Toronto driver's license—for Andrei Aksyonov; but the photos on the driver's license and the passport were of Sergei Antonov.

# CHAPTER 18

The two teams led by Romero and Potter finally arrived at the hunting lodge and rendezvoused late Wednesday afternoon. Exhausted from their trek, they were gratified to have the following day to recover.

Around dusk on Thursday, the team began to disburse around the military installation at Mezhgorye. When they were in position, they hunkered down to wait for darkness before assaulting their target. Winger asked Potter to put two men on patrol on each side. He and Romero each worked with one other man to cover their flank in rotating one-hour shifts, using night vision equipment. When Winger was not on patrol, he picked up enough of the conversation among those resting to hear an interesting tale about the local area. When he asked Potter about it, Winger expected the CIA operative to deny what he had heard, or at least laugh it off. So he was surprised at Potter's response: "Yes, honestly I was worried Yamantau Mountain was our target," he said quietly.

"What is it?" Winger asked.

"Well, it's a little like our Area 51," Potter replied. "Everyone knows the Russian Ministry of Defense is doing big things there, but no one knows exactly what."

Winger was skeptical about denials from an operative like Potter, especially one whose area of operations—AO—encompassed the area under discussion.

"So it's 'need to know,' then?"

"No, it's not like that, Billy," Potter replied. "We truly *don't* know—or at least *I* don't know. It may be just a relic of the Cold War, but it might not," he shrugged. "Locals say hidden inside Yamantau Mountain in the Beloretsk area there is a huge underground complex. It is supported by a railroad, a highway, and at one time it was populated by thousands of workers. Rumors say it covers an area the size of Washington, DC inside the Beltway. It's been reported there are provisions for living inside a network of man-made caves; an underground warehouse for food and clothing, and a shelter for the Russian national leadership in case of nuclear war. Some of our analysts believe the Yamantau Mountain project was associated with the 'Dead Hand' nuclear retaliatory command and control system for strategic missile engagements."

Winger emitted a brief, low whistle. "Never heard of it," he said, "which frankly surprises me. I've been away for several years now, but still ..."

"Yeah, I know what you mean," Potter replied. "They are said to have been working on the thing since 1996. I even saw an article in the New York Times about a 'mammoth underground military complex being built by the Russians in the Urals' back in '97, but then the trail went cold."

"Sounds like it would be almost adjacent to one of Russia's remaining nuclear weapons labs, Chelyabinsk-70," Winger said. "I wonder if that's where Shelepin draws his staff for this facility."

Potter nodded, "I wouldn't be surprised. But if the rumors about Yamantau Mountain were true, and it's still an active Ministry of Defense site, then ..."

"Then it's also a likely point of origin for a QRF—quick reaction force— when we make ourselves known down here," Winger finished Potter's thought.

About then, one of Potter's team appeared hurriedly from the woods to their north. "Sir," the man said, "we came across a patrol from the base below. Three men. We took care of them, but they will be missed as soon as they do not report in."

"Sounds like we'd better call in our own patrols and get started," Winger said to Potter. "It's getting close to time anyway." Potter nodded, and Winger keyed the mic on his radio three short bursts. Two bursts, a pause, and two more bursts came from Romero, then a similar three-burst pattern came from the remaining patrol of Potter's team members.

Romero signaled his partner and began to return to the rest of the group. Moving silently through the brush, Romero's head was on a constant pivot, relying on night vision goggles to scan the surrounding forest. His partner, the only female on Potter's team, had proven to be an experienced woodsman. She was as quiet and fast moving through the undergrowth as anyone Romero had ever worked with.

About a minute into their return, Romero smelled something on the breeze. Cigarette smoke. He signaled his partner to halt, checked the wind direction, and moved with extreme caution upwind, staying low and behind cover as much as he could. As they reached the top edge of a meandering wash, Romero could see the flares of two cigarettes below. The Russian patrol, two soldiers, had paused for a smoke. Below the rim of the wash, the smokers had correctly surmised they were hidden from view of the surrounding area. But the smoke itself had been lifted by the gentle breeze and carried to Romero, who was grateful once again he had never been a smoker, so he could detect burning tobacco readily—even in very small quantities.

Potter's team was not equipped with silencers for their AK-47 rifles. But Winger and Romero carried sound-suppressed M-4s. So Romero signaled his partner to "hold," and carefully scoped in on the two smokers. Lying in a prone position at the edge of the wash, he deliberately relaxed from neck to feet, drew in a breath, and exhaled slowly. As he exhaled, Romero squeezed the trigger of his rifle four times in almost perfect rhythm. Four muffled pops. One extra beat between shots two and three permitted him to shift from the head of the first man to the second. Within five seconds both targets were lying dead on the ground. After a quick check of the bodies, Romero's partner relieved the soldiers of their weapons, ammo, and uniform coats and hats. Then they resumed their return to rendezvous with Winger and Potter.

When Romero and his partner arrived back at their rally point, they found the rest of the team ready to deploy. "Sorry we're late, Boss," Romero said. "We ran into a patrol and took them out. Picked up a couple of AKs in the process, and brought these back in case you might find them useful." He and his partner tossed the uniform coats and hats on the ground. "Both guys were pretty good size, and since they were topple-over head shots, there's not a lot of blood on them."

"Nice work, Chief," Winger said. He glanced at Potter, who nodded in approval. Potter called over two of his men and instructed them to don the

Russian uniforms. He and Winger spoke with the two men as they dressed, and they indicated they fully understood their orders. Then Potter made sure the entire team grasped the changes they had just made to their plan, and they began to deploy around three sides of the base perimeter.

The installation was roughly rectangular, which was useful for surrounding and containing it during an assault. One of the devices Winger had carried in with him was a modified "Duke" radio signal jammer. Early jammer models, such as the "Warlock," wiped out everybody's communications for hundreds of yards in all directions. They could even crash remote-controlled drones flying overhead. In this case, merely blocking the signal from the overhead surveillance dirigible was adequate. Newer jammers, including the Duke device Winger was carrying, are more selective in their jamming, and with the modifications made by Tina Gosbee's team, were specifically tuned to impede the frequencies used by Russian military and intelligence operatives. It also covered cell phone signals for those frequencies utilized by commercial carriers in the Mezhgorye area. Winger's Duke was configured to be directional, fanning out the jamming signal in an inverted funnel shape.

At precisely ten thirty p.m., the two members of Potter's crew who had donned Russian uniforms appeared outside the front gate. One man appeared to be dragging the other, with his back turned toward the gate, and calling out in Russian as he grunted heavily: "I have a man down here. He was attacked by wolves! Open the gate!"

Immediately, flood lights illuminated the area. There was some clamor, and a half dozen armed soldiers rushed to the gate. Recognizing the uniforms and unable to see the faces of the men, the sentry hit the switch disabling the gate's locking mechanism and it began to swing open. When the gate was open about six feet, the first of the soldiers from the compound reached the two members of Potter's team. When Winger heard the first shots ring out, he engaged the Duke, and the rest of the team sprang into action.

As soon as Winger engaged the jammer, Romero sprayed the chain-link fence in front of them with a small aerosol can of compressed liquid nitrogen. The specially formulated chemical rendered the chain-link fence so brittle that a subsequent kick from the rubberized sole of Romero's boot produced a hole about four feet in diameter. Winger, Romero, and two others from Potter's team entered there, careful not to touch the edges of the remaining chain-link.

The fence had been electrified when Dawson's team was there before, and they were uncertain whether any electrical charge remained. The lights inside the compound continued to glow, so Winger deemed it better to be on the safe side.

The balance of Potter's team entered through the open front gate, assisted by some triangulated sharpshooting from Winger and Romero to disable the remaining sentries there. Additional soldiers, hearing the commotion and gunfire at the gate, poured out of two buildings; the barracks and another structure comprised the mess hall and off-duty recreation rooms. Between Winger and Romero's sound-suppressed sniping and the frontal assault of Potter's team coming through the gate, it took less than ten minutes to render the force defenseless.

As this transpired, Potter made his way into the headquarters and communications building. Two soldiers there, including the one remaining officer, had the presence of mind to seize their weapons, and Potter had to dispatch them immediately. They had obviously not prepared for this contingency, as both of the men were moving toward the door when Potter came through it. Potter's weapon was already raised in firing position, and he brought down both men before they could even shoulder their rifles. The remaining three soldiers looked like geeks to Potter; operators of computers, communications, and technical equipment. He wondered for a moment whether any of them even knew how to load and use their weapons.

Potter hustled the three remaining men into a small office and zip-tied them to various pieces of furniture and fixtures, rendering them immobile. Then he returned to the fray outside. Potter helped Romero sweep the mess hall and recreation building while Winger and his other team members went through the barracks. When they reached the technical building, comprising the R&D facilities, they found it unoccupied. Apparently, all of the technicians were in Prague, supporting the demonstrations and equipment at the auction.

One of Potter's men had sustained a flesh wound, which was rapidly dressed by the female operator who had been partnered with Romero on patrol earlier in the evening. Otherwise, the team survived the skirmish unharmed. The combination of depleted manpower, limited leadership, and the element of surprise had all worked to Winger's advantage. Now the mission came down to acquiring as much of the technology as possible and destroying the rest, then escaping the region.

"So far, so good," Potter remarked as he and Romero returned to the headquarters building. Winger was already pouring over the equipment and computers in the R&D center. By the time Romero rejoined him there, having pulled the hard drives out of the servers in the headquarters data center, Winger was climbing around some of the devices that had been subjected to the anti-gravity technology. The T-72 tank was a real challenge because of the tight spaces in which to work. The ICBM they had watched in their earlier visit, however, was much easier to examine. The gravitics device was embedded in a platform constructed for that purpose beneath the missile, where it lay cradled on the bed of its transport. Removing the mechanical fasteners along the edge of the device proved to be too time-consuming a process, so Winger took advantage of a nearby cutting torch and helmet. The process was ugly, and left extremely hot, red-glowing edges, but it was a few minutes to complete rather than the hour-plus alternative.

When he first got a look at the device, Winger thought he had damaged it with the cutting torch. Components appeared to be fused, as though they had become so hot they melted together. But when he thought more about it, he decided that made no sense. The effect was no more severe where he had cut away the housing—it seemed to be uniformly distributed across the interior, as far as his flashlight could illuminate. *No,* he thought, *it was the device itself that did this. But how? If it had gotten that hot, a lot of these components—especially the printed circuit boards—would have melted or caught fire. This is very odd.*

Before he began removing anything, Winger decided he would carefully videotape what was visible. He called Romero over and had him move slowly along the device in front of him with a powerful work light as he followed using the video camera provided by Gosbee. As nearly as he could determine, elements of the core mechanism included several printed circuit boards, a cooling plant comprised of a heat sink unlike any he had ever observed, and a device designed to spin up a stack of rotating disks.

The disks looked to Winger as though they were an unusual alloy, so he tested two of them with the device Dawson had gotten from Tina Gosbee. While Winger knew he didn't have time to examine each reading, he did verify the readings were indeed being uploaded. After sampling two of the disks, he noted they contained exactly the same levels of indium, barium, and copper along with other trace elements which seemed to be embedded in a ceramic substrate. The substrate material stemmed upward from this device, and flattened into a ceiling that ran along the length of the transport in a sheet about one quarter of an inch in thickness.

Working as quickly as he could, Winger removed three printed circuit boards that appeared to be central to the control unit, and managed to pry one disk loose from the array. He placed both into his backpack, stowing them carefully between thin, stiff bubble wrap partitions. He and Romero made similar videos of a truck they found that was equipped with a gravitics device, then headed back to the headquarters building. As Winger walked across the compound with Romero, he saw Potter's crew had been doing some intelligence gathering of their own among the paper-based files and communications equipment. But most of the operatives were moving bodies out of sight into the barracks and mopping up any overt signs of an incursion. Their purpose was to make it less obvious to airborne surveillance and any initial ground-based observers that something had gone very wrong. The rest, they knew, came down to luck.

The entire process of removing hard drives, photographing the gravitics devices, and extracting samples of critical components took several hours. In the wee hours of Friday morning, as preparations were underway for the auction in Prague, Winger and Romero were ready to depart the base in Mezhgorye. A substantial amount of the video and chemical analysis had already been uploaded via satellite link by the time they left the camp. Potter remained with his team at Mezhgorye, as they set explosive charges around the compound. The prisoners were moved to a position out of harm's way in a windowless cinder block room of the recreation building. In order to provide Winger and Romero with as much of a head start as possible, the charges would not be detonated until noon. Then Potter and his team would disband and blend back into the populations of nearby towns, planning to drift out again toward their home turf over a period of weeks following the assault.

When they had finished up with their work, Winger checked with Potter to verify his team was on schedule, and then activated the extraction plan they had devised before leaving the States.

At four a.m., the muffled sound of a helicopter began to be audible, and within five minutes a chopper was landing in the middle of the small parade ground on the base. It was much different than the helicopters they were accustomed to, with the most obvious differences being its nearly silent operation and its windowless cockpit. There were also no pilots or crew. This aircraft was an unmanned model of the Kaman K-MAX II helicopter, substantially modified for covert operations. With stealth shielding, radar jamming, and sound-canceling electronics as well as bullet-resistant armor, the aircraft still had a useful payload of nearly five thousand pounds. One of the most expensive characteristics of this particular aircraft was the absence of all markings indicating its origin, right down to serial numbers in the engine, drive components, and fuselage. The helicopter had a range of about three hundred miles, varying by payload and other factors.

As soon as the aircraft had touched down, the cargo door opened. Winger and Romero did the normal crouching trot to the bird, stowing their heavily loaded backpacks a bit more carefully than usual, in deference to the equipment and samples inside, and climbed aboard. Romero was the last man to get his over-shoulder seatbelt into position. As soon as the latch clicked, the cargo door swung closed and the bird lifted off. Both men were silent during the three-hour trip. It was too difficult to shout over the rotor sound, and there was nothing important to say, anyway. They would either be "painted"— spotted by Russian radar—or else they would land at their staging destination soon enough. At this point, there was nothing they could do to affect the outcome. Settling back into their seats with their hearing muffled by earplugs, they closed their eyes behind their goggles and got some badly needed sleep.

The helicopter, remotely controlled by a Special Ops contingent covertly housed in Western Europe, hugged the tree line and stayed over largely unpopulated areas en route. This required more time, of course, but the primary mission was to get Winger, Romero, and their cargo away from Mezhgorye as rapidly as possible without detection.

The staging area was almost due north from Mezhgorye, a field situated in the Perm Krai region, near the Kama Reservoir in the Ural Mountains. It was next to an ancient barn, overgrown with trees and nearly hidden by snow most of the year. As soon as the chopper landed, a flat-screen video monitor flickered to life on the front bulkhead, and a young civilian-clothed man appeared. "Sir," the young man said, "it looks as though you are safely on the ground. Please exit the aircraft. As soon as you get clear, I'll be taxiing her to her hangar."

"Roger that, Marine. Exiting now."

"Fair winds and following seas, Sir," the marine replied, smiling. *This guy is good,* he thought; *he knows a jarhead when he sees one.*

"Thanks. Out here," Winger replied as the cargo door began to swing shut.

The two men watched for a moment as the big barn door slid with remarkable quiet and efficiency to one side. The helicopter, resting on wheeled landing gear that had unfolded from its fuselage, began to advance toward the barn. Then they moved off, into the trees.

Winger and Romero moved carefully back through the Siberian forest, covering as much ground as they could, even as they lost the cover of darkness. Between the equipment and samples they carried in their backpacks, they were heavily burdened. That cargo slowed them from their normal pace, but they still made good progress considering the rough terrain and the need to pick their way through the rocky slopes. Even in late May, at this altitude the bitter cold of Siberia prowled like a ravenous wolf across the countryside. It seemed to descend from the mountains, enveloping all it encountered. It retarded much of the natural cover and left the forest a patchwork of thorny brambles, spotty stands of scraggly Siberian pine trees, and slippery rocks. They detected no signs of pursuit, but moved carefully anyway, regularly checking backward along the trail as they made their way through the forest.

Moving steadily west, they arrived at the reservoir around midafternoon on Friday. Both men were cold and exhausted, so the sight of Orlov's plane bobbing about on the waves was an enormous relief. When Romero signaled the craft, Orlov fired up his engines and swung in toward shore. Within twenty minutes, they were airborne again, and heading toward another out-of-the way water-based landing point where Orlov knew they could find food and rest for the night.

As they skipped over the treetops and mountain ridges, Winger looked down and wondered once again, as he had many times before, why people decided to remain and live in such conditions. He understood, of course, that family was a large part of it, and many people felt they simply had no other choice. But to deliberately remain in such harsh environmental conditions with so little human comfort struck Winger as profoundly sad. Yet here was Orlov, seemingly happy with his life of dodging authorities and entertaining his passengers with endless stories of life in Siberia. As long as he had some vodka, a place to set down for fuel, and a warm meal, he was content. Orlov was doing his part to undermine the Russian government, and that seemed to be enough for him. After a few hours, Winger and Romero smiled to see Orlov had broken out in song, though it was barely audible over the roar of the aircraft engine, as he prepared to land again for the evening.

# CHAPTER 19

Dawson and Gerard had rendezvoused with Bi-shou at the back of an obscure restaurant called Kolkovna around lunchtime on Friday. Following lunch, Dawson fished a document from his pocket, and unfolded it before them on the table. The drawing depicted an unmarked layout of the auction facility, developed from a combination of the building dimensions Mickey Wahl had gleaned from public records and the camera images Dawson had captured the previous day. Poring over the drawing and what they knew of the schedule, they developed a plan of attack for the auction later that evening. A great deal depended on timing and misdirection, but ultimately Dawson felt their odds were good.

Dawson and Gerard departed the restaurant and split up a couple of blocks away. Dawson diverged a few blocks to nail down a few last details while Gerard went on toward the hotel. Bi-shou left the restaurant last, lingering occasionally on the way to be sure she wasn't being followed. She could see Gerard a half block ahead and on the opposite side of the street.

As Gerard turned a corner passing a local branch of the HSBC Bank, a man waiting in the doorway of the bank stepped quickly out and shot her in the back at close range with a Taser. As her assailant switched off the device, Gerard fell heavily into his arms and was quickly supported by him and a partner who had followed him out. They were dressed in ordinary street attire and each of them sported a scruffy beard and sunglasses.

The two men bustled her into an old, white cargo van idling nearby, dumping her unceremoniously on the floor. The assailant removed the Taser probes and cast the weapon aside as the driver began to pull away from the curb. He leaned out to pull the sliding door closed before anyone else on the street noticed the event. But just as he touched the door handle, a slim hand reached into the van from the street and grasped his. Before he could get more than a word out, he found his already leaning-and-off-balance position had been amplified by a sharp tug, and he was headed facedown into a parked car as the van pulled away. At that point everything for the man went black.

Bi-shou swung gracefully up into the van just as the assailant's partner was moving from the rear of the van—where he had been retrieving a roll of duct tape and a black hood—toward the door to see what had happened. Bi-shou shot him in the right knee with her silenced .22 caliber pistol as she stepped into the van, and he collapsed on the floor beside the unconscious Gerard. Then she turned to the driver and said: "Drive!" He drove.

It took Bi-shou about three minutes to get the assailant's partner trussed up and gagged with duct tape, while she shouted at the driver to head for the river. She hoped it would work; the truth was, she had no idea where the river was as it related to their current location or how long it would take to get there. But she had to give the driver a destination and the river was all she could come up with.

Gerard regained consciousness after a few minutes, and by that time Bi-shou had extracted the truth about what had happened from the man she had shot in the knee. After taping him securely in place, she simply placed her full weight on the injured leg until he was crying freely. Then she pulled the duct tape away from his mouth enough for him to speak and he was quite loquacious. As it turned out, the three men ran a prostitution business employing heavily drugged women and a few young men, stolen off the streets and transported to other European cities as they were pumped full of heroine. They apparently worked for an organized crime boss named Puerto who was based in Cyprus.

Bi-shou returned the duct tape to its former position. All she really wanted to know was whether their cover had been blown, and she was relieved to hear the men weren't enemy operatives. They were just violent criminals who had chosen the wrong time and place to abduct a beautiful woman off the street.

Bi-shou directed the driver to a nearly empty parking lot a few blocks from the Charles Bridge. As soon as he had parked the van, she shot the man through his right temple.

Gerard was still a little groggy and sore, but the sound of the muffled gunshot brought her around just in time to see Bi-shou deliver a similar sentence to the trussed-up accomplice. While Gerard continued to get her bearings, Bi-shou exited the van. She used a knife from a small assortment of tools rattling around the back of the van to punch a hole in the fuel line along the underside of the van, and filled a Styrofoam cup she found along the street with gasoline. After getting Gerard out, she sloshed the gasoline around the van, went back outside and repeated the process, then created a path of spilled fuel from the interior out through the door and onto the ground to the point where gasoline was leaking out under the vehicle. Lighting a cigarette fished from the pocket of the van driver, Bi-shou flicked it into the van and got as far around the corner and down the street with Gerard as she could before the van's gas tank erupted in a ball of flame. *At least that takes care of fingerprints,* Bi-shou thought as they walked. In a few blocks, Bi-shou found a small hotel and a nearby queue of taxis. Ten minutes later, the two women alighted just a block from Gerard's hotel.

"I'm not sure what to say ..." Gerard started, but Bi-shou cut her off.

"There is no time right now. We need to get off the street," she said. "I did not see any security cameras or witnesses out where we left the van, but you never know. We need to get on with the mission and try to get out of here as soon as we can."

"Right," Gerard said, straightening to a fully erect posture. "I agree with you. See you tonight but—thank you."

Bi-shou met her gaze for a moment but didn't respond. She just hailed another taxi and disappeared into traffic.

When they had all returned to their hotels, it was time for Dawson to check in with Mickey Wahl and—by oblique extension—with Daniel Winters in India. Gerard waited until afterward to tell him about her adventure—what she knew of it, at least. Bi-shou would have to fill in whatever blanks she was willing to provide later. Somehow, Gerard felt, Bi-shou rarely divulged all she knew about anything.

* * * *

Near Lumbini Park in Hyderabad, Winters was prepping for showtime. He had a late dinner, then walked to his boat. He doubled back on his own path and waited for ten minutes, making sure he had no tail. It was a pleasant evening in Hyderabad, and even a moderate breeze did nothing to deter young lovers and a few families from strolling along the shoreline. Only when he was certain did he cast off and move his Sea Ray quietly away from shore. When he was near a midpoint on the lake, Winters dropped anchor and went below. His equipment was all set up, so most of the remaining work involved bouncing a signal to the satellite dishes at the leased residence on shore, reestablishing the uplinks from the residence to the satellites, and logging in to the accounts involved.

The more difficult—and completely illegal—work associated with actually hacking into the banking systems was largely done at this point, though it lay dormant. Winters would need actual bank account numbers and authentication codes to perform the necessary transactions, and that information had to come from Bi-shou. Once Bi-shou or her auction technician keyed the information, Winters knew, the clock would begin ticking. People would be tracking the signal back to its destination and a virtual net would start to close in on Winters. Then it was up to him to complete the transfers Dawson needed and get out of town before he could be discovered and captured or killed.

When he was ready, Winters returned to the main deck and simply sat there, listening to the waves lapping against the hull of the boat, and staring out at the gigantic Buddha impassive and erect. It was bathed in colored lights, holding its right hand aloft as though swearing an oath.

*Ah, that's it,* he thought. Suddenly, he knew what the statue reminded him of. Several years ago he had watched C-SPAN coverage of some of the congressional hearings related to one of the long list of scandals plaguing the Obama administration. The sight of the Buddha, so uncaring and cold in the middle of Hussain Sagar Lake, starkly brought to mind the image of then-IRS official Lois Lerner. Lerner had been at the heart of the controversy pertaining to abusing the powers of her office as the director of the Exempt Organizations Unit of the US Internal Revenue Service. In those hearings, Winters recalled, Lerner was found to be in contempt of Congress, and it was her seeming indifference and "I am above the law" attitude during the hearings that now resurfaced her image in Winters' mind as he gazed at the stony face of the Buddha. But it was the image of Lerner's swearing-in exercise that was invoked now, creating an uncanny and eerie sense of deja vu.

# CHAPTER 20

Since it would be unwise to return to their hotels following the event, Dawson and Gerard moved their extra clothing and travel items to the back of the van rented by Bi-shou, and drove around the neighborhood near the underground entrance. They finally selected an appropriate out-of-the-way spot where the van would be readily accessible. At the same time, they used the key provided by Kolář to let themselves through the gate to the underground, and stashed their equipment for later that evening. The large duffle provided by Connelly made it easy to transport, and fairly easy to conceal in the dark, damp interior of the abandoned underground.

As dusk fell, Dawson and Gerard returned to the spot they had scouted before. They parked and locked the van, and being careful to walk a circuitous route from there, returned to the underground entrance. A light rain was beginning to fall, which clouded over the skies, blotting out the moonlight and rendering the already murky cityscape even gloomier.

*Downright spooky in here now,* Gerard thought as she shook off the dampness of the first underground passage. Dawson could feel it too. Ever since he'd lost consciousness with the concussive force of a rocket-propelled grenade back in Afghanistan a couple of years prior, underground passages held a lingering effect; like an unseen malevolence, and he just couldn't completely shake it. Dawson would have found another way to do this if he could but he saw no other way; so he ignored it and pushed on.

The last sound they heard from the world above as they descended into the tunnel was distant thunder. Inside the caverns and tunnelways, the walls were becoming slick and oily. Their flashlight beams reflected from the patchy wet surfaces as though they were covered with cellophane. The ground was still solid enough, but Dawson and Gerard could now hear running water someplace—probably lots of places—throughout the underground system.

They made their way carefully back along the route they had established the day before, aided by phosphorescent markers they had deposited along their path. As they went along, they broke light sticks and left them in the spots where they had dropped the paint daubs the previous day. They left two sticks at each spot; seven locations in all. On their way back, they would be moving quickly and didn't want to have to be probing the tunnels with flashlights to find their way out.

When they arrived at the heavy door that opened into the underground chamber of the building, Dawson used a small can of spray lubricant to loosen some of the rust and debris from the ancient hinges. While it soaked in, Gerard held a flashlight on the work area where he used a small tool to carve two notches in both the stone floor near the door and in the surface of the door itself. Then he worked with Gerard to reopen it slowly, using their pry bars again. It was much easier now, having been opened recently, and with the application of lubricant.

As soon as they were inside, the sounds of equipment and people filtered through in muffled tones from other parts of the building. Final touches were being put in place, machinery was being tested, and there were dozens of people moving about overhead. Dawson and Gerard quietly set their gear bags down and got to work. They were dressed in black, and Gerard had her hair drawn back into a tight bun. Most of the cable and other materials had been moved from the small room at the bottom of the stairs, which meant there would be little foot traffic up and down the stairs during the events of the evening. There was still no guard posted on the stairway. *So far, so good,* Dawson thought.

Dawson and Gerard set up a small base of operations behind the room where the cables and other materials had been, and began to monitor audio and video feeds from the surveillance devices they had installed earlier. Audio was available to each of them through an earbud and the video was provided through devices that were essentially enhanced smartphones. The lighting wasn't optimal but it was adequate to pick up most activity within range of the cameras Dawson had installed.

At nine thirty p.m., Bi-shou was ushered into her observation point in the mezzanine office overlooking the main warehouse area, now converted into a space that would have been appropriate for a concert. All of the trappings of the old structure were covered behind deep blue draperies or engulfed in darkness, with a center "stage" area illuminated by a single spotlight. Bi-shou, realizing she would almost undoubtedly be surrounded by men for the evening, wore a moderately short skirt, heels, and a plunging neckline; a combination that always provided a disarming distraction. When seconds counted, she had often found such devices were as effective as a flash-bang grenade.

Bi-shou was escorted into the office that was to be her observation post by a man of almost indeterminable age and origin, though his accent indicated he was Russian. She had been driven to the converted building in a blacked-out limousine, and once inside she was led up the stairs to the mezzanine offices by a beefy man who looked uncomfortable in the suit he wore. She passed only one of the other offices, but noticed as she peered down the hallway that the doors to all of them were kept closed. There was one security person posted outside each of the doors. In the office she was to occupy for the event, Bi-shou was escorted to her seat and immediately offered a drink. When she was settled in, she asked one of two men who remained with her: "When will the presentation begin?"

"Approximately fifteen minutes," he replied. "May I have your bank identification information, please? We will, of course, allow you to make the actual funds transfer yourself, once it has been determined you are the successful bidder. But the bank's identification information will enable us to speed the process along by setting up the lines of communication in advance." Winters had provided this information, and Bi-shou repeated it from memory. The second man, a small, wiry figure with a troubled complexion and round wireframe glasses, entered Bi-shou's information into a computer from the corner of the room. After about twenty seconds, he smiled slightly and nodded to his partner; the man who had provided Bi-shou with her drink.

"Good," the man said to her, "everything seems to be in order. We should begin in just a few moments now."

\* \* \* \*

On Hussain Sagar Lake in Hyderabad, Winters was alerted that someone had keyed in the bank routing number and account combination. He prepared to begin his work. He had already cloaked the account and the web front end, which provided the "mask" over the particular bank and account number involved. It reflected an account balance of fifteen million US dollars. The actual transactions—transferring funds to the auctioneer's site, reversing the transaction, then emptying any additional funds from the destination account—were the most difficult aspects. It required him to "become" the destination bank for a short time, and once the clock started ticking, his actions would be discovered and stopped in less than a minute.

\* \* \* \*

About ten minutes later, the soft classical music emanating from speakers in the rear of the room faded away, and a figure appeared in the spotlight below. Bi-shou sipped the last of her drink, leaned forward in her seat to view what was about to unfold, and handed the empty glass back to her host. The man on stage had the bearing of a military officer, but wore a civilian suit. He was a short, rotund man, with polished diction and a German accent. His face conveyed intelligence and purpose. Many of those in attendance recognized the man as Professor Jürgen Bleckhaus from the Technische Universität Berlin.

Although Bi-shou was fluent in multiple languages, she was relieved when her host explained the presentation would be done in English. In her left ear, hidden by her hair, was an earbud through which she could hear Dawson, Gerard, and Winters as well as a tiny microphone. She carried no firearms but

Bi-shou knew she'd have no trouble obtaining one if she needed it. The bulge under the jacket of her host made that clear.

"Good evening, everyone," Bleckhaus said, facing the gallery formed by the mezzanine offices. "I will be your host tonight. First, we will have a brief presentation from the scientist who brought about the technology you have come here to observe. Then we will see the technology demonstrated. Next, I will permit one or two questions from each of our bidders, and finally, we will commence with the auction."

The young computer operator in the corner of the room asked Bi-shou whether all was acceptable, and she nodded in ascent. He tapped a couple of keys on his keyboard, and waited impassively. On the floor of the demonstration stage, a small bank of five lights each flickered from red to green.

"Very good," Bleckhaus announced, "all of the bidders are ready to begin. So I will now introduce our special guest this evening, the chief scientist responsible for the development of the technology you are about to observe."

Bi-shou noted Bleckhaus did not introduce Sergei Antonov by name, but suspected many—or perhaps all—of the bidders would know who Antonov was from the work of their own intelligence agencies. He spoke with a thick Russian accent, but enunciated each phrase slowly and carefully, so his English was understandable. "The technology we are about to demonstrate here this evening has been named 'Icarus,' after the mythological character whose father fashioned wings for him to fly like a bird. With Icarus technology, we are able to defeat the effects of Earth's gravitational field in a localized area, essentially making almost any object weightless for a period of time. As you will see, even very large and heavy objects can be made to levitate. The period of time is a function of the availability of energy provided to the Icarus device—as long as the device is powered, it remains effective."

Antonov was perceptibly nervous, and the spotlight amplified the fact by generating enough heat to cause visible beads of perspiration to appear on the man's face. Now sixty-two years old, Antonov was nearly bald and wore large, round wireframe glasses. "This technology has its genesis in work performed by Dr. Eugene Podkletnov in Finland between 2000 and 2004. The purpose of the technology is to achieve what we call 'Gravity Shielding' or sometimes 'Gravity Field Modification.' I have been instructed to provide limited information this evening about the technology itself for obvious reasons, but I am permitted to tell you this: The science involved has been enabled by high-temperature superconductors which have been developed through the application of Bose-Einstein condensates, which create high-frequency magnetic fields. The resonant frequencies of these fields are critical. The next breakthrough built upon this initial work was performed at the Marshall Space Flight Center, funded by the United States National Aeronautics and Space Administration. It was called the 'Breakthrough Propulsion System.'"

Antonov paused at this point and took a drink from a bottle of Evian he had brought with him to the stage. Then he continued: "That work was defunded at NASA and moved to clandestine facilities after the results produced more radical solutions than the United States government was willing to pursue. It was split off into individual channels of research then, to slow and control the development by isolating individual components. One such component became known as the field of 'Polarized Space' and the most publicized area of research in that area was later done by the Boeing Phantom Works. The work was called 'Impulse Gravity Generation,' specifically the Gravity Research for Advanced Space Propulsion—GRASP—Project, and it caused a significant stir in the scientific community. Then subsequent work around electrical discharges generated at two million volts was performed, and superconductors emitted a gravitational field—for one millionth of a second—that was propagated at sixty-four times the speed of light. This field could bend metal and punch holes through ceramics and bricks by 2014. Most of what I have just revealed to you can be verified easily by Internet searches. The 'secret sauces' involved in our Icarus technology include the production of miniature and portable superconductors, electron density maximization—the processes we use to polarize space around materials—and specifically the polarization of vacuum, dealing with particles that are several orders of magnitude smaller than electrons."

"Thank you, Doctor," Bleckhaus interrupted, huffing and puffing back to Antonov's side on stage. "Now I believe we will proceed with our demonstration. If our audience will be so kind as to permit us a few moments to bring out our equipment, we will begin momentarily."

The mercury vapor lights began to illuminate, adding their orange pallor to the air, and revealing the cavernous nature of the structure's high-bay ceiling. Bleckhaus and Antonov both exited the stage area, and the growl of an 840 horsepower V-84 engine starting up drowned every other sound in the building. Moments later, the building shook as a Russian T-72 tank, heightened by the addition of the Icarus technology, lumbered onto the stage.

The tank stopped at the middle of the stage area and the two Russian soldiers who had maneuvered it into position climbed out. As Bi-shou and the other bidders watched, a faint glow appeared around the tank. It was almost a shimmer, barely discernible in the mercury vapor lighting. The tank slowly and unceremoniously levitated to a position of about four feet from the floor. One of the soldiers moved to the front of the tank and the other to the rear. The soldier at the front of the tank shoved on the front corner of the tank track with the sole of his boot, and the vehicle began immediately to slowly spin in position. When it had rotated twice, the Icarus technology was carefully disengaged by an operator behind a screen in the control area, and the tank descended gradually back to rest on the floor. The tank was left where it rested and the two soldiers retreated from the stage.

A similar exhibition was performed using a military transport truck filled with Russian soldiers who had been brought in from the Mezhgorye facility for that purpose. Again, the truck was left in position following the demonstration and the soldiers walked away into the shadows. Shelepin realized this use of the soldiers depleted security at Mezhgorye for the period they were in Prague, but it was a chance he was willing to take. He could not afford word getting out about the new technology, and so he used soldiers he knew would remain loyal. All of these men recognized that anyone revealing the nature of the work at Mezhgorye would be hunted down and killed, along with any friends or family who might have been told about it.

Shelepin's decision couldn't have been better for Billy Winger and the team in Siberia.

# CHAPTER 21

Just as Antonov was winding up his presentation, Shelepin was approached in the wings by a member of his staff. "I have an urgent call for you, Sir," he whispered. "It is Captain Yuri Dressen in Yasenevo."

Shelepin stepped even further back into the shadows, accepting the mobile phone from his subordinate and pressing it to his ear. "Make this quick, Dressen," he growled. "I am in the middle of something very important."

"Yes, Sir," the officer replied, "we have found two border security officers murdered near the route Orlov seems to have taken back into Siberia. We believe Orlov may have landed someplace near Mezhgorye."

"How certain are you of this information?" Shelepin asked.

"Absolutely certain about the border security officers, and about seventy-five percent on the destination, Sir. But given Winger's involvement, I thought it was important to alert you."

"I understand, Dressen. I will look into it," Shelepin said, and ended the call. He wasn't terribly worried. *After all,* he thought, *what could two or three men do?* Then he turned to the officer who had brought him the phone and said, "Contact the base at Mezhgorye and find out if there has been any unusual activity. Tell them to be alert, and contact you every thirty minutes to confirm security."

Then he wheeled and returned to the demonstration where Antonov was answering a few questions from the bidders. As the last question was answered, Shelepin's lieutenant reappeared. "Sir, we have been unable to reach our people in Mezhgorye."

Immediately, Shelepin's mind began to calculate the potential loss if the intellectual property at Mezhgorye was stolen. The impact of such a loss was almost incomprehensible, but it was still of far less value without Antonov. It was also virtually impossible to get backup onto the base because of the secrecy of the operation. Calling in a quick reaction force would alert everyone upward from him in the command chain that there had been a serious breach of security on his program—a program into which over fifty billion rubles had been poured by the Russian government. Within hours, the inquisition would begin: Where was Shelepin during this time? What exactly had been stolen, and by whom? How could this have happened?

Shelepin, his staff, his family, and virtually everyone who had ever supported him in his career would be brought under suspicion, and many of them would not survive. No, Shelepin could not let that happen. He needed to complete this auction with success, return unnoticed to Mezhgorye, and destroy it—blaming the attack on Winger and the CIA. With Dressen's corroborating evidence, and whatever he could fabricate on his own, he might just pull it off. But the key was to move quickly now. If he could make this auction successful, he could build a nest egg that enabled him to disappear—and he knew if things didn't work out back at Mezhgorye, then that was exactly what he would have to do.

Just as he was completing that thought, the same officer approached him again. "Sir," the man said, "something else has come up. An American operative ..." He turned his mobile phone so Shelepin could see the grainy image displayed on it, "... was spotted on hotel security video today."

"At *our* hotel?" Shelepin demanded.

"No Sir, at the Four Seasons. It looks as though he has been there for at least a couple of days."

Shelepin was turning red at this point, even in the shadows of the cavernous building. He knew in his gut this could be no coincidence; he was staring at a photograph of Ben Dawson. Shelepin knew Dawson by reputation, and his presence in Prague just as this auction was happening could be no accident.

When America needed to acquire a new technology, especially a technology like Icarus, Dawson was the man they turned to. He had been a thorn in the side of China, Russia, Iran, and North Korea for years. Shelepin could hardly believe the man was even still alive.

There was one incident in particular in Dawson's past Shelepin remembered better than the others; something about an attack on the American research facility in Virginia, the Brystol Foundation. Dawson thwarted an effort by the MSS to capture a breakthrough naval technology, capturing a feared MSS assassin and killing the rest of the assault team. Something about all of this bothered Shelepin. It was at the edges of his mind, but he just couldn't pluck it from all the information swirling around. *It will come to me later,* he thought. *I just need to think about something else, and it will come to me.*

The auction was underway now and Shelepin mentally reviewed the bidders; the North Koreans, the Chinese, the Iranians, and an independent organization he thought was probably an ISIS front. The truth is he didn't really care who tendered the winning bid. He just wanted it to be at least six million US dollars, and preferably more. The greater the take, the better his chances were of disappearing when the time came. He had over a million dollars in his Caymans account now and about three hundred thousand in the Swiss account, but that wouldn't be nearly enough when it was time to truly disappear.

"Alert the security team this man may be in the building, and he is extremely dangerous," Shelepin said to his subordinate. "If he is seen, I expect him to be brought to me—dead or alive."

As Shelepin uttered these words, Ben Dawson was emerging from the stairwell in the darkest recesses along the wall near the receiving dock. Dawson and Gerard, dressed in black and wearing black balaclavas, were nearly invisible in the shadowy edges of the building. They moved rapidly from point to point around the perimeter of the building, setting up tripod-based light sources as they went. The light source they set up nearest the stairway from which they'd emerged would flash a red strobe when engaged. The others—there were a dozen in all—switched their strobes randomly from blue to white to green to yellow. All of them were activated remotely by a switch Gerard carried. A few feet to the left and to the right of each strobe, Dawson and Gerard set up smoke bombs—also triggered by the remote switch in Gerard's pocket. On two occasions, Dawson and Gerard had to belly-crawl through an area that wasn't quite dark enough to walk through. But after about an hour, they had set up their devices and were ready to go. Dawson clicked his mic once, paused, and clicked twice more. In her bidding room, Bi-shou pretended to adjust her earring; clicking twice, pausing, and clicking once more.

"Ms. Wen?" the security man was saying to Bi-shou, as she returned her attention to the matter at hand. She had appeared lost in thoughtful consideration, pondering her bid.

"Yes?" she replied.

"Do you wish to place your bid now?" he responded. "There is no hurry; you have four minutes remaining in this first round. There will be three rounds."

"Yes, I have an opening bid," she said. "The bidding is to be in US dollars?"

"Yes, that is correct," the man replied politely.

"My bid is seven and one half million dollars," she replied, gazing directly into the man's eyes.

To his credit, the man barely registered his surprise at the size of the opening bid. He simply turned to the computer operator and repeated the number. "Seven point five million is the opening bid from Ms. Wen," he stated evenly.

The computer operator entered the amount in his console. Three more minutes elapsed and then a sign appeared across from the bidding offices. It had been suspended from the ceiling for this purpose, and it showed a value beneath lighted headers reading bidder one, bidder two, bidder three, and bidder four. Bi-shou was bidder four. When the values appeared, Bi-shou was not surprised to see she was the high bidder by one and one half million dollars. Bidders one and two each bid six million. Bidder three had bid five million.

On the second round, Bi-shou held her position at seven and one half million. Bidder three simply stopped bidding. Bidder one came in at seven million, eight hundred thousand. Bidder two jumped to eight and one half million.

There had been a five-minute break between bidding rounds one and two, and there was a ten-minute interval between rounds two and three. One minute into the interval, after refilling her glass, Bi-shou beckoned the security man to her side. Softly, she spoke into his ear as he knelt beside her chair. "I am prepared to make a very large final bid," she said. "Very large. But before

I do, I want to speak to this scientist of yours. I have only two questions for him, and I do not want the others to hear my question, or his answer. Unless I speak with him in the next few minutes, I will not raise my bid from its current value. Do you understand?" She smiled sweetly, but the security man knew she was completely serious.

"Please excuse me for a moment," he replied, and stepped hastily out of the room. Bi-shou could hear him in muffled conversation outside the door, and then footsteps as he walked away down the makeshift hallway. It took about four minutes for three men to return through the doorway again; the security man, Sergei Antonov, and Vadim Shelepin.

"Ms. Wen," Shelepin said in a very businesslike tone, "you have made a request which requires me to violate the rules of our auction here. I am generally opposed to departing from the rules in business transactions. It confuses the people involved and it rarely ends well. However, my colleague has explained that you are an unusually motivated bidder, and under such circumstances, I sometimes make allowances." *I have seen you before,* he thought, *but where?*

"Thank you," Bi-shou said. "I believe you will find your flexibility is justified." Then she turned to Antonov and said: "You are Dr. Sergei Antonov?"

"Da, uh, yes, this is true," the man replied. His eyes darted between hers and Shelepin's, trying to understand what was going on.

"And you understand more about this technology than anyone else in the world, is this correct?"

"Yes, this is also true. It is my work, and … it has been my life."

*He looks profoundly sad,* Bi-shou thought. *A man who has struggled against impossible odds throughout his adult life, only to watch the magnificent thing he has developed being traded like a pack of American baseball cards at auction, with himself—his very life—thrown into the bargain.*

She turned back to Shelepin. "My final bid," she said, "is fourteen and one half million dollars."

Shelepin forced himself to refrain from smiling, and glanced at the computer operator. "Enter the bid and compare it to the others when they become available," he said.

Bi-shou didn't really need to ask the two questions; she just needed to get Antonov into the same room with her. But the ploy had worked.

In the final round of bidding, only bidder two's offer of eleven million dollars provided any real competition. When the bidding was completed, all bidders were asked to remain in their places while the winning bid was confirmed. The computer operator watched his screen as Bi-shou made a cell phone call. The number she called was a shill, a redirected number networked through a CIA switchboard in Zurich. The operative on the other end of the line was Ron Meriwether, a member of Dawson's team.

After identifying herself as Sheryl Wen and providing an account number, Meriwether provided Bi-shou with a numeric code. She walked over to the computer monitor, already displaying the appropriate window for code entry as a result of her initial instructions when she entered the room. When the operator had removed himself so he no longer saw the screen—an unnecessary courtesy since the numeric code could ostensibly be used only once, and was valid for only forty-five seconds—Bi-shou entered the number which had been provided. She motioned to the operator, who then returned to his keyboard, and—as she watched—completed the transaction.

* * * *

Aboard his Sea Ray in the middle of Hussain Sagar Lake, Winters watched the transaction occur. As soon as the computer operator hit the "Enter" key, Winters started the timer on his watch. This initial transaction shouldn't trigger a rapid response, because the private bank being utilized in the Caymans was much slower to recognize a problem than more established firms in other parts of the world. But when money began to move in the opposite direction, he knew international banking authorities would begin to see alerts from their systems. The transaction in Prague took less than two minutes to complete, reflecting a transfer of fourteen and a half million dollars into Shelepin's account in the Caymans.

There was no money in the fund from which the transfer originated; the domain naming system—DNS—address had been compromised by Winters, and the mask generated by the web front end had literally created money where there was none. The ability to do this, in the wrong hands, could cripple the world economy. It was one of the secrets Teng-hui most ardently desired, and the reason he was sacrificing pawns like Patrick Burke. He needed to determine who at NSA could covertly execute such an action.

Winters would wait fifteen minutes, or until he received positive confirmation from Dawson, before he triggered the reversal.

*   *   *   *

At the confirmation of the transaction, Shelepin turned to Bi-shou and thanked her for her participation. "Congratulations on your winning bid this evening, Ms. Wen," he said. Mentally, he was furiously working on where he had seen this woman before, but to no avail. "Since you are the successful bidder, you and Dr. Antonov will be escorted from the building first. Right this way, please."

"Thank you," Bi-shou responded.

Dawson had posted himself as close as he could to the bottom of the stairs where Shelepin and Bi-shou would emerge. Gerard had managed to work herself carefully under one end of a long set of tables used by the sound and lighting technicians at the far end of the stage, closest to the receiving docks and where she also had a clear view of the stairs from the bidding offices where they emptied onto the main floor. A wooden speaker case at the end of the table offered some added concealment, and provided an excellent stabilizing bench for her sound-suppressed Beretta.

Dawson figured there was something less than a fifty-fifty chance Shelepin actually planned to allow Sheryl Wen and Sergei Antonov to leave the facility alive, and an even slimmer chance he planned to allow them to leave the country in that condition. So he had decided to take the choice away from Shelepin. As Bi-shou descended the stairs, she said aloud: "It is very dark behind these stairs."

Dawson and Gerard understood Bi-shou's signal, which meant Antonov was with her, and behind her in the group coming down the stairs. They had worked out two other phrases to describe situations where Antonov was in front of her, and where Antonov was not among the group emerging from the stairs. When they came into view, the security man from Bi-shou's office was first, followed by Bi-shou, then Antonov, and then Shelepin. As planned, Gerard waited until she could see Antonov and triggered her remote switch.

Suddenly, all power was cut from the facility and it was plunged into darkness, except for the dim and fading light of the mercury vapor lamps high up among the girders. Smoke bombs spewed dark billows from around the perimeter of the enormous room, and bright pencils of strobe light pierced the smoke from various positions in an erratic pattern of color and intensity. Bi-shou immediately ducked and practically tackled Antonov, dragging him off to one side while cupping her hand over his mouth. As soon as she had him clear, she spoke into his ear. "If we are going to get out of here alive, we need to move toward the red light—NOW!" She jerked him in that direction and moved quickly along behind him, shoving him urgently as she went.

Since there was only one red strobe among all of the others, picking it out was no problem. As soon as they passed his position, Dawson fell in behind them. He pivoted from left to right, weapon drawn, ready to engage pursuers as they moved toward the ancient stone steps leading into the lower level. Gerard remained another fifteen seconds, watching figures stumble around as Shelepin tried to get security people into pursuit of Antonov and the woman he knew as Sheryl Wen.

The last mental image he had of her was a murky view of her in profile as the smoke grenades exploded and the lights were rapidly extinguished. Then it hit him; he had seen this woman in a grainy news photo around the time of the Brystol Foundation shootout a couple of years earlier. She was the MSS assassin Dawson had thwarted. Apparently, she had gotten free somehow, and was now in the employ of the MSS again.

Suddenly, he wasn't sure his original plan of simply killing Ms. Wen and returning Antonov to work in Mezhgorye. It seemed less plausible than simply letting them go. He didn't like having his hand forced like this, but it wasn't such a bad outcome. He had to trade Antonov for fourteen and a half million dollars, and he'd have to make the loss of the work at Mezhgorye look like a CIA assault, but it could be done. His career as the Chief of the Soviet Operations and Technology Directorate would probably be at an end; perhaps his career at the Federal Security Service would be over entirely. If his superiors failed to press him on why he was in Prague during the attack, he would survive this. He might even be able to retire with distinction, in a dacha along the Black Sea. And if it looked as though he needed to execute his backup plan, then the funds he had acquired this evening would enable him to disappear in quiet opulence for the rest of his days.

The security man from Bi-shou's bidding office seemed to be the only person who had a clear sense of the direction Bi-shou and Antonov had fled. He could see shadowy figures disappearing in the direction of the red strobe light, and so he followed it as well. His weapon was drawn, and he moved forward in a cautious, crouched manner, probing the darkness and smoke. He thought he discerned movement at one point so he fired off two rounds in that direction. It didn't appear he had hit anyone, and he kept moving.

Gerard had moved from her position and was also headed toward the red strobe. Suddenly, the figure of the security man loomed in front of her just as he fired off the two rounds. Realizing she probably didn't have to kill the man, she reversed her weapon and brought it down forcefully on the back of his head. The man staggered and fell heavily, but held onto his weapon. She jumped into the air and landed with her right heel on the hand holding the weapon, crushing the hand between the weapon—pinned to the floor—and her boot. He screamed in pain, releasing his pistol. Gerard kicked the weapon away and continued on, finding the stairway and disabling the red strobe before disappearing behind the others into the lower level of the building.

As she descended the stairs, she could see flashlights were beginning to appear on the main floor, and shouts were ringing out. Gerard figured they had perhaps three minutes before pursuers would be closing in on them.

When she caught up with the others, Dawson was collecting their remaining gear and Bi-shou was explaining in rapid, imperfect Russian that they were going to help Antonov get away from Shelepin and the Russian government, and get him to a place of safety and freedom. He just needed to trust them now, for a short time, and they would get him to a much better place where he and his work would be respected and not sold to the highest bidder. She must have been convincing because Antonov cooperated, following Dawson and Bi-shou through the heavy wooden door and into the Prague underground.

As soon as they were on the other side of the door, Dawson turned and wedged two of the pry bars they had used in previous days into the slots he had fashioned at the base of the door. Though primitive, he knew they would be a substantial deterrent to any brute-force methods employed from the other side. While they paused for Dawson to install his makeshift barriers to pursuit,

Gerard handed Bi-shou a pair of hiking shoes, in trade for the stylish heels she had been wearing.

"Thank you," Bi-shou said. "I was wondering how I was going to manage this."

"OK," Dawson said, "pick up the light sticks as we go. No point leaving a trail for them to follow." Then he spoke into his mic: "India, do you copy?"

"I copy," Winters' reply came back. "Showtime?"

"Roger that; it's showtime. Good luck."

"Copy that. India engaging. Safe travels, Sir."

# CHAPTER 22

Winters took a deep breath, looking at his watch. He had no indication the initial transfer had triggered any alerts. So far, so good. But he knew full well the next step would enjoy no such obscurity. He reset the timer and then hit the "Enter" key on his keyboard. Sitting in his gently rocking Sea Ray in the middle of Hussain Sagar Lake, Winters watched the funds being withdrawn from Shelepin's account; not only the fourteen and a half million that had been transferred in, but the remaining million dollars as well.

About the time the transfer reached ten thousand dollars, the first alarms were triggered on computer screens at nine different international banking oversight organizations, most notably the Federal Bureau of Investigation.

One million dollars' worth of the balance had originated somewhere in the Russian government—probably skimmed from R&D funding somehow over the years. So it was real money there, and Winters needed to make sure that transfer was visible to all the right people. He routed the transaction through several countries. He tunneled through servers and made the transaction appear to originate from the Russian military IP address of the computer in the Mezhgorye base commander's office. Winters had to make the string of transactions difficult, but not impossible, to follow. It was going to make the future very uncertain for the Chief of the Soviet Operations and

Technology Directorate. *A million dollars is hard to explain, even in rubles!* Winters chuckled to himself.

The first fourteen and a half million was, of course, fictitious at the outset. Winters had created money from mere electrons faster even than the US Treasury could have printed it. He made it disappear just as fast. The magnitude of the transfer out of an account and across international boundaries would have been more than enough to put it on the radar. When the transaction showed a transfer out with no corresponding transfer into a receiving account, it would make everyone very suspicious indeed. The fact that the remaining million landed in Shelepin's Swiss bank account rendered the entire matter a focus of serious attention. Within a few hours, questions would begin to be raised at the highest levels of the Russian Federal Security Service. It was going to be a very bad day for Vadim Shelepin.

*Now,* thought Winters, *how do I avoid having a very bad day as well?* Dawson had explained that organized crime was always scouting for large monetary transfers like these. Other organizations such as government agencies like China's MSS watched for them as well. Only extremely rare individuals possessed the technological know-how to perform these transactions, and criminal organizations wanted those people. Their tactics were far more aggressive than law enforcement agencies, and their networks of operatives were often second to none. Larger criminal organizations had managed, over the years, to place operatives inside of banking institutions and the computer systems providers that support them. When transactions like this—which made millions of dollars simply vanish into thin air—occurred, these organizations moved on them with uncanny speed.

Winters knew, even as he packed up his equipment, people in telecommunication rooms somewhere had already tracked his signal and, using GPS coordinates, had essentially discovered his location. That's what Dawson had warned him about while he and Wahl were finishing up the last of the pizza back at the NSA. The question now was: Who was closest, and would they be able to find him before he could disappear?

The organized crime groups in India are most often headquartered in Mumbai. But the Ibrahanni Group operated in Hyderabad as well as several other major cities, controlling its activities from a headquarters in Dubai.

Its legitimate businesses in stock brokerage provided this organization with a strong platform from which to launch projects such as the acquisition of hacking technologies. Technologies that could produce results like the ones Winters performed were too tempting to ignore, and as soon as the withdrawal transaction began, operatives based in Hyderabad were dispatched to the coordinates triangulated by technicians in the Ibrahanni Group's headquarters.

The decision to push these transactions through a Wi-Fi setup came with benefits and penalties. The obvious benefit was that people trying to quickly identify the source would find it originated from the middle of a very large lake. The fact the lake was in Hyderabad also helped; the signals from his computer were awash in an ocean of other Wi-Fi traffic. One of the downsides, especially in this case, was the sophistication of the equipment required and the time it took to process these specific transactions.

Winters pulled out the hard drive from his laptop and tossed it overboard. The balance of the equipment also went over the side at various points as he turned toward shore. By the time Winters returned to dock the Sea Ray, the boat looked like any other pleasure cruiser on the lake. As prescribed in the rental agreement, the boat rental company would pick up the vessel the following morning.

Once inside the condo, he methodically broke down the equipment there and repackaged it in shipping containers. Arrangements had already been made for pickup, and the containers were affixed with address labels to—the late—David Volmer in Salt Lake City. The entire process took him just over an hour. He knew there were international banking authorities trying to trace his transactions on the Internet, but with current technology he estimated it would be months until they even found the Russian military point of origin he had built. If they broke through the facade, which Winters considered unlikely, it would probably take more than a year to get back to the IP address, and longer still to close in on the physical location in Hyderabad.

Unfortunately, there were almost certainly organized crime and/or nefarious government agencies in pursuit of him by tracing his activities through the origin of his Wi-Fi signal. None of them knew who he was, at least yet, but they would be coming for him nonetheless. The faster he could get out of India the better.

*  *  *  *

Shelepin's decision to allow Bi-shou to escape with Antonov unaccosted seemed prudent for nearly forty minutes. During that interval, Shelepin quickly oversaw the rapid cleanup of the smoke, made sure the minor injuries among his staff at the warehouse were effected, and explained it all away to the other auction participants as a minor malfunction in some of their lighting equipment.

He had just shaken hands with the last of the losing bidders and tucked him neatly into a limousine returning to the hotel when the technologist who had confirmed his wire transfer from Bi-shou's account appeared at his side. "Sir," he said, "did you make additional arrangements for funds transfers I am unaware of? The funds transfer has been reversed. In fact, all funds in the account, including the funds already residing there, have been transferred out. Did you authorize this?"

"What are you saying?" Shelepin demanded, his hands clenching into fists. His eyes seemed to bore holes through the skull of the technician, and cause perspiration to drench the man's clothing in spite of the damp, cool warehouse air.

"It is all transferred out, Sir," was all the stricken young officer could think of to say. "It is gone. The entire 901,092,500 rubles has been transferred out of the account; not only the transferred amount from tonight, but also the amount that was already in the account. It is all gone."

"And where, *exactly*," Shelepin said, as his face reddened and contorted in rage, "did all of my money *go*?"

The technician could barely speak; his voice cracked as he replied: "The funds transferred in this evening appear to have evaporated, Sir. They left your account with a destination of the account from which they were received—the account of Ms. Wen. But they never show arriving there. The entire account has disappeared, including every historical reference. It is as though the account never existed at all."

Shelepin stared blankly at the technician for almost ten seconds. "And the rest of my money?" he asked in a detached tone. "Where did the *rest* of it go?"

"We did trace the transfer, Sir," he replied. "It was deposited in an account under the custodianship of the Resource Policy and Planning Board for the

Council on Resource Policy and Allocation. This is the funding oversight organization of the ..."

"The North Atlantic Treaty Organization—NATO," Shelepin finished. His eyes were now closed, as though he was trying to make everything in front of him disappear. Shelepin realized he himself would disappear soon, along with his family, his friends, and his closest allies in the Russian government. "How long will it be?" he finally asked quietly.

"I do not understand, Chief Shelepin," the technologist said. "How long until what?"

Shelepin's gaze, which had lost its target, refocused on the man. "How long until the Central Committee becomes aware of this?"

Now the technician understood. He began mentally running through the process he knew would unfold once the transactions began to be investigated. He was sure they had already been detected. His assumption, however, was that international investigators monitoring such transactions would have no immediate way to identify the owner of Shelepin's account. The process should take months, perhaps even years, to work its way through international courts. He thought about the last such cases he'd heard about, and offered Shelepin his best estimate. "I would estimate at least six months," he replied, "perhaps even one year." The technician was unaware Winters had left a trail—faint but distinct— that would lead directly to Shelepin. It would take mere days to follow.

"All right then, we have some time," Shelepin said, regathering his wits about him. He turned to his second in command. "Have a team sent to watch approaches to the Chinese embassy, and other teams to watch the airport and the railway stations," he said. "Kill or capture Antonov. No excuses. He must not leave our custody alive. In the meantime, I will return to Mezhgorye. If we cannot recapture Antonov, we can at least continue the development of Icarus without him."

\* \* \* \*

Friday night found Winger, Romero, and Orlov in a small lakeside port called Krasnorechenskoe Farm. The tiny town was situated at the southern end of Lake Vozhe, where Orlov was able to secure his aircraft to a dock without difficulty.

Although the village was a tourist draw in the winter, the late spring and summer months left the village sparsely populated, which suited Orlov's purposes well.

When the men had secured their aircraft, they walked into the village and Orlov took them to a small inn where he knew the owner, a fellow hater of the Russian government who had assisted Orlov in the past. The inn had a few rooms on the second floor along with the owner's residence, but generated most of its revenue from the small bar and restaurant on the first floor. Winger, Romero, and Orlov were brought large plates of steaming beef Stroganov and steins filled with dark ale. They ate gratefully, and then retired to their rooms upstairs to get some sleep.

The following morning, Orlov's aircraft lifted off just as dawn broke across the horizon. He assured them, "If we do not encounter any more Russian border patrols, I will have you in Helsinki tonight. I have established a route that is most likely to avoid both ground-based and airborne security. It takes longer, but it is the safest way." Winger and Romero hoped he was right.

The trip into Helsinki, as Orlov expected, was dangerous. On two occasions he was nearly spotted. The first time it was a ground-based border guard who happened to be patrolling in an unoccupied area because of recent problems with poachers crossing along the Estonian border. The second occurrence was close to that same location, but it was a Russian Border Security aircraft. Fortunately, Orlov flew so close to the tree line as he approached, he was lost in the ground clutter from the perspectives of both land and airborne radar. With skillful maneuvering, he was able to come in over the water at the mouth of a river passing by Ust-Luga, and his glide path got him onto the water just outside Helsinki, where Winger and Romero could get commercial transport to the airport.

Orlov decided to make a holiday of it, and secured his aircraft to the dock as Winger and Romero were unloading. "Пока!" he said, as he bid them goodbye. "I will see you next time, maybe for fishing. Good fishing in Siberia! Tell Ben Dawson hello from Orlov!"

Again, Winger marveled at the sheer happiness of the man. *A modern nomad,* he thought. *This guy wouldn't have it any other way.* Winger and Romero checked into a Helsinki airport hotel for the night.

# CHAPTER 23

The dark streets of Prague outside the gates where Dawson, Gerard, and Bi-shou emerged with Antonov revealed no signs of pursuers. Gerard had emerged first and quickly scouted the area around them and around Dawson's rental van. A light rain was falling but the streets were quiet. Only a few lights glimmered in the buildings around her, and the streets were wet but not yet slippery. When Gerard was satisfied all was clear, she radioed Dawson and the others. Then she started the van and pulled it into position in front of the gate and waited while Dawson and Bi-shou shepherded Antonov aboard. Fifteen minutes later they had cleared the Charles Bridge and were headed out of town.

Dawson weighed their alternatives for getting out of the area and finally decided to shift to the Dresden option. "Let's try to get across the border into Germany," he said. "I know a country road just outside of Altenberg that I'm pretty sure will get us across the border without explanations. When we've gotten that far, I'll alert Charles; we already have commercial tickets for a flight out of Dresden anyway. I'll feel better if we put some distance between us and Shelepin's crew."

Gerard nodded. "We're heading up E55, then," she said. "What do you think; about two hours?"

"Yes, at least," Dawson confirmed, settling into his seat. "I'll help with navigation. I don't think it will be more than a few hours all the way to Dresden if nothing goes awry."

He was right. The border was violated by an old farm road that deteriorated at one point to a pair of dirt tracks through the corner of a meadow, and it was perfect for an unauthorized crossing. Along the way, Dawson explained what was happening to Antonov. The Russian seemed greatly relieved that his future would be in America, although he remained concerned about arrangements for his family to meet him there.

"I understand your worry, Dr. Antonov," Dawson said. "It is a difficult situation. I can only tell you that the United States government will do whatever they can to secure their safety."

The scientist was clearly distraught—the entire experience had been harrowing on a level that was almost unimaginable to most people. Dawson was worried for the man as well—but he also refused to make promises he knew he couldn't keep. Finally he said: "Dr. Antonov, if we had left you there, to be sold to the highest bidder along with the technology you developed, what would have happened to your family?"

Antonov thought about it and realized almost immediately that they would have no future in those circumstances either. Even when he was working for Shelepin he had never been allowed to return home. Shelepin just kept promising he could return home "in great glory" when his work was completed. But Antonov knew in his heart it wasn't going to work out that way. This way, he realized, at least there was a chance.

A small bed-and-breakfast called The Klosterwitz was happy to receive guests without reservations when they paid cash in advance, and they took two large rooms. Dawson suggested they get some sleep and a decent meal before heading to the airport.

As they settled in, Gerard parked the van in the least conspicuous location she could find, and Dawson placed a note in the drafts folder of Jennings' email account. He explained they would be traveling through Dresden. Then they began to get some badly needed rest, with Dawson, Gerard, and Bi-shou taking shifts monitoring a window overlooking the entrance and driveway into the bed-and-breakfast.

\* \* \* \*

Winters would be on his own until his return to US soil, and would only be comfortable when he was back at work, surrounded by the security of a US government agency. As scheduled, his commercial taxi arrived at five thirty a.m. Traffic was much lighter than usual at that time. But the combination of motorcycles, trucks, pedestrians, garish neon lights, and the occasional cow wandering along the road, made the ride through Hyderabad a bizarre experience. Winters had already used his fake passport—identifying him as David Volmer—to purchase airline tickets to Mumbai. Then from Mumbai to Pune, he would travel by train on the Sinhagad Express. He would fly again, then, from Pune to Ottawa, Canada. Finally, from Ottawa he would travel back into the United States. It was a long journey with a lot of connections, but it made him more difficult to track.

\* \* \* \*

In Dubai, a data center occupied several floors of one of the newer office buildings where the Ibrahanni Group headquarters was established near the Dubai International Financial Center. Legitimate investment and brokerage activities were carried out on the first three floors of the building, and less transparent activities were performed on the fourth and fifth floors. The sixth floor was filled with offices for the company's senior management. In the data center on the fifth floor, Indian Wi-Fi traffic associated with banking transactions was mirrored and analyzed by extremely skilled technicians. They all held advanced degrees in computer technology, and had been sponsored for additional education and training at some of the most advanced schools in the world, including MIT. They specialized in "Big Data," the mining of huge amounts of transactional information to identify and understand patterns and anomalies. Several of the technicians had been hired away from Google and other similar search engine firms.

Prabhu Yadav was one such technician. Yadav was born in Mohali in 1975, displayed a gift for mathematics and equations, and was fortunate enough to have parents who could sponsor his educational development. Recruited to Yahoo! just after graduating with his advanced computer science degree, Yadav was lured away by the Ibrahanni Group only two years later and earned more at age twenty-six than both of his parents combined. When asked what he did for a living, Yadav merely shrugged and said: "I work in the IT department at an international bank."

Around nine a.m. Saturday in Dubai, Yadav's computer alerted him of an anomalous transaction within an international funds transfer. The message had been generated by an Ibrahanni Group operative in the Indian Central Bureau of Investigation—CBI. The CBI agent's membership on an international task force provided him with access to ongoing investigations coordinated with law enforcement agencies such as Interpol and the FBI. In situations like these, the operative communicated that information to his contact at the Ibrahanni Group at least one hour before taking any official action himself. The delay usually provided Ibrahanni operatives enough lead time to determine whether there was an opportunity for them to exploit before law enforcement could arrive on any scene to interfere. Because it was the weekend, the Ibrahanni Group operative inside the CBI hadn't discovered the funds transfer for several hours.

The transaction was an anomaly, and Yadav was able to compare the currency transaction amounts and determine there might well be a connection between the anomaly and a Wi-Fi signal in Hyderabad. The possibility the Wi-Fi signal was a trigger made it far more interesting, and it was something no law enforcement agency would know simply because they weren't looking for it. Only the largest and best equipped organized crime families were monitoring Wi-Fi activity in their "territories," screening it as part of its "Big Data" research, and comparing it to anomalous international financial activity.

If someone was operating out of Hyderabad and affecting funds transfers on an international scale, Yadav's boss would want to know. Not only was criminal activity being undertaken in his "territory," but the talent and technology involved were sophisticated. His boss would want a big piece of whatever action this was. If possible, he would want to recruit the individual. If money didn't work, coercion probably would, and the Ibrahanni operatives were skilled in coercion. But the Hyderabad office would have to move quickly to find this person before he or she got away.

Yadav flagged the message as urgent and sent it directly to the head of special operations in Hyderabad, Ravikumar Singh. Singh had proven relentless over the years and he got results, especially in delicate matters such as this one. Singh immediately shot back a status: "I have people on the way now, but do you realize these GPS coordinates designate a position in the middle of Hussain Sagar Lake?"

Yadav responded, "Yes. I know. Please do whatever you can. This could be very big."

"Understood," Singh replied, and signed off.

*  *  *  *

Just about the time Winters was boarding his flight from Pune to Ottawa, Ravikumar Singh was beginning his survey around the perimeter of Hussain Sagar Lake. He had commandeered a commercial tour boat that was being refueled for afternoon excursions. After offering the fueler a substantial wad of money for the private tour without success, he finally resorted to flashing his pistol at the man to secure the cooperation he needed.

Singh had spotted the Sea Ray but hadn't had any luck identifying who had chartered it as yet. He wasn't even sure this was the platform from which the transaction had been performed, but it made sense to him. It had clearly been used within the last several hours because the cowling around the motor was still warm. He saw no evidence of the specialized electronics Winters had been using, of course, since it was at the bottom of the lake. But it seemed to Singh to be the kind of vessel someone might use for this purpose. It was fast, quiet, and comparatively easy for a single individual to maneuver. Continuing on foot, Singh looked for a likely residence close to the dock where a land station might be situated to support communications, and possibly even provide land-based surveillance of the lake.

Singh was joined after an hour by two additional operatives. The difficult part for him was explaining exactly what he was looking for. He didn't know, precisely; he just knew he would recognize it when he saw it. Finally, he just told the men to look for a private residence with a line-of-sight to the statue in the middle of the lake, especially anything with unusual antennae on it, or unusual movement around it. Two hours went by as the three men scoured nearby neighborhoods.

Around three p.m., one of Singh's operatives decided he should look for a coffee shop in the area. He began to poke around the streets about two blocks away from the shoreline. Suddenly, he heard the loud revving of a truck engine and saw a mid-size cargo truck pulling away from a residence that faced the lake from a small hill to his left. Trotting to the street in front of the building, he thought he could see a Federal Express logo on the back of the vehicle as it disappeared into traffic. He turned back to look around the residence. It was nothing special; there were many such buildings in the area. They were often rented to tourists in the spring and autumn. This one looked like a two-residence building, and both residences seemed vacant. There were no vehicles visible, but a resident's car might well be parked on the street; that would not be unusual either.

Pulling a small spotting scope from his pocket, the operative examined the doors and windows of the building. Peering through his scope, he caught the tiny reflective glimmer of freshly installed staples attaching a wire along the edge of one side of the building and leading up to the roof. By walking backward a few yards, the operative was able to see what looked like satellite TV dishes attached to the roof. *Again, nothing unusual about that*, he thought, *but ...* "Ah," he said aloud to no one but himself, "what is this?"

One of the dishes was pointed upward at an angle plainly designed for satellite communications, similar to all the other satellite dishes in the neighborhood. The other dish, however, which was slightly different in size and shape, pointed out directly at the lake—nearly parallel to the surface of the water. The operative pulled out his cell phone and engaged his speed dial.

"Singh," came the greeting at the other end. "What do you have for me?"

∗   ∗   ∗   ∗

When Dawson's team awakened late Saturday afternoon, they set out to find a place for dinner. The Haxenhaus, a small restaurant not far from their hotel, provided an excellent meal, and all of them began to feel some of the tension of the mission dwindling.

When they arrived at the Dresden International Airport, Dawson was surprised to be greeted in the lobby by Gary Pellar—the CIA staff member Dawson had met with in Deputy Director John Deering's office. Although Dawson didn't know him well, he was pleased to see the Agency had sent someone to support them.

"We have a charter jet warming up for you now," Pellar said, smiling.

"I'm surprised to see you, Gary," Dawson said. "We already have commercial tickets outbound from here."

"I know," Pellar replied. "What can I say? My boss is a worrywart. When Charles told him about your route, he insisted we give you a security detail on your way home. So here I am."

He directed them through a secured doorway, past two armed security personnel, and into a plush conference room with a US flag placard on the door. Dawson, Bi-shou, and Gerard set their duffels and backpacks down as they entered the room. "Your bird should be wheels-up in under thirty minutes, Ben," Pellar said. Then he turned and introduced himself to the others. "Dr. Antonov, it's a great honor to meet you in person at last," he said when he finally turned to the scientist.

Antonov, who spoke English haltingly, replied: "I thank you. But I am a little confused about what is happening."

"Yes, Sir," Pellar said, "I'm sure you are. If you will have a seat, we have about fifteen minutes and I will try to explain what I can. I understand you drink tea, not coffee; is that correct?" And as he spoke, a young man brought in a silver tray with tea service. Dawson, Gerard, and Bi-shou gave the men some privacy, stepping to the opposite end of the room and speaking quietly among themselves while Pellar did his best to reassure Antonov about his future, and about the arrangements that would assure the safety of his family.

While they were talking, Dawson decided to check his Gmail inbox to see if Winger, Winters, or Wahl had left him a message. Finding none, he left a short message of his own in a drafts folder named "Jennings." It simply said: "Outbound shortly. Debriefing with Pellar from the Agency now. Any updates?"

Normally, since this folder was flagged to alert Charles Jennings' admin immediately, Dawson received a response within a couple of minutes—especially when he was in the field. This time it took nearly five minutes and his phone buzzed. The text message said: "Check mail immediately." Dawson popped back into his email account and clicked on the Jennings folder. The message there said: "Just talked with John. Be advised: No idea why Pellar is there. He is on PTO. Something is wrong!"

Dawson handed his phone to Gerard, who was closest to him, and motioned for her to share what she was reading with Bi-shou. As they were reading, Dawson whispered: "Follow my lead. We need to see where this is going." Dawson then began to move toward his backpack, where his sidearm was secured.

Bi-shou cleared the message and handed the phone back to Dawson. He pocketed it and as he reached down to open his backpack, the door to the conference room opened and four men entered. The first was Todd Connelly, who had delivered Dawson's equipment to the Four Seasons Hotel in Prague, followed by three others. They all wore civilian clothes, but carried .40 caliber Smith & Wesson M&P Pro semi-automatic pistols with sound suppressors on their barrels and their safeties disengaged.

Dawson was angriest at the moment because he hadn't seen something like this coming. All the microexpressions, body language, and verbal queues he'd observed in Pellar back at Deering's office should have set off alarm bells. Instead, Dawson had chalked them up to petty jealousy and inter-agency rivalries. Again, as he had several times over the last few years, Dawson wondered whether he was simply getting too old for this game.

Almost instantly though, Dawson started producing a mental list of questions: *Is Pellar really after Antonov for his own purposes? Is he trying to obtain and resell the intellectual property involved, or acting on behalf of another buyer? If it was indeed another buyer, then who: a foreign government, a terrorist organization, or a private enterprise?* Without these answers, there was no way of understanding how deep, how wide, or how high the corruption at CIA was, and no way to be certain about who had authorized this action.

As soon as Pellar's men entered the room, they had collected the phones and weapons of Dawson and his team. All three of them were frisked and told to sit at the conference table while Pellar explained to Antonov that he should not be concerned. He would be safe and allowed to work in freedom at his new location. However, he was not told for whom he would be working, nor where, or to what end.

Turning to Dawson then, Pellar said: "You and your team will walk with us through the airport lobby and to our vehicle. As you can see, my people all carry silenced weapons. I need Sergei here, but I do not need *you*. If you resist or try to raise an alarm of any kind, you will be executed on the spot and left for the Dresden airport authorities to deal with. I will have to kill you eventually, of course, unless someone decides to pay me an outrageous sum to release you. But it would have to be an obscene amount because—I have no doubt—I'll be looking over my shoulder for the rest of my life if I let you go. Any questions?"

"Only two, I suppose," Dawson replied. "Who's bankrolling you? I can't imagine you're doing this on your own. You don't have the organization to do anything useful with the technology as it stands today." Dawson was fishing and both men knew it.

"Well," Pellar grinned, "if you don't force me to kill you before my 'banker' arrives, I'll let you see for yourself. You're right, of course; I have no interest in developing the technology. That's for geeks like Brystol. I'm interested in the kind of wealth that puts me beyond reach. What's your second question?"

"How did you know we were coming out through Dresden?"

Pellar's self-satisfaction was evident. "All your travel arrangements for this mission were coordinated through Deering's office since it's a joint operation. It was easy once we determined you were a no-show at the train station in Prague. Shall we go now?"

Pellar made sure the smartphones belonging to Dawson, Bi-shou, and Gerard were all left in the waste bin. Two of his operatives carried the backpacks and duffels, and they all walked calmly out through the front lobby of the airport—where they were monitored through the airport security cameras by Mickey Wahl back at NSA headquarters.

# CHAPTER 24

"Have you got them?" Jennings asked as they exited the building. Wahl had been called frantically by Jennings about thirty minutes earlier as he was just about to pull into the parking lot at work. Within ten minutes, he had identified the exact position of Dawson's phone and identified the IP—Internet Protocol—addresses of the half dozen smartphones within twenty feet of Dawson. So when the smartphones of Dawson, Gerard, and Bi-shou were shut down and discarded, Wahl continued to track the balance of the mobile phone signals as they moved through—and then away from—the airport. He popped them up on a two-dimensional grid map of Dresden.

"Yes, Sir. I guess the Agency folks don't know we can do this?" Wahl said as he worked, while Jennings literally peered over his shoulder in the lab.

"We are often criticized for failing to share information between the various agencies, Mr. Wahl," Jennings replied without taking his eyes off the screen. "You're seeing one example of why, at times, we do not. Checks and balances work for all of us, and people at the top of all of these agencies constantly try to balance the level of collaboration against the level of risk associated with complete transparency."

"Looks like they are headed out to a semi-industrial part of Dresden, similar to the warehouse district in Prague where the auction occurred," Wahl said.

*  *  *  *

Winters had made it through the first legs of his journey and most of the way through his flight to Ottawa when Singh finally determined who owned the property near Hussain Sagar Lake. Determining whose name was on the rental agreement took more time, and obtaining that information required a personal "interview" with a rather stubborn agent at the leasing office. It would be almost two weeks before the leasing agent recovered from his "accidental fall." The admitting physician at the local hospital marveled at how so many injuries had been sustained in just one tumble down the stairs.

Singh conferred with the Ibrahanni Group analysts in Dubai, and they eventually unraveled the travel plans of David Volmer through the Pune-to-Ottawa flight. But the closest operatives of the Ibrahanni family to Ottawa were stationed in Toronto. The flight time between Toronto and Ottawa was only an hour, but assembling operatives, briefing them, and getting them on an aircraft before Winters landed in Ottawa turned out to be more than the Ibrahanni Group could manage. The operatives in Dubai were unable to track Volmer's return to the United States because there was none. Volmer became Winters again as soon as he passed through Customs in Ottawa, and the trail disappeared.

When he appeared for check-in at the Ottawa airport and boarded the aircraft for Washington, DC, Winters encountered no issues at all. For all intents and purposes, he was home free. Sitting aboard the Canada Air jet, he mentally checked off items he'd need to complete in order to close out the adventure. Among them were disposing of the remaining equipment shipped back to Salt Lake City, and then hacking the Canadian Customs and Immigration database again to reflect Volmer's return trip to Utah.

Winters knew from Dawson's description two weeks earlier that things could have been much worse. Although he was unaware of how close he had come, any significant delay getting through the airport in Ottawa might have proven fatal. Waiting for his bag at the airport in Washington, DC, he left a note for Dawson in his Gmail drafts folder which simply read: "Safely returned from vacation. Will check in at the office on my way home."

It was 8:30 p.m. on Saturday when Winters arrived at the NSA. Jennings had left word with campus security that Winters was being reinstated—coming back from official leave—but since they weren't expecting him until the following Monday, it took about thirty minutes to track down his badge and other credentials.

"Holy cow, Mickey," he joked as he walked into the lab. "I'm gone for a couple of weeks and you have the boss here working on a Saturday night?" Then he saw the expression on their faces and realized something serious was underway. His manner quickly adapted to their more serious tone. "What's up?"

"We have a bit of a situation here, Daniel," Jennings said, barely glancing at Winters. "A rogue officer at CIA named Pellar has taken Ben, along with Bi-shou and Ms. Gerard as hostages. I believe that may be my fault; I contacted John Deering to get Agency assistance, and that appears to be the way the CIA officer intercepted Ben in Dresden. Pellar seems to be preparing to trade Antonov for cash, and they are all headed into an industrial area of Dresden by land transport. Mr. Wahl has been able to isolate the mobile phones of some of the captors, and we are tracking their location as they move."

"Winger and Romero are in Helsinki," Wahl added, "and we need to re-route them to Dresden."

"I want to use Winger and Romero to lead the hostage rescue team in Dresden," Jennings said. "I have informed John Deering so he can move his operatives in to assist."

"I'm not sure I understand what happened, Sir," Winters said. "Bi-shou and Lily were there with Ben, right? And they let themselves be taken hostage?"

"Yes, I think there is more involved here," Jennings agreed. "I am surmising that Ben has decided to find out who is behind all this. Unfortunately, of course, he gives up almost all tactical advantage this way. I'd have preferred to interrogate Pellar after Ben's team was back here."

"Mickey," Winters said, "can you mirror your display on the big monitor over here? I'd like to see this too, and having all three of us crowded around your console doesn't make much sense."

"Oh, sure," Wahl said, and with the stroke of a few keys, the flashing red light moving through the streets of Dresden was displayed on the wall-size smart board. Winters immediately sat down at his old desk and got to work. Interrogating the database with records from the mobile phones involved, he identified one of the phones as belonging to CIA operative Connelly in less than two minutes.

*   *   *   *

As soon as he arose on Sunday, Winger checked in via his smartphone. He was surprised to see both a text message and a message in the Gmail drafts folder asking him to contact Daniel Winters at the NSA immediately. They appeared to be urgent so he responded to the text message simply by saying: "Winger here." He began to receive an encrypted message within seconds.

About five minutes later, Winger walked down the hall to Romero's room and tapped on the door, saying quietly, "It's Winger, Chief."

Romero was already up, Winger could see. He had just been doing crunches and pushups. "What's up?" he asked as Winger slipped inside.

"I got a message from the NSA. Ben, Lily, and Bi-shou were taken hostage by a rogue CIA officer named Pellar. Evidently they made it out with Antonov, but now Pellar has them all. Walked them out of the Dresden airport a few hours ago. We need to get a move on. We're going to Dresden."

"Damn!" was all Romero could come up with.

"Yeah," Winger replied. "Pellar must be on drugs or something. For a guy at his level—evidently he reports directly to Deering—to go off the reservation like this is darned near suicidal. There must be an unbelievable payoff. The Agency has operatives out looking for them now, but nothing yet."

"You know, Billy, this makes no sense," Romero said, scratching his bristly head.

"What do you mean, Chief?"

"Well, unless they kill them almost immediately, they're in for a world of hurt. Can you imagine? Assuming they aren't injured or something, I just think the three people you probably *don't* want most as captives are those three. Even if we get there in time, I'm betting we end up rescuing this guy Pellar from *our* team."

"I see your point, Chief," Winger replied. Thinking about it, Winger realized that a martial arts champion trained in police methods, a highly skilled assassin, and an experienced international operative like Ben Dawson were just about the last three people anyone would want to try to capture and keep as hostages. "Still, Ben got blindsided here by somebody who was supposed to be on our side."

"Yeah, I gotta believe he was pretty pissed about that," Romero said, the traces of a smile tugging at the corners of his mouth. "It's about the only way they could have taken him by surprise. And Lily is there. Can you imagine what will happen if they start roughing up *either* one of those two?"

"It would get ugly fast, that's for sure."

"So why leave the airport with them?" Romero asked.

"Probably wants to see whether Pellar is at the top of this thing or who's bankrolling him," Winger speculated aloud.

Romero nodded in reply. "It's the only thing that makes sense to me," he said. "Still, it's a helluva risk."

\* \* \* \*

Wahl had been right; the destination of the large passenger van in which Antonov and Dawson's team were transported was an industrial park comprised mostly of warehouses and small logistics firms. The building was a 1950s brick and stucco structure that originally housed a warehouse on the lower level and both offices and a residence on the second floor.

Dawson and his team, along with Antonov, were hustled inside and shown to a room with an old sofa and a few overstuffed chairs. It looked as though it had been some kind of customer waiting room or reception area. There was one dull overhead light, a long, low sofa table in front of the sofa, and little else in the room. Two of Pellar's operators remained behind in the room with Dawson, Gerard, and Bi-shou. They sat several feet apart in the overstuffed chairs, across from Dawson and his team on the sofa.

"Just to make sure we all understand the ground rules here," Pellar said, "these gentlemen will keep their pistols at hand with a round in the chamber and safeties in the 'Off' position. At the first inkling of trouble from any of you, they will shoot you. There is no particular reason to keep you alive, from my perspective, other than the possibility Jennings would pay handsomely for your return, Ben. Frankly, I doubt it's in the cards. So if you'd like to remain alive to find out, I recommend you just sit quietly. Take a nap or something. Are we clear?" Dawson and the two women nodded, and settled back into the sofa.

Pellar looked at his two operatives, who also nodded, and then left the room. He closed the door behind him but didn't lock it.

Once outside, Pellar directed Connelly and another operative to put Antonov in an adjacent room and watch him while Connelly made some phone calls. Pellar's first call was to Charles Jennings' office at NSA. Since Jennings was in the computer lab with Winters and Wahl, his office phone was forwarded to the mobile phone of his admin, Gloria Treadway. Treadway explained that Jennings was not in his office at the moment and asked if the matter was urgent enough to require her to track Jennings down.

"That won't be necessary," Pellar replied. "Could you just give him a message for me, please?"

"Of course."

"Please tell him Thomas Pellar called. The price of the three assets is twelve million dollars. The price of only his primary asset is ten million dollars. Payment must be available by wire transfer at ten a.m. or his opportunity will expire. After the transfer has been made, the assets will be available to him, in good condition, by five p.m. The routing and account numbers will be sent by text message to Jennings' mobile at nine a.m. All of these times are in Dresden time. Could you read that back to me please?"

Treadway did as he asked, and then Pellar rung off. He had little hope of actually receiving the funds but it would be a very nice bonus if he did. *Nothing ventured, nothing gained,* he thought. Then he turned off the burner phone he had used, broke it, and discarded it in the waste bin. Reaching into his pocket, he withdrew another smartphone, turned it on, and dialed from memory. It went to voicemail and he left a message: "We are on schedule and awaiting your arrival." After disconnecting the call, he waited three minutes to determine whether there would be any return call and then, receiving no callback, powered off his device.

Everything was in motion now. He had a few hours to relax. For Pellar, it had been a long journey but he could clearly see the end approaching. A career US State Department employee, he had never married. Pellar had been a close friend of like-minded individuals who ended up in the CIA after the initial withdrawal from Afghanistan in 2011, but after a few years most of them had retired or moved on. Pellar had worked very hard to curry favor and identify potential opportunities to enrich himself over the years. He did well in the State Department when it was led by Hillary Clinton. But, although he rose steadily in rank, he never discovered an opportunity to acquire a great deal of wealth.

Those opportunities were certainly available. After all, Pellar knew that although the median household wealth of freshman House members was only around half a million dollars, by the time they spend a few years in Washington the picture usually changed dramatically. He recalled one recent news report describing the US Congress as a "club" comprised of "245 millionaires," saying opportunities for members of Congress to obtain wealth are abundant. It went on to explain that members of Congress are not prohibited by "insider trading" rules when the information they have access to is not "public information." So lawmakers, who learn of upcoming government contracts to be awarded to a publicly traded company, are free to buy shares of the company's stock before news of the contract award is made known to the public. Pellar didn't really mind this kind of privilege among the elite; he just wanted in.

Then, when he moved over to the CIA, his own department's work provided the first glimmer of hope. The CIA had been in possession of the Kammler "Bell" device, which was captured in 1945 along with Kammler himself. The Agency had tried to move the related research into development several times, but without success. Kammler died late in 1946 of an unusual illness; the medical doctors attending him concluded it was an anomalous form of cancer brought on by radiation poisoning. Pellar had been approached—cautiously— several times over the years by both the Russians and the Chinese about selling whatever information the Agency had on the device, and the device itself. Each time he had declined the offer, but he did not report any of the overtures; an act of treason by omission if not by commission.

When Dawson's team returned from Mezhgorye with evidence the Russians had obviously made a breakthrough in operationalizing the technology, Pellar saw his chance. Since Brystol and the NSA were planning to wrest the technology away from Russia anyway, he only needed to build on their covert operation with one of his own. He decided he would allow Dawson's team to take the responsibility and do the work. He would simply take it away from them at exactly the right moment, using Connelly—with whom he had become friends while they served together in Islamabad—and private contractors loyal only to him. He had already worked out an agreement with a broker of black market technologies like Icarus, and expected to live out the rest of his days in a beautiful villa on the southern tip of Bali, far from the attentions of any significant government. All was ready for his escape; he just needed the money. And now, in a matter of hours, it would be within his grasp. *It's all finally coming together,* he thought.

Treadway dialed Jennings' mobile and passed along Pellar's somewhat cryptic message. She was only mildly surprised when Jennings said: "I understand. Please get through to John Deering, Gloria. I am working on an urgent matter here that I will need his help with. Tell him I am leaving Fort Meade in twenty minutes and will meet him at his office in Langley."

Before he departed for CIA headquarters, Jennings ensured Winters understood what he needed to do to get the emergency funds transfer executed. Jennings knew—although he could authorize the transfer—there would be a detailed explanation required on Monday morning.

# CHAPTER 25

The time went by slowly for Dawson and his team. Dawson was seated in the center of the long sofa. After a few minutes he slid down into the sofa, leaned his head back, and closed his eyes. While he appeared to the security staff to be napping, he was actually running through candidates who might be bankrolling Pellar. One by one, he tried to confirm or eliminate them based on various facts at his disposal, inferences, and deductions.

Gerard and Bi-shou were both too edgy to relax as Dawson had appeared to do. Gerard fidgeted and moved around as best she could while seated in order to keep her muscles loose for what she knew must inevitably lie ahead. Bi-shou was the very picture of poise and serenity, though her eyes were as cold as ice. She spent her time calculating distances, estimating response times of each guard, and reviewing the magazine capacity of the weapons they held.

Around nine a.m., there was some muffled talking outside the room, and Connelly entered the room with a large brown bag. He set the bag down in front of them along with three bottles of water. "The boss says you can eat if you want. If you don't, it's fine with me. I'll be back to collect the stuff in thirty minutes." Then he wheeled and left the room. The bag contained several breakfast pastries from a local restaurant. Bi-shou wasn't interested in the food at all, but used the opportunity to test the patience and responsiveness of the guards. She deliberately allowed her bottle of water to tip over and roll to the floor, and then abruptly stood to retrieve it. All three of the captives noticed it took at least a full second—perhaps a second and a half—for the guard to wave his pistol and order her back to her seat, after which he stood and retrieved the bottle himself. A one-and-a-half-second response time was something she and Gerard could work with. She met Gerard's eyes momentarily and saw the recognition there of what she had done. Now if they could couple that delay with even the briefest of distractions, they would have their opening. The three of them picked at their food until the operative returned and collected the remainder of food and trash. Both guards remained alert throughout that process, so the distraction they were looking for didn't appear immediately.

Bi-shou decided the best opportunity would likely be when the guards swapped out positions with the other two operatives. During the event, there would be the natural distractions associated with the changing of the guards and all four of the operatives would be in the room. While this made the odds more challenging, it minimized the likelihood of someone coming through the door with guns blazing. Bi-shou correctly surmised Pellar was an office type; he exhibited no evidence of knowing anything about tactical field operations. He assumed four armed operatives would be sufficient to control three unarmed operatives, so he hadn't even directed they be zip-tied. Errors in judgment like that would never have permitted him to survive in the field.

Gerard continued to flex her muscles in place. At one point, she reached into a small pocket of her blouse and retrieved a hair tie. The guards watched her but didn't respond as she pulled back her long, auburn hair and made it into a ponytail. She decided if no other opening arose within fifteen minutes, she would ask to use the restroom just to see what opportunities it might produce.

They all knew they had to remain vigilant in order to act quickly when an opportunity presented itself.

\* \* \* \*

As soon as they arrived at the airport in Helsinki, Winger and Romero were swept up by US officials and taken directly to a chartered Gulfstream.

"Quite a change from Orlov's buggy," Romero remarked.

"Holy moley, guacamole!" Winger said, staking out a big leather chair for himself. "I wonder if this thing has a bar. Can't drink much anyway with work ahead of us, but a cold beer would be nice."

They were wheels-up within five minutes after Winger and Romero were in their seats. While they cruised at altitude, Winger's phone buzzed. *Wi-Fi on board,* he thought, *nice!* "Winger," he said into the phone. It was Winters.

"Sir," Winters said, "we have coordinates for the location where our people are currently being held. I am texting you the street address and GPS coordinates now. You'll be met on the ground by the CIA Chief of Station, Lyle Richardson, and driven to the site personally. You'll have to provide him with the address; the boss wasn't comfortable sharing that before you got there. He said something about it being hard to know who to trust these days. Anyway, I assume you still have the samples and artifacts from Mezhgorye with you?"

"Affirmative," Winger said. "We have two backpacks of 'souvenirs,' our sidearms, and not much else. Traveling pretty light at this point."

"Understood," Winters said. "Stand by, please."

Winters was away from the phone for a minute and when he returned, said: "Keep the 'souvenirs' with you. Do not release them into anyone else's custody until you return to DC. Roger that?"

"Yeah, I got it," Winger replied. "Do you know what the situation is on the ground?"

"Honestly, no," Winters replied. "We think Ben is trying to find out who's behind this latest snatch. There seem to be only four operators and Pellar, but I'm going on electronic intel here so it's sketchy. In the meantime though, the boss authorized a $12 million transfer of funds to Pellar's account for the safe return of Ben and his team. We're waiting for his account numbers now and will try to learn more using that information. It's probably a kite though—flushing straight through to other places, and I will be trying to track it in the background. Of course, even when the ransom has been paid it doesn't guarantee anything, so be careful."

"OK, let me make sure I understand," Winger said. "Ben and the two ladies are being held by Pellar. We know where they are but the Agency doesn't. You've told them I will have the location when I arrive and they are to support us when Romero and me go in after them. Sound about right?"

"Yes, you've got it," Winters replied.

"Crap," Winger said. "You don't really think the Agency guys are going to want to support a couple of private contractors working for another agency, do you?" Romero, who had been listening to Winger, was also sporting a deep frown.

"They are receiving orders to that effect right now from the highest levels of the Agency, which is why I'm talking to you instead of the boss, Sir. He's down at Langley," Winters said.

"I'll bet *that's* an interesting conversation," Winger said through a mischievous grin. "OK, Danny boy, we're on our way. They tell me we'll be on the ground in less than two hours. Sure hope they wait to start the party 'til we get there. Anything else?"

"No, Sir," Winters replied, "that's it. Good luck."

"Roger that. Out here," Winger said, and disconnected the call.

*  *  *  *

It was nearly ten a.m. local time when Winger and Romero touched down in Dresden. Winger had assessed the situation correctly; Richardson—an Agency lifer—was not a happy man but he cooperated grudgingly. On balance though, Richardson realized that since he wasn't in charge of this operation, he should be absolved of any responsibility for the outcome. *But if those desk jockeys at Langley hadn't hired Pellar in the first place,* he thought, *and then allowed him to go off the reservation, they wouldn't have this mess to begin with.* Richardson remembered a similar incident with other Agency operators pretty high in the organization over recent years—*Was it Kessler and Hubbard?*—and wondered how so many bad apples had gotten into the mix.

The men introduced themselves and shook hands. "You've got the address?" Richardson asked.

"Yeah, we just got it during the flight," Winger replied, "from elint—electronic intelligence—so we're not a hundred percent sure."

"OK, let's roll," Richardson said. "I have four more operatives and my driver. I'll call this in to them and they will meet us a couple of blocks away."

"Sounds good," Winger replied. He and Romero carefully stowed their backpacks in the trunk of Richardson's Mercedes sedan, and they got under way. Richardson predicted about a thirty minute travel time.

*  *  *  *

About the time Richardson's car was leaving the airport, Pellar reentered the room and spoke to Dawson from just inside the doorway. "Good news," he said. "Jennings has decided to fork over the cash to get you all out. The funds have already been transferred so if you behave yourselves, I *might* let you live; we'll see." His face broke into a broad grin as he turned and left the room. Dawson could hear him remark over his shoulder: "This day just gets better and better! Too bad there are only a few hours left."

Another hour went by. It had become clear to both Gerard and Bi-shou that Dawson wasn't interested in making his move until they knew who was funding Pellar's operation.

About thirty minutes into that hour, Winger and Romero—backed up by four CIA operators—arrived and took up positions at the site. Dark clouds filled the sky and Romero could smell an impending rainstorm. *Sure hope it holds off in case I have to take a shot,* he thought. Romero set up a sniper's nest on the roof of a building across the street, back away from the edge of the building and behind a small facade. He was provided with a sniper rifle by one of the Agency operatives, and connected to the rest of the team by radio. Two of the CIA men then concealed themselves along the street, surreptitiously covering the building from different angles.

Winger scanned the setup from the street behind the building and saw one possible entry point to the structure on the second floor. A low, commercial building adjacent to the one where Dawson was held displayed a sign that read: "Autosklo." It appeared to Winger to be an automotive repair shop, and there was an ancient iron-pipe-style fire ladder attached to the back of the structure. No exterior surveillance cameras were suspended from the target structure. Picking their way carefully along the stucco surfaces of the building, Winger and two of the CIA operatives made their way to the ladder. One operative remained on street level behind the Autosklo building to provide cover in case someone appeared suddenly at the window and the other operative followed Winger up to the roof. Standing on top of the building, after dodging a solar panel mounted on the side of the adjacent building, Winger could easily reach up to the sliding glass window. The room on that corner of the second floor was dark. Hoisting himself gingerly, Winger could hear no sound when he pressed his ear against the corner of the glass. He briefly examined the edges of the window. No alarm wires were visible. Then he gently tried sliding the window aside, but—as he anticipated—the lock was engaged.

Finally, Winger pulled his KA-BAR knife from the inside of his combat boot and cut away the glazing from the edges of the glass. The process took longer but made very little sound and allowed the sheet of glass to simply fall forward into Winger's gloved hand. Poking his hand in through the opening, Winger unfastened the latch and slowly moved the frame aside. This left enough room to squeeze through. Winger carefully entered, then turned and assisted the CIA operative following behind him. Winger and the operative unslung their weapons, took them off "Safe," and began to move. Just as they did though, activity began to occur in front of the building.

Stepping back, Winger glanced carefully out of the window toward the street. He saw two black SUVs roll slowly up to the curb. They were shiny new Navigators—unusual for Dresden—with darkly tinted windows. Where they stopped to unload their passengers, Winger could not see who they were. He quietly whispered into his radio: "Chief, can you tell me who it is?"

"Negative, Billy," came Romero's reply. "They have their backs to me. Six men—I'd guess four of them are operators; they have that manner about them. Big guys, but light on their feet. The other guy is shorter and looks pretty heavy. Obviously pretty overweight; he moves like a sumo wrestler."

*Bleckhaus,* Winger thought. *But who is the other guy?* "Roger that," he whispered. "We're inside now so I'm going quiet."

Winger and the Agency operative made their way slowly and carefully around the perimeter of the room, deliberately placing each footstep to avoid squeaks in the floorboards. The room was devoid of furniture, which helped, and looked as though it had been unoccupied for some time. The door was closed but not locked. But the handle was old and loose, so Winger had to move it very carefully to avoid rattles. The next problem was the hinges which squeaked badly. All Winger could do was wait until he could hear sounds from the lower level. In this case, that sound was provided by the arrival of the new visitors from the vehicle outside. As soon as he heard the voices and shuffling below, Winger opened the door just enough to squeeze through. The squeak wasn't good, Winger knew, but it didn't result in any obvious changes in the sounds and activity on the first floor.

"Boss," Romero's voice came through Winger's earbud, "they left two operators on the door. The other two are inside now."

"Roger that," Winger whispered in reply.

Winger and the Agency operative crept carefully toward the stairway, and Winger slid his head quickly into the stairwell and back. The stairs were made of a thin concrete cast which was another bit of luck; there would be no squeaks there. The stairs appeared to open toward the front of the building but offset to one side from the building's entrance, and was unguarded. This made some sense since the second floor was unoccupied. Winger figured correctly that Pellar didn't plan to be there for long. Followed by the CIA operative from Richardson's team, he slowly started down the stairs.

# CHAPTER 26

As soon as the arrival of new visitors reached Dawson's ears, he sat erect and slid forward to the front edge of the sofa. Gerard and Bi-shou understood the signal and subtly braced themselves to spring from the sofa. After about two minutes of muffled voices out in the entry area, Pellar entered the room followed by Bleckhaus and the guest of honor. Behind Bleckhaus two additional operatives entered the room, posting themselves at each side of the interior door. Dawson was certain he had never before seen the man accompanying Bleckhaus. He was a dark, powerfully built man with thick ebony hair and a Fu Manchu-style beard and mustache.

Bleckhaus stood speechless, studying Bi-shou closely. He knew he had seen her before but was obviously having trouble placing her.

"It was Shanghai," Dawson said to him. "In the bar at the Hilton during the conference last year."

Bleckhaus drew in a sharp breath. Continuing to stare at Bi-shou, he said: "Ja, the conference. You dropped your badge near our table in the bar! Ja, I remember now!"

Dawson studied the other man carefully for a moment and then said: "RAW?"

The stranger smiled slightly and replied, "I knew we would meet eventually, Mr. Dawson. I hoped it would be under different circumstances though. Yes, my name is Rajinder Kao and I work with the Research and Analysis Wing—RAW, as you say—of India's Foreign Intelligence Agency."

"I must confess I'm surprised at your candor, Mr. Kao," Dawson said.

Kao shrugged. "I have no objection if these gentlemen want to kill you. But I do not expect to remain undiscovered by your colleagues for long in any case."

"Interesting," Dawson said, "and well played, if I may offer a compliment."

"Thank you," Kao replied. "I appreciate that, considering the source."

"How are you hooked up with our friend, Dr. Bleckhaus, here?" Dawson asked, nodding toward the increasingly uncomfortable-looking German.

"Ah. Yes, Dr. Bleckhaus," Kao replied. "It seems the payments to Comrade Shelepin disappeared after they were deposited."

"I suspect you had something to do with that?" Pellar interjected with a snarl. Dawson and Kao both ignored him.

"This means the comrade had no way to pay our friend the professor," Kao continued. "So he has offered, once I have implemented our primary application for the product, to market derivative capabilities. In the mean-time, he will assist me in assuring the technology is brought successfully into production."

"I see," Dawson said. "May I ask you one other question? I realize you may not wish to answer."

Kao glanced at Pellar and said, "Of course. Unfortunately for you and your beautiful colleagues, I do not believe it can matter at this point anyway."

Dawson saw a half-smile again and the sneer developing on Pellar's face as he asked: "Why does India want this technology so badly? I understand there is a great tactical advantage vis-à-vis the Pakistanis, but surely more conventional and less costly technologies would serve you better."

"The answer is quite simple, Mr. Dawson. The answer is MIRVs."

Dawson thought for a few seconds and then said: "Ah. I should have seen that; thank you. It was the missing piece."

"Yes, I think you really should have, or at least the American CIA should have," Kao responded, smiling more broadly now as Pellar's expression be-came less gleeful.

"MIRVs?" Pellar asked. "What do MIRVs have to do with it?"

"Mr. Dawson can explain," Kao said.

"For many years—at least a decade, I think—India has been trying to solve the problem of how to launch Multiple Independent Reentry Vehicles—MIRVs. Everyone who knows about MIRVs understands the main rocket motor pushes a carrier into a free-flight suborbital ballistic flight path. After the boost phase, the carrier maneuvers using small on-board rocket motors and an on-board inertial guidance system. It takes up a ballistic trajectory that will deliver a reentry vehicle containing a warhead to a target, and releases a warhead on that trajectory. Then it maneuvers to a different trajectory releasing another warhead, and repeats the process for all warheads. MIRVs provide greater first-strike effectiveness, more damage on target, and render countermeasures such as anti-ballistic missile systems much less effective. The problem for several nations, especially India, has been detection when such a vehicle is launched. Almost everyone—even the United States—would have to try to ascertain the trajectories of the warheads and intervene if any of them target US interests. But we can intervene in such a launch today because we can see it easily from space and even from the ground. It's like Cape Canaveral. Now, if no one could detect the launch because there *was* none, and the MIRV carrier simply floated silently into position one night like a dirigible, life for India's enemies would suddenly become much more interesting. India is about to leapfrog the rest of the nuclear community in their hemisphere. Is that about it?"

"I could not have explained it better, Sir," Kao replied with a slight and momentary bow. He shifted a small briefcase he had been holding from his left hand to his right as he made ready to depart.

Dawson looked at the briefcase and asked: "The technical specification for the new device, I presume?"

"Precisely so," Kao responded. "And now if you will excuse me, I really must be gathering up Dr. Antonov and be on my way."

As Kao said the word "way," there was a mechanical coughing sound and Connelly, who had moved into the doorway, sunk to his knees; his eyes rolling back in his head as he dropped his weapon clattering to the floor. The other operative belonging to Pellar who had been posted outside the room was monitoring the exterior of the building. He had been keeping his eyes on the street out front, and by the time he half-turned toward the noise, he was dead as well. Both men had been killed by Winger as he swung out of the stairway and spun to the opposite side of the door frame. The CIA operative who followed Winger in replaced him at his initial position.

Bi-shou was the first among Dawson's team to respond when Winger's initial shot was fired. She leapt across the distance between the sofa and the overstuffed chair containing Pellar's closest operative before the man could bring his weapon up and into position. Bi-shou had already worked out a half-dozen ways to kill the man, and had settled on breaking his neck. Using the forward momentum of her body, she performed what one of her early instructors had called a scissors vault. She careened off of her left hand, placed flatly on the sofa table, landing with her legs wrapped tightly around the man's neck where it extended above the top of the overstuffed chair, and twisted her body—hard. It was almost as graceful as it was effective, and Gerard would have appreciated it if she'd seen it.

Gerard was almost a half-second slower to respond than Bi-shou. She simply launched forward, taking a full step to bring her left hand down on the man's gun hand while driving her fist as forcefully as she could into his Adam's apple. The operative was bringing his weapon around by the time Gerard hit him, and fired prematurely under the force of Gerard's blow. The man's errant shot punctured the sofa precisely where Dawson's chest had been seconds before, launching bits of stuffing and wood into the air. The man Gerard struck died seconds later from asphyxiation resulting from his collapsed windpipe. But by that time, the room was a blur of bodies and bullets.

Several events were unfolding simultaneously at that point. Outside, the sound of gunfire alerted the Indian operatives of trouble and they began to draw their sidearms to head inside. Romero killed them both in less than five seconds from his sniper's position across the street.

Gerard's forward motion carried her into a loose summersault during which she picked up her victim's pistol and shifted as quickly as she could into a prone firing position facing the door. She was the first to see Pellar diving to the floor behind the sofa. Since she was in a prone position anyway, it was a simple matter for her to roll to her left and follow his descent visually as his body appeared beneath the edge of the sofa. The sofa rested on six squatty, round wooden legs which left the bottom of the sofa frame about three inches from the floor. It took her just over a second from the time Pellar's body hit the floor, resting on his right side, until she had her weapon in position. She fired three rounds, "walking" them straight up the sofa at the position she judged to be the center of his chest. Beneath the sofa, she could see Pellar had appeared to roll onto his back and then remain still. A coroner would determine some time later that Gerard's first round had killed the man.

Bi-shou, having dispatched the man guarding her, didn't spend time trying to locate his weapon in the milieu; she simply engaged the closest Indian operative by hand as he closed in and began to swing his newly-unholstered weapon toward her. The expression of surprise still registered on his face as she practically climbed up his body in two steps, using his knee as a foothold to launch a vicious kick that landed beneath his chin, snapping his head straight backward.

Kao pulled a nine millimeter Glock from his jacket, but not in time. Dawson had hit him like a linebacker and sent the weapon skidding away on the floor. Kao kicked savagely at Dawson in order to get back to his pistol, only to find Winger standing over him with the barrel of his weapon pointed at a spot directly between his eyes.

Bleckhaus had literally backed up until he was against the far wall of the room, trembling and sweating profusely. Bi-shou had recovered her recently deceased guard's handgun and was calmly holding him in place there.

When he got free from Kao, Dawson said, "Wow. I think you may have cracked one of my ribs. And you seem like such a pleasant guy." Wincing, he got to his feet. "Thanks, Billy," he said to Winger. "We gotta stop meeting like this," and motioned to Gerard. "Lily, you and Billy had better see how Antonov is doing."

Gerard was already racing that direction. "Way ahead of you," she called back over her shoulder. Winger had to hustle just to catch up with her before she reached the appropriate room.

Antonov was unharmed, but clearly nervous. The room where he was being held was no longer guarded by the time Gerard and Winger reached it. Agency operatives had already taken the sentry at that door without resistance and were moving him toward the door of the building.

"Everything is fine now, Dr. Antonov," Gerard smiled. "We have the kidnappers in custody and we will see you safely to the United States."

The CIA operative who followed Winger down the stairs was somewhat disappointed at having never gotten off a shot. He zip-tied Kao and Bleckhaus, then marched them out to the street. There they found Bleckhaus' driver already secured and waiting in the back seat of a CIA SUV.

Winger called Romero down from the sniper's perch and then found time to beckon Bi-shou aside and greet her personally.

"I am a little disappointed in you, Billy," she scolded, even as he swept her into his arms.

"And why is that?" he asked, finally releasing her gently back to the ground.

"Because you did not use your new birthday gift."

"I needed a sound suppressor, Kid. I can't even get one of those without a Class A license, and the barrel needs to be threaded."

"Don't worry," she smiled, "it is already on your Christmas list."

# EPILOGUE

Dawson had been right; one of Kao's kicks had indeed cracked a rib. It wasn't fractured, so there wasn't anything much to do by way of treatment except allow it to heal and minimize upper torso exertion for a few months. Gerard thought that was just fine. "A little office time and R&R won't hurt you at all," she said.

As a result, Dawson spent several weeks catching up on technical journals, expense reports, and email. During that time, he attended enough of Brystol's sessions with Antonov to know the Icarus technology still had much further to go than some of its predecessors.

Antonov said as much almost immediately, and the samples Winger and Romero collected at Mezhgorye confirmed it. The application of multimillion-volt charges required to modify even local gravity fields had a "confusing" effect on the materials exposed to that level of energy. The molecular structures of the materials became entangled in such a way as to fuse them, which—until that problem was resolved—rendered most of the mechanisms involved useless after they had been levitated. There was also an extraordinarily high rate of radiation sickness and other maladies associated with the work, which made Brystol extremely cautious about proceeding with development.

News of the demise of Vadim Shelepin leaked out of Russia through backchannels shortly after Dawson returned to the Brystol Foundation, with the Soviet Operations and Technology Directorate announcing their leader had succumbed to a sudden illness and would be sorely missed by his comrades.

When Dawson met with Jennings one evening over dinner at the Taft Dining Room in the Washington University Club, Jennings told him about the fate of several of the players involved in what Jennings called "your recent adventure."

"It seems Professor Jürgen Bleckhaus has lost his attraction to the media, as well as his position with the Technische Universität Berlin," he said. "They don't really like international arms dealers representing their university. Since he is a German citizen, the CIA turned him over to the German BND, Bundesnachrichtendienst. So he has dropped off the grid for now, which is unfortunate. The Agency would like to chat with him, and they are negotiating with BND for an opportunity to do so. Deputy Deering is pretty frustrated about being overruled; he wanted to hold Bleckhaus until we were able to complete our interrogations. And Rajinder Kao, as you pointed out, is a very interesting man."

"How so?" Dawson asked between sips of iced tea.

"It remains a mystery to me how he stayed off the radar for so long over at CIA," Jennings said through a brief scowl. "He is obviously a very capable fellow and someone we should have been aware of. It appears Kao and Pellar became acquainted while Pellar was in Islamabad, but he was obviously successful keeping Kao invisible to the Agency. It was Pellar, evidently, who deployed the operatives in Ankara to get a homing beacon installed on your friend Orlov. But the really interesting part about that gambit was the young woman involved. Apparently, she is a double agent. Looking back at the signal traffic surrounding the events in Ankara, Daniel determined she identified your operatives, Winger and Romero, and alerted both Pellar at the Agency and then her handler at the Russian Federal Security Service."

"Hmm. Yes, I have been wondering about that. How do people like Kessler and Pellar keep surfacing at CIA, Charles? It could be my imagination, but it seems as though staff members who joined the Agency between 2008 and 2016 have an unusually high frequency of—well—defective moral compasses."

Jennings nodded. "It hasn't gone unnoticed, Ben. Deputy Deering is trying to do something about it—internal reviews, more extensive background checks, that sort of thing. But he can't afford a witch hunt over there. It's been a pretty demoralizing environment since …"

"Since Benghazi?"

Jennings nodded again. "Your friend Mr. Kao is still in custody, but not for much longer I suspect. The State Department is pressing for some kind of international arms trafficking charge, but the entire matter is a political football, and aside from conversations, we have no hard evidence."

"So it's likely I'll be running into him again at some point," Dawson remarked.

"I'd say so," Jennings replied. "And Daniel is making progress in recovering the ransom we paid for you and your team. I think we'll have it all back by the end of this month. He has turned out to be remarkably knowledgeable about international banking; I'm not sure where he picked that up."

"I discovered years ago that Daniel is an unusually versatile young man, Charles," Dawson replied through a suppressed smile. "He's going to grow into an excellent leader for you one day soon."

"By the way, Benjamin, I wanted to ask you about another matter," Jennings said, switching topics. "There was a chap tailing you at one point here in DC. A Patrick Burke, I believe?"

"Yes, Sir, there was. But he wasn't tailing *me,* precisely. He seemed to be more interested in Winger and Bi-shou. Never did figure out exactly why." Dawson speared another bite of prime rib and before putting it in his mouth, continued: "He seems to have given up on them when they left the country, though. No one has seen him since we got back." At that moment, their server appeared and refilled Dawson's iced tea. Dawson added a fresh packet of Splenda and slowly stirred it in.

"A loose end, then," Jennings mused aloud. "I'm not a fan of loose ends."

When the server had retreated, Jennings looked thoughtful for a minute and asked, "How is your newest team member performing for you?"

"Bi-shou?" Dawson asked in confirmation. "She's doing well, I'd say. I have seen no signs of relapse and she has performed extremely well in the field since joining us. Have you heard something different?" *What is he getting at?* Dawson thought.

"No, nothing at all. But as you'll remember, I had a rather frightening encounter with that young woman back in the days of the Salacia project. I just want to make sure she is remaining on the straight and narrow."

"Yes, I'm watching that, Sir," Dawson said. "But there is at least one other 'loose end,' as you put it, I'm wondering about."

"Bertha Lyman?" Jennings asked.

Dawson nodded as he began to sip his tea.

"The Agency has asked us to closely follow Ms. Lyman's activity but leave her unapproached until they have collected whatever intelligence may be useful, and we have agreed. For now, we will continue to monitor her communications and see whether we can hook some other large fish."

The conversation went on for another twenty minutes and then Dawson finally asked: "So what's next? Kenneth has several projects underway at the Brystol Foundation, but is one of them more likely to cause trouble than the others?"

"Indeed there is, Benjamin, indeed there is. It's called the Lethe Project, and I think you'll find it a bit of a departure from most of your recent work. No less dangerous, though. Let's give it a little while before you get embroiled in this next one, eh?"

"Fine with me, Charles. I have plenty to keep me busy at the Foundation, and even if I didn't, Lily would have no trouble filling my time."

Jennings smiled at this. "And how is Miss Gerard these days?" he asked.

"Oh, she's pretty disappointed in herself. She seems to have lost—literally—half a second in her response time, according to her, and she means to get it back. Something about losing her edge. Still fighting martial arts above her weight class and winning, but that's my girl. She's made reservations for us to spend some time on the beach over the next couple of weeks, so I'll be largely incommunicado."

And on it went, the conversation eventually waning and ending as dinner conversations usually did between Dawson and Jennings. "A toast to the late Max Kelly and fallen comrades everywhere," Dawson said, and Jennings finished it: "and God bless these United States of America."

* * * *

The following week, Dawson sat on the deck of the Hotel Laguna, gazing out over the water as the setting sun dissolved into the Pacific Ocean. Lazy beachcombers drifted by below him, slowly waltzing between the surges of waves spending themselves in foamy arcs against the sandy shore. The weather was perfect, and after only a day along the water, he could almost feel stress lifting away into the salty ocean breeze.

About thirty minutes earlier, he and Gerard had finished dinner. Gerard had slipped out of her sandals and beach dress, revealing a bright blue bikini, and strolled out to the water for another swim. Dawson smiled as he watched her returning to the deck. He noticed the stolen glances of admiration from other male diners, trying not to make their appreciation obvious, especially to their respective dinner partners. Dawson met her at the edge of the wooden steps with a beach towel and the rest of her paraphernalia, and they made their way around the side of the building to head inside.

"Work off your dinner?" Dawson asked.

"Yes, I think so," Gerard smiled at him. "In fact, I was thinking that after I get changed, you might escort me down the street for an ice cream cone."

Another twenty minutes found them strolling hand in hand down South Coast Highway, admiring beautiful works of art by Wyland, Pitre, Warren, TerBush, and others in the gallery windows.

"Makes me wish we could sail off to some tropical paradise and forget everything we do for a living," Gerard sighed.

"I think you'd be bored pretty quickly, don't you?" Dawson replied.

She thought about it for several paces and said, "I think it would take me a long time to become bored if you were there." She walked closer then, her arm against his.

"That's nice of you to say," he grinned.

He felt Gerard shrug a bit as she said: "It's certainly true, but not only because I love you. Things just seem to happen around you no matter where you go. There hasn't been a boring day since I met you. Between the intrigue, the crazy technologies, and the rather colorful company you keep, I don't really expect that to change anytime soon."

Then it was Dawson's turn to shrug. "I'm not getting any younger, Lily."

"Neither am I," she chuckled. "But we still manage rather well, I think."

"No argument there," he agreed as they stepped into the pool of light at the snack shop.

Carrying their cones away, Gerard noticed Dawson was shaking his head and smiling ruefully. "Penny for your thoughts," she said.

Dawson licked another side of his cone and said: "Sometimes it's all just hard to believe. What was it—six weeks ago—we were digging through the tunnels below Prague together? In my case, I'm an old beat-up operative just slogging his way through another mission. No mystery why I'd be sneaking around in a sewer someplace, breaking into an enemy hideout. But then there's you. I'm climbing through century old ruins full of rats and who knows what else, on the verge of being discovered and killed or maybe even worse. Suddenly, I get close enough to my partner to realize that under the coveralls and gloves and boots is the woman I love. A beautiful woman who smells like Sand & Sable, who is probably more lethal than most of the operators I know, and chooses to be there with me when she should be somewhere far less dangerous and far more lucrative. You should be doing private security work for some CEO someplace swanky, and ..."

Gerard stopped in her tracks and turned. Forgotten for a moment was the ice cream melting in her hand. "Wait a minute!" she said. "Rewind a sentence or two there. What was that right after the coveralls and boots? Just before the Sand & Sable thing."

"See, that's the problem with older guys like me. The memory just isn't what it used to be." He began to take another lick from his ice cream cone, but found that—for some reason—it was planted firmly in the middle of his forehead.

Gerard just stood there, licking hers and smiling. "Ice cream headache?" she asked.

# THE LETHE PROJECT

If you liked *The Icarus Project*, you'll love *The Lethe Project*! Ben Dawson and his team are back, intervening again as another bleeding edge technology threatens the international balance of power. As a bonus, here is the first chapter from the next installment in the Brystol Foundation series. Enjoy!

# CHAPTER 1

The Bethlehem Chapel in Washington DC's National Cathedral was deserted, except for a solitary figure seated in the front row near the center of the room. Daily services had ended on this Tuesday in February, and the place was shrouded in silence. The man was perfectly still, his expression sober, fixed somewhere between a question and a frown. His eyes were locked on the alter screen staring at the figure of the baby Jesus, serene in the arms of His mother Mary, as angelic figures watched over them from above.

When he had been there nearly two hours, another figure appeared at the back of the chapel. The woman was dressed in a warm leather coat and an off-white scarf over a dark green woolen suit. Her auburn hair spilled in waves over the scarf around her shoulders. Her boots were leather as well, a stylish

Italian pair that softened the sound of her footsteps on the stone floor as she moved up the aisle.

As she reached the third row from the front, the man spoke to her. "Hello, sweetheart," he said, turning toward her as he smiled. Ben Dawson was a man of average height, with brown hair and brown eyes—a man who easily blended into a crowd.

"How did you know ..." she began to ask, and then stopped short. "Ah, I see. Sand & Sable, right? But I'm not wearing that much. It's not as though I bathe in it, you know."

"I know," Dawson said. "But it's pretty distinctive, especially in an empty cathedral, and I'm very fond of it. Brings back a lot of memories."

Lily Gerard slipped into the seat next to him as he wrapped his left arm over her shoulders, and she laid her head against him.

"Sorry to disturb your reverie," she said quietly.

"No problem; I was finishing up anyway," Dawson said. "Think a little, pray a little, think some more, pray some more. It's my way of talking with God, I guess. After a couple of hours I usually either run out of things to talk about or fall asleep. What brings you here?"

"You weren't at the Foundation and your mobile phone is off. This is where you usually are when your phone is off, and since your phone is off ..."

"Clever girl. Is something wrong, or did you just miss me?"

"Both, I guess," she said with a shrug. "Diane called. She left a message on the machine at the condo, then called me. She says Dr. Brystol would like to see you when you have time, but it didn't seem urgent."

Dawson sighed and said "OK," but seemed uninterested in moving from his seat at the moment.

Lily Gerard ran a small security company, and was Dawson's lover and confidant. Dawson, as security director for the Brystol Foundation, was Gerard's primary client. The Brystol Foundation—founded by Dr. Kenneth Brystol—developed, protected, and deployed new technologies. Brystol still led the organization. Much of the work done at the Foundation was top secret, and most of it was for the United States Government. Dawson had come to work for the Foundation nearly a decade ago, after he left a promising career at the National Security Agency. His work had taken him all over the world, and partnered him with almost every US intelligence agency and branch of the US military at one time or another. Now in his fifties, Dawson knew he was slowing down physically. Fortunately, his mental faculties were Dawson's real strength, and he had been assured many times that he wasn't likely to find himself without gainful employment anytime soon.

"I see why you like it here, Ben. The quiet is so much deeper and the still-ness is almost palpable."

"And then there's the sheer beauty of the place," Dawson nodded in agreement. "The Gothic arches and the stained glass evoke a special kind of reverence, I think. And the marble. There is something about marble. I watched them harvest marble from the foot of the Alps just outside of Turin once. They cleave it away in gigantic twenty-five-ton blocks, and the Italian marble is so white—especially the statuary marble—it seems utterly pure. I stood there one day, in one of the enormous marble quarries, and understood for the first time how truly small we all are compared to the majesty of God's creation. The only thing I've ever really seen like it is the Grand Canyon, I guess."

"The ocean is that way for me," Gerard replied quietly without lifting her head. "But it still seems a little strange."

"How's that?" Dawson asked, beginning finally to shift in his seat.

"You're not Catholic," Gerard replied with a shrug. "You were raised a Baptist, right? So why not do your meditating in a Protestant church? I've seen some around the DC area."

"Ever been in one?" Dawson smiled.

"I don't think so," she admitted. "I mostly went to community churches growing up. Why?"

"Most of them aren't anything like the churches I grew up in," Dawson said. "Many of them are huge buildings now, cavernous inside and filled with speakers, projection systems, and band equipment. They're more like concert arenas than places of worship. There's nothing reverent about them. Nothing that helps to quiet the soul and let a person be alone with God."

"We've never talked about this, have we?" Gerard said. "God, I mean. We're always tearing around the world, shooting people and getting shot at, and we never really talk about the value of human life."

Dawson stood, and Gerard followed. "No, we haven't," he agreed. "And more important, I guess, what the purpose of life really is. Sounds like a good topic for dinner or one of our after-dinner strolls."

Dawson pulled on his coat and they left the cathedral hand-in-hand.

"Thinking of converting to Catholicism, then?" she asked as they walked. She suspected she already knew the answer.

"Nope. Nothing against Catholics, but I just see things differently. Our theologies overlap in some areas, but where they don't, they *really* don't. How did you get here, sweetheart?"

"I took a cab over from the office," Gerard replied.

"Well then, how about riding with me out to the Foundation? I'll see what Kenneth wants on our way home tonight."

"Sounds good to me," Gerard said as she pushed her arm further inside of his, drawing them closer as they walked.

Dawson's car was about a block away. The February sky was the color of smoke, and pedestrians were few. Most of them were bundled up to their faces, and they squinted against the cold wind as it shoved them in harsh gusts along the sidewalks.

As they reached Dawson's car, he thumbed the power switch on his smart-phone. By the time he and Gerard were belted in with the heater engaged, the phone registered three voicemails, two text messages, and a half dozen new emails. "Well, it *has* been a couple of hours, I guess. More than enough time for something to fall apart," he muttered resignedly.

Before he backed out from his parking place, Dawson checked his text messages and scanned his voicemail traffic. Then he sighed perceptibly and scrolled down to a contact listing for Tom Bradley – office, and clicked on it. The name was fictitious, but a lot of calls occurred between Dawson's phone and that number. On the other end of the line, the phone rang once and then was disconnected. About thirty seconds later, Dawson's phone buzzed and he hit "Accept." The voice of the caller was mellow and seemed unperturbed at the time it had taken Dawson to reply.

"How are you this evening, Benjamin?" It was Charles Jennings, Dawson's former boss, a deputy director at the National Security Agency.

"I'm well, Sir," Dawson responded. "How are you?"

"Very well, thank you," Jennings replied. "Are you able to speak?"

"Yes, Sir, I am in my car, and Lily is the only person with me."

"Ah, Miss Gerard is with you. Well, I am sorry to interrupt, then. I do need to speak with you about a matter of some importance. Could you possibly meet me at the George Washington University Hospital? I'm already here. You can bring Miss Gerard along with you, of course, though it might be better if she waited in the lobby. I need to show you something, and I'm afraid it's rather confidential. I don't think it will take more than an hour, and probably less."

"I understand. Yes, I think that would be fine. I'm her ride home so I expect Lily will be willing to wait for me. I was just going to head over to the Foundation; evidently Kenneth has been trying to reach me."

"Don't worry about that," Jennings said. "Kenneth is here with me, and he was trying to reach you about the same matter. Please come by as soon as you can and offer my apologies to Miss Gerard—oh, and assure her your dinners this evening are on me. It's the least I can do."

"All right, Sir. In that case, we'll be there shortly."

"Very well. It is the psychiatric hospital located in the 900 block of 23$^{rd}$ Street," Jennings said. "I will meet you in the lobby."

"Oh, the psychiatric hospital," Dawson said. "That's even closer—I can be there in just a few minutes."

"Wonderful! See you then," Jennings said, and the call ended.

Dawson explained the situation to Gerard as he drove, and as he suspected, she had no issues with the change in plans. "The psychiatric hospital? How odd," Gerard said with a puzzled expression. Then she shrugged and smiled. "I think perhaps we should go somewhere a little nicer than our usual haunts this evening since Charles is footing the bill. I can make reservations while you and Charles and Dr. Brystol are doing whatever it is you'll be doing."

"Ah, dinner with a beautiful woman. Now you have my attention," Dawson grinned as he slowed for a traffic light.

Gerard sighed and said through her smile, "I don't mean to be immodest, dear, but I rarely have trouble getting your attention."

"Touché," Dawson replied. "Truer words were never spoken."

*  *  *  *

When Dawson and Gerard entered the lobby of the psychiatric center, Jennings and Brystol were both waiting for them. Greetings were cordial and Brystol was charming as usual. "My dear," he spoke to Gerard, shaking her hand and then patting it gently before he released it, "you look lovely as ever." Then he looked at Dawson and said: "When Charles told me Lily was with you, I finally understood why you were out of touch, Ben." His smile was genuine and there was a twinkle in his eyes.

Dawson had mentioned to Gerard at some point that Kenneth Brystol reminded him of the character played by Christopher Lloyd in the movie *Back to the Future*, and Charles Jennings looked to him like Donald Sutherland. She always smiled involuntarily when encountering these men because she just couldn't shake the images from her mind.

Even in his late seventies, Brystol was full of life and seemed as vital as any man twenty years his junior, leaping about from technology to technology and managing to add value everywhere his relentless curiosity dragged him. Jennings, the Sutherland look-alike, gave the air of an Ivy League college professor, frequently right down to the tweed jacket. Like Brystol, Jennings was pushing well into his seventies. He was considering retirement, and for years he had harbored a hope that Dawson might backfill him one day at the NSA. But John Deering, his colleague at the CIA, had been throwing broad hints at Dawson for a few years as well, and Jennings knew anything could happen.

Dawson was officially the Chief of Security at the Brystol Foundation, which would have been challenging enough, but he was also acting on behalf of Brystol's friend, Charles Jennings—who had recommended Dawson to Brystol in the first place. In that role, Dawson had been in the field as an unofficial operative for the NSA almost as much as he had been at the Foundation, and as he sometimes remarked, he wasn't getting any younger. But the Brystol Foundation often became involved in the development and deployment of cutting-edge technologies. Those innovations drew the interest of multiple countries, criminal organizations, and wealthy private investors who wanted to use them for their own purposes. They frequently became hotly contested objects of pursuit with political and kinetic battles along the way.

When Gerard had been comfortably installed in one of the hospital lounges, the three men walked down the hall to an elevator bank and ascended to the sixth floor. As they stepped off the elevator, Jennings went first and waved his credentials at one of two plain clothes security guards. The guards clearly recognized Jennings and Brystol, but eyed Dawson. *These guys are serious,* Dawson thought, *and both are armed. Probably former military, judging by their posture and haircuts.*

The guard Jennings had approached took a few steps forward to meet him. "This gentleman is with us," Jennings said. "His name is Ben Dawson and he works for Dr. Brystol."

"Very well, Sir," the guard replied, and resumed his previous position. Dawson nodded at the two guards as he passed by them but neither returned the gesture. He noticed the rooms they passed while walking to the end of the corridor were all empty, and suspected it was not the normal situation. The remainder of the psychiatric center, as far as he could tell from what he had observed, was a beehive of activity.

Their destination was room number 604. But just before they reached the room, Jennings pulled up short, turning to his right and waving Dawson and Brystol into a small anteroom. The dimly lighted space had been outfitted with desktop computers and one window—apparently connecting it to room 604. When Jennings drew the heavy curtain back, Dawson could see the window wasn't a window at all—it was a two-way mirror. On the other side of the mirror, sitting at a desk and hooked to an IV line and at least two electrodes, was a young man Dawson knew well from the NSA. The man was black, and the dim lighting in his room made it difficult to clearly see his facial expression, but he seemed to be frowning at the text on some papers lying in front of him. There was a desk lamp shining directly on the papers but not much other light in the room.

Mickey Wahl, an employee of the NSA, had assisted Dawson with some of his most challenging recent projects. He was an exceptional technician specializing in computers and telecommunications with a strong background in cryptography and cyberwar techniques.

"What's Mickey doing here?" Dawson asked, incredulous. "Is he ill?"

"Possibly," Jennings replied. "How much do you know about Mickey, Ben?"

Dawson took a little deeper breath than usual and said: "I know we'd have had a very difficult time pulling off some of the most important things we've done in the last few years without him. I think he just had his thirty-first birthday a few days before Christmas. I met his girlfriend, Cecelia, at the party—an insurance actuary, I think. He's from Grand Rapids, Michigan. Computer Science Ph.D. from Cal Poly, where he was also a basketball star. Loves computers, statistics, cryptography, sausage pizza, and Diet Coke. Works for your IT department head, Daniel Winters. Intelligent, a little immature in a geeky way, but a solid citizen. I guess that's about it. Why?"

"Mickey has been leaking information to people outside the NSA, Ben," Jennings said. Dawson began to respond—loudly—with a single compound word, but Jennings held up his hand in a stopping gesture. "I know what you're going to say. I didn't want to believe it either, but there's no doubt about it. The extraordinary aspect of this is we're pretty sure he has no idea he is doing anything wrong."

"In fact, he may not know he's doing it at all," Brystol added. "Watch this," he said as Jennings turned and left the anteroom.

On the other side of the glass, Dawson and Brystol could see Jennings enter room 604 and pull up a chair next to the desk.

"Hi, Boss," Wahl said with a smile. "Any word yet on when I can get out of here?"

"Not yet, I'm afraid," Jennings replied. "I don't think it will be too long now, though. Have you had any luck with the message traffic on these communiqués?"

"Not really," Wahl replied. Dawson could see Wahl was pretty frustrated. "If there is something in particular you're looking for, I could help you better back at the office with my computer—or at least with a laptop from here—if you're worried about someone at the office seeing what I'm working on."

"You just finished reading these papers, didn't you, Mickey?" Jennings asked.

"Yes, Sir."

"And what do they say?"

Wahl looked at Jennings, frowned hard, looked down at the papers, and looked back up at Jennings. "I don't remember, Sir," he said.

"Well then," Jennings continued gently, "just read me the first paragraph aloud."

Wahl picked up the top sheet and began reading. The paragraph was a message intercepted between a high-level ISIS commander and one of his lieutenants. It was only a few sentences long and instructed the lieutenant to move his forces from one city to another. As soon as Wahl finished reading the paragraph aloud, Jennings said. "Thank you, Mickey. Tell me, what did that paragraph say?"

Again, Wahl was stymied. He couldn't reproduce anything about it at all. Then Jennings pulled a folded paper from his inside jacket pocket. He unfolded it and placed it in front of Wahl. "Could you read this first paragraph for me, Mickey?" he asked politely.

Wahl read the paragraph which seemed to be an excerpt from a recent congressional hearing on funding for preschool activities. When he had finished, Jennings asked him again: "Now, what did that paragraph say?"

Wahl responded immediately. "It's about government funding for preschool programs, Sir," he said. "The question it was addressing is related to priorities of three different programs recently presented to a congressional subcommittee, and the subcommittee is apparently trying to determine which one it will recommend to the full body of congress."

"I don't understand," Dawson said to Brystol. "Why can't he remember the first document after he reads it when he is able to do such a great job on the second one?"

"Someone has tampered with Mickey's brain, Ben," Brystol replied. "They have selected specific information and events, and conditioned Mickey so he has absolutely no recollection of the information or of handling that information. It's a technology we have been exploring for several years now, but as you can imagine, the ethical aspects of this are as knotty as the technology is dangerous, so we have been moving very slowly with human trials. Apparently, someone out there is now ahead of us and they want something the NSA has; perhaps *everything.*"

Dawson turned from the two-way mirror and looked Brystol in the eye. "How far has this gone, and in what directions?" he asked.

"We can selectively erase human memories, Ben. And that means the guilt, remorse, and inhibitions associated with any of those memories are expunged as well. There's a lot more, but just think about that for a minute. Someone out there is ahead of us; they can actually keep a person from even processing information related to specific topics, or related to specific actions they perform."

"And the Foundation has been doing this kind of thing?"

"Our work in this area at the Brystol Foundation is called the Lethe Project, and as I said, we've been proceeding very slowly and carefully. There is a lot of potential benefit from a technology like this, treating diseases like Post Traumatic Stress Disorder. I'll go into that with you later. But for now, you need to understand the profound danger here. Someone has already managed to infiltrate the NSA. We don't know where else they may have found a crack or crevice to get into. But the clock is clearly ticking and we need your help."

# ABOUT
# THE AUTHOR

Bill Duncan worked in Iraq in 2006–2007 and in Afghanistan in 2010–2011 as a Special Assistant to the Deputy Undersecretary of Defense for Business & Stability Operations. At the completion of his work in Iraq, Duncan was honored by Deputy Secretary of Defense Gordon England at a ceremony in the Pentagon's Hall of Heroes. At the conclusion of his work in Afghanistan, Duncan was awarded three medals from the Office of the Secretary of Defense and the US Joint Chiefs of Staff. Details may be viewed at: www.billduncanscareer.com.

Before and after his work in the Middle East, Duncan has been a member of executive management teams at major manufacturing companies such as John Deere, McDonnell Douglas, Boeing, JDS Uniphase, and Emerson. He is the author of several business books and dozens of business-related articles. He has earned a bachelor of arts degree and a master's of business administration/technology management, as well as multiple professional certifications. Duncan currently lives and works in St. Louis, Missouri.

More information, photographs, and background about the author's experiences that inspired the Brystol Foundation series can be viewed at: www.bill-duncan.com. Additional copies of these books can be purchased there as well.

www.ingramcontent.com/pod-product-compliance
Lightning Source LLC
Chambersburg PA
CBHW071328250626
47159CB00004B/1513